Tonight he looke

He'd obviously come to the reception on his own. She'd heard about his divorce—hard not to when it had been splashed across the media. Not that there had been anything salacious. Just the usual bland statement about him and his wife separating, no one else involved and a request to respect their family's privacy. Still, on a slow sports day during the summer hiatus, it had filled column inches.

As if he felt her studying him, Scotty looked up and their gazes met. Held.

Her heart double skipped. Was that a flicker of interest widening his pupils?

There was something about the recently retired captain that drew her to him. His dark hair, flecked with gray, was still short, like it had been when he was playing. His tanned face bore the scars of his career. The one that had always fascinated her was the white line that marred his otherwise perfect lips. Left side, near the corner. The result of a high stick—one that hadn't been penalized—it had taken twenty-five stitches to close the cut.

He gave a half smile, raised his glass to her, then returned his attention to his drink.

Wow. Talk about a look that packed a punch.

Suddenly, she wanted to make that half smile full-blown.

Dear Reader,

The New Jersey Ice Cats are back and ready for action! This time though you'll get a sneak peek at what it's like behind the scenes, when retired captain Scott "Scotty" Matthews takes on a new challenge in the team's front office. Can he be as successful off the ice as he was on it— especially when he has to face off against sexy business consultant Sapphire Houlihan?

When Sapphire appeared in *A Perfect Compromise*, I knew that finding her the perfect hero would be complicated. Not because she's a confident, successful woman, but because she's actually happy with her life as it is. It would take a special man to stand up to her and make her reconsider her "no strings" philosophy. Scotty wasn't the obvious choice, but he was definitely the right one...in the end!

Aside from helping these two get their happy ending, writing this book was fun because I got the chance to use knowledge from my former career in business. It was great to be able to combine marketing, hockey and romance in one story.

I love to hear from readers. You can get in touch with me via email at anna@annasugden.com or via my website, www.annasugden.com. You can also find me on Facebook and Twitter.

Anna Sugden

ANNA SUGDEN

A Perfect Strategy

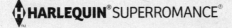

HARLEQUIN® SUPERROMANCE®

Recycling programs
for this product may
not exist in your area.

ISBN-13: 978-0-373-64014-0

A Perfect Strategy

Printed in U.S.A.

Former marketing executive **Anna Sugden** loves reading romance novels and watching films with happy endings. She also loves watching hockey and football, where she prefers a happy ending for her teams. When she's not researching hockey players (for her books, of course), she makes craft projects and collects penguins, autographs and memorabilia and great shoes. Anna lives in Cambridge, England, with her husband and two bossy black cats. Learn more about Anna, her books and her shoes at annasugden.com.

Books by Anna Sugden

HARLEQUIN SUPERROMANCE

A Perfect Compromise
A Perfect Distraction
A Perfect Trade
A Perfect Catch

Other titles by this author available in ebook format.

For Marcela, with love.
For Keith, love always. xxxxx

Acknowledgment

Jill Marsal, my fabulous agent!

Victoria Curran, for helping me
make this book the best it can be.

PROLOGUE

Fifteen years ago

"MAN, IT'LL BE good to finally play a game for real."

Scott "Scotty" Matthews hefted his bag over his shoulder, shut the hatch of his SUV and followed the small group of teammates toward the arena.

"Yeah, the preseason just doesn't cut it," grumbled Cam "Bullet" Lockhead. The New Jersey Ice Cats' much-feared enforcer slammed his palm against the security bar to open the door into the building's lower ground level. "Pansy-assed friendlies aren't worth the effort to strap on my skates."

"You're only pissed because Coach banned you from hitting and fighting." Ryan Grey punched Bullet on the arm. "He wanted you to save it for tonight's home opener."

"We've had the entire freaking summer off. I want to get back to work." Cam hip-checked his friend into the door frame. "But how can I do my job if I can't drop the gloves?"

Scott pushed them ahead of him into the wide, concrete area where all the behind-the-scenes magic for the arena took place. The cold air was filled with the low hum of the ice-making machinery, the grinding of skates being sharpened and the throaty rumble of the Zambonis. He inhaled deeply, enjoying the smell of buttered popcorn and the acrylic tang of heating sticks. Yeah, it was good to be back.

"You can make up for it tonight," he reassured Bullet. "Plus you'll keep the crowd happy. They always bay for blood at a rivalry game. With Philly here, our fans will definitely expect you to put their fourth line out of business."

Ike Jelinek, who'd recently been promoted to the role of starting goaltender for the Cats, cuffed Bullet on the back of the head. "I don't know what you're whining about. You didn't play more than five minutes in each game. I was out there for the full sixty in four of the six."

"And you sat on your butt wearing the ball cap for the other two." Cam stuck out his lower lip and flicked it up and down with his forefinger. "Aww, did the poor, little net-boy get tired standing in his crease for so long?"

Scott grinned as Ike told his friend to do an anatomically impossible sexual act. Much as he loved Celine and his kids, he'd missed hanging out with these guys over the summer. They were more like family to him than his real siblings.

One of the problems with not making the postseason was that he'd finished playing in April.

Which meant he'd had too long a break from hockey. Sure, the family vacation in the Caribbean had been great. He'd loved having the time to play with Angela and Wayne, who were growing up way too fast, and to chill with Celine. But by the time the Conference Finals were done in May, he'd already been itching to get on the ice. He'd been working out and training even before the Cup had been lifted by Tampa.

Scott had volunteered to help out with the younger guys at prospects camp in July and had counted off the days to training camp.

"You can— Oomph." Scott ran into Grey's back. His friend had halted abruptly. "What the hell?"

Grey had a strange grin on his face as he stepped aside and gave Scott a clear view of the locker room. Most of the team was already inside, getting changed for the pregame skate. A heavy rock beat pounded. As he walked in, the music switched off and the guys stopped what they were doing and started to whoop and applaud.

Scott frowned, confused. It wasn't his birthday, he hadn't done anything dumb that the media was gnawing over and he hadn't even played in the last preseason game. Shaking his head, he walked forward a couple of steps, heading to his stall. He was surprised to see the room was full of coaches, trainers, equipment guys and other backroom staff.

They must be as excited as he was about opening night and…

His brain froze. His steps faltered.

His gaze narrowed to the red jersey with the snow-leopard logo hanging in his stall. More specifically to the left shoulder. To the letter stitched there.

He blinked, thinking he must be dreaming. But nothing changed. Instead of the *A* he'd worn last season, there was a *C*. "Holy crap."

Scott had known that there would be a new captain, since Johnny "Bruiser" Bruskowski had retired at the end of last season. As one of the alternate captains, Scott had figured he'd be on the list of possibles to lead the team but had assumed he was still too young. That it would go to one of the veterans. In his mind, next time around was more likely and he was good with that.

Clearly, the coaching staff and management had had a different idea.

Before he could process that, Scott was surrounded by people slapping him on the back and congratulating him.

"Hail the new captain," Bullet said, with the right mix of deference, respect and mockery. "Best man for the job."

"Only because none of you bozos wanted it," Scott retorted good-naturedly, trying to hide his awe at the faith the organization and his team had put in him. "You'd have to toe the line too much."

"Damn straight."

"Come on, guys. Stop jawing and get suited up. Ten minutes before you hit the ice for warm-ups." The trainer nodded at Scott. "Be good to see you leading the boys out there."

"Thanks, man." He raised his voice above the hubbub. "And thanks to all of you. I'll do my best to fill Bruiser's skates, though he's a tough act to follow. Luckily for me, this is the best freaking hockey team in the world and I look forward to proving it to those other suckers, when we lift the Cup next June."

A rousing round of cheers echoed through the locker room before everyone turned to the serious business of getting ready for a game. Scott strode to his stall, opened his bag and began his pregame routine, starting with placing the latest photo of Celine and their kids in pride of place—on the shelf above his sweater. He looked forward to celebrating his good news with them tomorrow. If she wasn't too tired, there might even be a private celebration with Celine tonight. Especially if the Cats won.

He allowed himself a few seconds of heady anticipation before clearing his head and getting himself into game mode. By the time he'd changed into his gear, his mind was 100 percent focused on the task ahead.

It wouldn't be easy tonight. Philly had made a lot of changes over the summer and were hot favorites to win the East coming into the season. They hadn't lost a single preseason game, so were riding high on confidence. Scott planned to ensure the Cats knocked that cockiness out of them. They would not win in his barn, or at his first game as captain.

"You ready?" Grey called out from across the room.

Scott gave him the thumbs-up before reverently lifting his sweater off the hanger and slipping it over his head. On only two other occasions had the action meant as much to him—the day he was drafted by the Ice Cats and the night he made his first appearance in the show.

Putting on his helmet, he headed to where his friends were waiting. Then he led the way out, through the short tunnel and into the brightly lit main bowl of the arena. As his skates hit the ice, he looked over behind Ike's goal to his seats. His heart swelled to see Celine, Angela and Wayne going crazy clapping and cheering him from behind the glass. He saluted them with his stick, then began his warm-up.

The rest of the pregame routine passed in a blur, no matter how hard he tried to imprint it all on his brain to preserve the memory. He couldn't remember heading to the locker room, what Coach said or even what he'd said in his first captain's speech. The next thing he knew, he was standing by the famous snow-leopard logo, with Ike ahead of him and Grey behind him, ready to lead his team out.

When the doors swung open, he cleared his throat. "Let's go out there and show them the Ice Cats play the best damn hockey in the world."

As he strode toward the ice, he allowed his mind one small lapse in focus to acknowledge that life couldn't get much better than this.

CHAPTER ONE

Present day

"THE HOCKEY NETWORK, New York, isn't renewing my contract?"

Scott paused, steak-laden fork halfway to his mouth, to look at his agent.

"They want to go in a different direction. They want a more 'three-sixty' coverage." Andy added air quotes.

"You mean they're changing *me* because I suck at color commentary." Scott had never been good at running his mouth off and THNNY seemed to want to fill every second of the game with talk. He didn't mind commenting on plays and stats, strategy and tactics, even guys' college or juniors careers. But the network wanted him to gossip about the players, as well.

Sharing in-depth information about the men he'd been teammates with less than a year ago was something he had no interest in. He'd been on the butt end of that kind of intrusion enough this past season, between his retirement and divorce, to be real uncomfortable with sharing details about guys' personal lives. He didn't even like repeating locker-room tales.

Besides, who cared? Scott sure as hell didn't. The only thing that mattered was what happened on the ice.

"I wasn't sure I wanted to continue next season, so I guess that makes my decision for me."

"You're sure you don't want to coach?" Andy patted his mouth with his napkin. "I've had feelers from several GMs about you. A future Hall of Famer is always of interest."

Scott ate the piece of steak, using the time to mull that over. He'd done some work with the Cats this past season, helping the younger players tighten up their defensive tactics. He liked to think he'd played his part in helping the team win the Cup, even if he hadn't been out there on the ice with them.

Getting his name etched on the silver chalice one last time had been cool, though it hadn't made up for losing it the previous season. For sure, it hadn't been the same as winning it as a player.

"I enjoy stopping by practice to work on drills with the guys," he said finally. "But I don't want to do it full-time. Or have the responsibility for running the team, day in and day out. I don't have the patience. It drives me nuts to work on plays and then see it all fall apart come game time because they forget how to execute in the heat of the moment."

Andy gave an exaggerated shudder. "You and me both. That's the problem when you're naturally talented. You can't teach what's in your gut."

"I hope your gut is enjoying my food." Ryan Grey clapped a hand on Scott's shoulder. "Good to see you, bro."

"You, too, man." Scott stood and greeted his friend and former teammate.

Ryan's career had been cut short by repeated concussion issues. After a troubled few years, he'd decided to turn his love of cooking into his next career and now ran one of the most successful high-end steak houses in the tristate area, if not the whole East Coast.

"It's been a while." Ryan topped up Andy's red wine. "How's retirement treating you?"

"Still finding my feet," Scott admitted. "If I was a better cook, I'd give you a run for your money."

"You could try." His friend grinned. "But I won't be losing sleep over it. You're a better D-man than chef."

"True." Scott didn't take offense. He had enough culinary skills to survive without starving and had a sharp dialing finger for takeout and delivery. "Still, I can grill a mean burger."

"Maybe you should open a sports bar." Grey relit the candle on the table and straightened the centerpiece. "Don't you have a business degree, too?"

Scott nodded. It was a bit clichéd—retired pro athlete putting his name to an eatery—but it could be fun. "That's a good idea. I may look into it."

"Anything I can do to help, give me a shout. I'm happy to share what I've learned." Grey's head lifted. "I have to go—my maître d' is signaling. Don't be a stranger."

"I have a guy in my organization who specializes in second-career investment opportunities. He's helped some football players with bars and nightclubs. I'll put you in touch with him." Andy pointed his wineglass toward Scott. "No pressure, but he'll give you the facts and figures of what's involved."

"I'd appreciate his insights. But I'd still like to keep my hand in hockey somehow."

Even though he knew his body couldn't take playing at the highest level anymore, he didn't feel old enough to be retired. He kept in shape and skated regularly. After so many years playing, he couldn't give up hockey completely.

He wasn't really part of the Ice Cats any longer. He was like an honorary uncle: included and indulged, but not a true family member. And he hadn't felt like part of the commentating group— they'd been together a few years and it had been hard to slot into their tight-knit circle. Since his divorce one year ago, he sure as hell hadn't felt like part of his family.

Andy signaled for the check. "You could join

me and become an agent. Some of my best guys are former players. You definitely have what it takes."

That was a major compliment. His agent didn't bullshit or give praise lightly.

Driving home, Scott kept Andy's advice front of mind. A couple of the opportunities they'd discussed made more sense than the commentating. In truth, the network had done him a favor by not renewing his contract.

Scott pulled into his garage and parked. As the door rumbled closed behind him, he took his time getting out of the car. Putting off the moment when he'd have to walk into the dark, empty house. Something he'd dreaded for the past year.

The divorce had come out of left field. Hell, it had been a freaking fastball from another freaking ballpark.

He'd assumed when he retired, he and Celine would spend more time together, especially now that both Angela and Wayne were in college. Since Scott and Celine wouldn't be driven by the brutal schedule that had dictated their lives from September to June every year since they'd met, they would finally be able to do the things they'd always talked about. Instead, she'd left him.

His bitter laugh echoed around the garage. That was one play he hadn't read at all.

Scott walked through the house, turning on lights. He kicked off his shoes in the front hall, then went into the living room and flicked on the flat-screen. Relieved to have noise—he didn't care what channel was on—he padded to the kitchen and poured himself a glass of wine. Then headed for his den.

The silence was the worst. For the past couple months, his kids had hung out here a lot, particularly while their mom was traveling. But this week, they'd both headed back to college early— Angela had wanted to get a head start on her third-year projects and Wayne had football practice.

Leaving Scott alone in a house he'd never really felt was home. He'd bought it for Celine when he became captain. A thank-you for all the sacrifices she'd made and the fantastic job she'd done with their kids. While his responsibilities at the rink and with the team had taken up more time, she'd decorated, extended and remodeled, until it was *perfect*.

And it was. Perfectly color coordinated. Perfectly furnished. Probably perfectly freaking feng shuied, too. All he knew was that other than in his den—where she'd given him free rein—he felt like he was in a show house.

He'd have been happy to give it to her when they split up, but she'd wanted a sleek apartment in the city. Less bother while she was traveling. Not wanting to get rid of the family home while his kids still technically lived there, he'd agreed to hold on to it until Wayne graduated. But he couldn't bring himself to use more than a few rooms.

In his den, he dropped onto the sofa and turned on the Yankees game. Top of the fifth, and they were beating the Red Sox by four runs. Good news, but not enough to distract him. Maybe he'd sit in bed and read. The latest Robert Crais was next up on his nightstand; Elvis Cole was always good for taking his mind off things.

Scott walked back through the house, turning off lights and the TV in the living room. The thick vellum invitation on the mantel caught his attention.

Crap. He'd forgotten all about J.B. and Issy's reception. The pair had been married during the play-offs in a quickie civil ceremony but were having a full-blown celebration now that the successful Cup run was over and players were heading to New Jersey for their preseason preparations.

Scott was glad for J.B., but he wasn't looking forward to attending yet another function stag. At least there would be plenty of Cats and their families there, so he wouldn't be stuck making small talk with people he didn't know.

That brought to mind the earlier conversation over dinner. He was out of a job.

He'd never not known where he was headed. He hated feeling rudderless.

Damn it. Why hadn't he seen this coming?

As he walked upstairs, he stopped to look at the

family pictures that lined the wall. One for each year he and Celine had been married. For the first time he noticed that the writing had been on this wall, literally, if he'd bothered to notice. The happy smiles had become stilted over the years. The body language more brittle. He and Celine had been wrapped in each other's arms on their first anniversary, but by the final picture, taken last summer, they were as far apart as physically possible, with their kids almost like a buffer between them.

The truth was that he missed his kids and hockey more than he missed his wife.

Scott sank onto the top step and rested his elbows on his knees, staring into the glass of red wine like it held all the answers.

Unfortunately, it didn't.

SAPPHIRE HOULIHAN'S LIFE WAS, to quote Mary Poppins, practically perfect in every way. She had a fabulous career, running her own successful management consultancy. She was healthy and fit and had finally lost the extra ten pounds she'd been carrying since college. Though after the one or two…okay…several to-die-for desserts she'd eaten at this wedding reception, she'd probably put half of those pounds back on. She had a busy social life and an active sex life, with absolutely no strings attached to either.

Everything was just how she liked it. Simple, straightforward, easy to manage.

So why did she feel so…restless? Unsettled?

Sapphie sipped her champagne and looked around the glittering ballroom. Her Louboutined foot tapped to the rock beat of an oldie but goody. The party was in full swing.

Her heart warmed to see her childhood friend Isabelle Brandine—no, Isabelle Larocque now—dancing with her husband, Jean Baptiste. Issy looked so happy. Who'd have thought a playboy hockey player, and a vacation fling at that, would turn out to be The One for conservative Issy.

Of course, there was the little matter of baby Sophia—currently being cooed over by J.B.'s mom—the result of that fling and an unfortunately timed bout of food poisoning. Sapphie believed her goddaughter was the catalyst for bringing Issy and J.B. together. So, despite a troubled path, their story had a happy ending.

If anyone deserved that happiness, it was Issy. Inseparable from the time they could crawl, Issy and Sapphie had grown up in a poor town in North Carolina. Because their parents had preferred partying over responsibility, the two friends had had to be the "grown-ups" in their respective households: looking after their siblings, making sure what little money their folks brought in kept a roof over their heads and food on the table.

When they'd escaped at eighteen, headed for college and better things, Issy had done everything she could to build a stable, financially secure life for herself, with the hope of settling down with a nice, responsible man to raise a family. Everything she hadn't had as a child.

Sapphie deposited her empty glass on a passing waiter's tray and snagged a fresh drink. She sighed.

That definitely wasn't the life Sapphie wanted. Marriage, kids, a mortgage—no way. She'd had enough of responsibility and commitment growing up and was determined never to be tied to any person or any place. She depended on no one but herself. She controlled her life and cherished her freedom.

Sapphie didn't own an apartment but kept three serviced condos—one on each coast and another in Chicago—convenient pieds-à-terre for when she flew back and forth across the country to see her clients. No cleaning, no maintenance, no worries.

As for dating, Issy teased her about having "a guy in every port." Not quite true, but Sapphie didn't go out with any man for long. That way she didn't encourage expectations that she couldn't, or wouldn't, fulfill. Like the apartments, it suited her perfectly.

Sapphie pushed away from the pillar she'd been leaning against and sat at an empty table. The late nights she'd put in recently for her biggest client, Marty Antonelli—not to mention the red-eye she'd taken from LA to get here to help Issy with the party—were catching up with her. She had a room at the hotel until Monday and planned to take advantage of the spa to pamper herself.

Perhaps she'd sneak away and get an early night. Eight hours' sleep sounded heavenly.

Taylor "Mad Dog" Madden sat beside her. "How soon can I cut out of here without offending the happy couple?"

The Ice Cats' defenseman was a close friend and also one of J.B.'s groomsmen.

"I was wondering the same thing. Do you think we're getting ol—" Sapphie broke off when she saw his face, tight with anger. "What's put a bug up your butt?"

"Nothing." He slammed his beer bottle on the table, then stared out at the dance floor, arms crossed.

She followed his gaze and spotted a familiar, pretty blonde talking to a slight man with thinning dark hair. "Oh. Lizzie came with someone."

"Apparently, she's been dating him for a few weeks." Taylor's lip curled. "Pompous jerk. He keeps touching her ass."

"And that's your business, how?"

He tossed her an irritated look. "It isn't. I just think he should have better manners."

"Uh-huh. Not jealous, then."

Taylor had a thing for Lizzie Martin, though he was loath to admit it. The pair had dated briefly, a few years ago. That had been before Sapphie had met Taylor last summer when she and Issy had taken a trip to Antigua to celebrate her thirtieth birthday. He and J.B. had been getting some R & R at the same resort. Sapphie and Taylor had hit it off straightaway.

Their time in the Caribbean had been fun, and once back home, they'd become friends with occasional benefits. There was never any thought of a serious relationship, on either side. More recently, they'd dropped the benefits and simply enjoyed each other's company.

Sapphie wasn't upset about his feelings for Lizzie. He was a good person and he deserved a good woman. Especially if she kept him on his toes.

"You don't freaking slow-dance to Bon Jovi, idiot." Drumming his fingers on the table, Taylor looked ready to storm the dance floor and yank Lizzie's date away from her by the scruff of his neck.

"I think Lizzie made that point," Sapphie said as the blonde moved out of her partner's arms. "So relax."

Taylor drained his beer. "I'm fine. As long as he stops pawing her in public."

"Because you want to be the one who paws her."

"No." He sighed. "Yes. But that won't happen. She's mad at me for embarrassing her at the Cup celebration a few weeks ago. I don't know what's wrong with me. Every time I open my mouth around her, I'm eating shoe leather. I don't have that problem with you."

"Because our relationship is simple."

"Maybe we should date instead."

"Right." Sapphie rolled her eyes. "I don't want to spoil what we have."

"You're right." He sighed again.

"Go sort things out with Lizzie. Apologize, then ask her to dance."

"Even if she accepts I'm sorry, I'm the last person she'll want to dance with."

"It's not like you to give up because it's tough."

His lips twisted. "Me and Lizzie isn't tough—it's impossible."

"I wouldn't be so sure." She'd seen Lizzie surreptitiously watching Taylor. "Anyway, you've got nothing to lose by giving it a shot."

"I guess. Anyone ever told you you're bossy?" he grumbled good-naturedly.

"All the time. It's how I earn my money. You're lucky I don't charge for my advice."

"You'd be worth every penny." He kissed her cheek, then stood. "Wish me luck."

She held up crossed fingers. "You can do it."

Taylor strode off purposefully, but his body language changed as he approached Lizzie. He was nervous.

Lizzie straightened the moment she saw Taylor heading toward her. Though Sapphie couldn't hear what was said, the pair's reactions were enough to get the gist of their conversation. As it grew more heated, Sapphie hoped Taylor would back off, but he didn't. Soon Lizzie stalked out, with Taylor hot on her heels. It would end either in tears or with them tearing up the sheets. There was too much passion for anything else.

As Sapphie made her way across the room, she spotted Scotty Matthews at the bar, nursing a drink. Sapphie had always had a fan-girl crush on the former Ice Cats captain. Her favorite player since she'd started following the team, he'd been a powerhouse on the ice and, from what she'd heard, a great leader and a mentor in the locker room. He was a nice guy but hard to get to know. She'd seen him at several Ice Cats parties and he'd seemed pretty self-contained. Watching everything, saying little.

She'd found it hard to be her usual chatty self with him. He'd look at her with those serious blue eyes and she'd become tongue-tied. Because she'd never been fazed by a gorgeous man before, she'd assumed it was because he was older than her—in his early forties. Though he'd never said anything overtly disapproving, she'd felt she never quite measured up to his standards.

Tonight he looked lonely.

He'd obviously come to the reception on his own. She'd heard about his divorce last year; hard not to when it had been splashed across the media.

As if he felt her studying him, Scotty looked up and their gazes met.

There was something about the recently retired captain that drew her to him. His dark hair, flecked with gray, was still short, like it had been when he was playing. His tanned face bore the scars of his career. The one that had always fascinated her was the white line that marred his otherwise perfect lips. Left side, near the corner. The result of a high stick—one that hadn't been penalized—it had taken twenty-five stitches to close the cut.

He gave a half smile, raised his glass to her, then returned his attention to his drink.

Suddenly, she wanted to make that half smile full-blown.

Sapphie sauntered to the bar and settled on the stool next to him. She was pleased to notice him checking out her legs as she crossed them.

"I suppose a dance is out of the question, Captain?" Her question came out slightly husky, giving it an unintentionally sultry note.

He didn't answer immediately but looked at the crowd on the dance floor doing their best impression of John Travolta to "Stayin' Alive." "Not really my thing."

Yet his toe tapped on the rung of the stool.

"I always find it amazing that you guys have perfect rhythm and timing on the ice, yet you claim not to like dancing. Me, I love it." She wiggled in her seat.

He frowned. "That's completely different. One is a sport. That—" he pointed to the dance floor with his glass "—isn't."

"True. And some people should probably stick to hockey. Bless his heart, Monty has two left feet."

A step behind the music all the time, Chaz "Monty" Montgomery made up for his lack of skill with enthusiasm.

"He's a goaltender," Scotty said. As if that explained everything.

The music slowed. Couples drifted together.

Sapphie wrinkled her nose. "I never did like this song."

"That was my ex-wife's favorite."

Way to go, Sapphie. "I'm sorry."

Scotty shrugged. "Everyone has different tastes."

They sat silently, watching the light from the disco ball send sparkles over the dancing couples.

"Honestly, I never liked this song much either."

At his dry words, she whipped her head around to look at him. A hint of a smile played around his lips.

She was tempted to lean over and kiss them. To taste that scar. But this wasn't the time or place for that behavior—especially from the maid of honor.

That didn't stop her wanting to.

Willing herself to sound casual, she said, "I'd offer to give you new memories for the song, but we should pick something that won't make us wince every time we hear it."

"Good thinking. Plus the singer has the same name as my ex."

"We'll definitely choose another song, then."

With impeccable timing, the DJ segued into the next track. Unfortunately, it wasn't any better. She looked questioningly at Scotty, hoping this wasn't one of his favorites.

For several seconds he appeared to be enjoying the music. Then he said solemnly, "Sorry, but we can't have our song being about a dying woman. Too morbid."

She grinned, relieved. "I love Bette Midler, but this song always grates on me. Perhaps because I hate movies with sad endings. Life's hard enough."

"For sure." His smile faded.

Way to bring the evening down, dodo. Determined to cheer things up, she said brightly, "Next song, whatever it is, love it or hate it, we dance. Deal?"

For a moment, she thought he'd refuse. But he nodded. "Okay. Deal."

They waited as the current song reached its climax. Then the DJ's deliberately deep voice washed over the crowd. "Last slow song before we take up the tempo again. So grab your favorite girl or guy and smooch."

The moment of truth. Sapphie and Scotty looked at each other.

She was surprised by how much she wanted this dance. Even a little nervous.

He held out his hand, palm up. "A deal's a deal."

"It certainly is." She laid her hand in his. "Luckily, I like this song," she said as they joined the other couples. "I've always liked Christopher Cross. This one's a little corny, I know, but there's something romantic about the lyrics. Especially given where we live." Jeez, she was babbling like a teenager on her first date.

"I like the idea of being caught between the moon and New York City." Scotty pulled her gently into his arms.

Without saying anything, they slipped into the old-fashioned way of slow dancing. Her right hand clasped in his left. Her left on his shoulder, while his other hand rested against the small of her back. They started with a respectable gap between them, but the number of people made them draw closer together.

At least, that was her excuse.

Her thighs were pressed against his. Solid, hard muscle. Her breasts crushed against the broad wall of his chest. The heat of his body seared her, despite the barrier of their clothing.

He brought their joined hands in and rested them against his chest. She could feel his strong, steady heartbeat beneath his tuxedo jacket.

Her left hand slipped across his shoulder to his neck, delighting in the smooth skin and corded strength. The hand at her back began to caress her, slowly moving up and down her silk dress before edging toward her hip.

Their feet barely moved as they swayed to the music.

His cheek rested against her temple. His breath stirred her hair and whispered against the sensitive skin beneath her ear. If she turned her head slightly, her lips would be pressed against his jaw. If he turned his head slightly, his lips would be pressed against hers.

She wanted his kiss very much.

Slowly, tentatively, she started to move her head. At the same moment, he began to move his. Their mouths were so close. So tantalizingly close. One slight movement and they'd meet. She lifted her gaze to his.

Oh, those serious blue eyes. She could lose herself in them. They would be her downfall tonight. How could she resist him?

CHAPTER TWO

Scott was as nervous as a geeky teenager dancing with the homecoming queen.

He hadn't held a woman, other than his wife, in his arms for...hell...too many years to think about. For sure not since he was eighteen. Even before then, he'd been more interested in hockey than girls, so he was as green as a rookie when it came to women. What little he knew was as outmoded as a cassette tape in the world of music streaming.

Slow-dancing with the prettiest woman in the room... Staring into her clear blue eyes.

He angled himself slightly so that his groin wasn't against her thighs, then shifted his hand on her back.

Even he could read the invitation in Sapphie's expression. The way she moved their joined hands to link their fingers. How she tilted her head so her mouth was barely a breath away from his.

Sapphie wanted to kiss him.

He'd never wanted anything so much.

The thought startled him. His heart thudded against his ribs. It sounded like something his always-in-love, everything's-a-drama daughter would say.

He was a grown man. He'd seen Sapphie a few times over the past year and each time he'd felt guilty about how he'd reacted to her. He'd put it down to his divorce, his retirement—anything but the fact that it was Sapphie herself who sent his pulse skyrocketing.

Kiss the woman already.

He lowered his head, brushing his mouth over her lips. Getting the sweetest taste.

A lightning bolt shot through his body, headed straight for his groin.

He wanted more. Much more.

Start me up.

The intro to a Rolling Stones song blasted him out of the sensuous moment. Scott jerked his head up. At the same time, he tightened his hold on Sapphie. Not wanting to let her go. But they couldn't remain on the dance floor making a spectacle of themselves by continuing to slow dance while everyone around them bopped to Jagger.

He and Sapphie eased apart, but he didn't let go of her hand. She tightened her grip. They headed toward the back of the ballroom, where they found an empty space near a table to stand.

"So…" Sapphie cleared her throat. "Probably not the best place for kissing."

The tips of his ears grew hot.

"Uh, no."

Sapphie looked him straight in the eye. "Do you want to find a place to continue this or get a drink?"

He knew what his answer *should* be. "I'm not thirsty."

Sapphie's smile lit up her face, making him feel like he'd scored the game-winner. Which, given he was a stay-at-home defenseman, would be as much of a miracle as this evening was turning out to be.

"There are gardens out back," she suggested. "We could take a walk, get some fresh air."

"Fresh air's good."

She tilted her head toward the door. "We can make a break for it before the song ends."

Like naughty schoolchildren, they slipped past the caterers replenishing the buffet and paused in the foyer to adjust to the brighter light.

Scott half expected Sapphie to change her mind. What would a bright, bubbly and beautiful woman like her want with an out-of-work, out-of-place old guy like him?

Instead, she tugged on their joined hands, pulling him into a side corridor that ended at a glass fire door. He pushed open the door for her, then let it close behind them.

The night was surprisingly still, even though crickets and tree frogs chirped. The balmy air felt good after the chill inside. A rain shower earlier in the day had lowered the blazing late-summer temperatures and cleared some of Jersey's notorious humidity.

Scott and Sapphie strolled along the brick path, their way lit by old-fashioned lanterns that cast pools of soft light at regular intervals. They crossed over a wooden bridge that spanned a shallow stream and continued toward a stone gazebo. Turning a corner, they took steps leading down to a jetty, which stretched out into the dark water of the lake.

Sapphie slipped off her shoes and held them by the heels. "Come on. Let's dangle our feet in the water."

She didn't wait for his answer before dashing to the end of the jetty.

Scott followed, smiling at her infectious enthusiasm. "Wait. You'll ruin your gown if you sit there." He shrugged out of his tux jacket and spread it out on the planks. "Now you can sit, my lady."

She grinned, clasping her hands to her chest. "My hero. Thank you, Sir Galahad. Or should that be Sir Walter Raleigh—protecting my silk dress from damage by laying down your coat?"

"Either way, you're welcome. Can't have you going into the ballroom with a dirty patch on your backside."

Flirting wasn't one of his skills, because he'd never needed to play those games.

Thankfully, Sapphie laughed at his inept response. "That would be hard to explain." She dipped her bare feet into the water and wiggled her toes. "Oh, that feels good."

Man, was he out of his depth when he was turned on by dainty feet and cute toes.

She patted the space beside her. "Won't you join me? There's enough room, so you won't get mud on your great butt either."

He sat beside her and was about to put his feet in the water when he realized he still wore his shoes. Hoping Sapphie hadn't noticed, he removed them and his socks, then put them behind him on the jetty. He also remembered to roll up his pant legs.

"You're right. That feels good," he said.

They sat quietly, watching the play of moonlight on the rippling water. For a woman who exuded energy and life, she was surprisingly good at handling silence. She didn't rush to fill it with chatter. The only movement was the swish of her feet making little whirlpools.

Scott managed not to jump when her hand slipped into his. Instead, he kept staring forward as he entwined their fingers, then rested their joined hands on his thigh. His thumb mimicked her feet, stroking her soft skin in circles. His pulse kicked when she copied his action, her thumb drawing circles on his knuckle.

He turned to look at her. Only to find her studying him.

The silence became charged. Like the electricity in the air before a storm.

Sapphie gently touched his mouth with her finger. She lingered over his scar, making it tingle. "I know this doesn't hurt anymore, but it makes me want to kiss your poor lip better."

He almost couldn't breathe. "Feel free," he managed to say.

She didn't need a second invitation. She kissed her fingertip and pressed it to his lip.

He tried not to be disappointed. He'd expected—

Her mouth replaced her fingertip. She brushed a soft kiss against his scar. So fleeting it was over almost before it started. Yet it sent fierce need pulsing through his body.

Her second kiss was firmer, lasting a fraction longer. Her third, longer still. Then her tongue traced his scar.

He hardened instantly, spurring him to action. Two could play this game.

He reached up and rubbed his thumb over her full lower lip. Back and forth, gently parting her lips.

She responded by nipping his thumb, then flicking her tongue against it. Her mouth curved into a teasing smile. A satisfied glint lit her eyes.

So she thought she was in control? That she had him where she wanted him.

Not quite.

He swept in and took advantage of her parted

lips. No teasing or flirting. No hesitation or asking permission. His hand cupped the back of her head, anchoring her to him.

Her grip on his other hand tightened. Her free arm wound around his neck, pulling him closer. She met his desire and upped the intensity.

Suddenly, it wasn't enough. He wanted to feel her against him. To touch her.

He released her hand and stroked her arm. Was her skin as soft everywhere? While he massaged her neck, he ran the fingers of his other hand over her bare shoulder and down her back, until they met silky fabric. He'd admired the strapless, knee-length sheath earlier—the way it emphasized her delicious curves and showed off her amazing legs. Now it was an unwelcome barrier.

Pulling his lips from hers, he kissed his way across her cheek to her ear. She inhaled sharply as he nipped at her earlobe. When his mouth trailed down her neck, she tilted her head to give him better access.

Sapphie sighed as he continued his journey across her shoulder, paying particular attention to the hollow of her collarbone. When he reached the curve of her shoulder, his mouth took a lower path, toward her breasts.

He licked a moist trail along the top of her dress, following the rise and fall of the blue fabric over the swell of one breast, into the valley between, then up over the other.

He nudged aside the silk and retraced his path.

He wanted more. He ran his hand along the back of her dress, searching for the zipper.

He tried again.

Where the hell was the damn thing?

Sapphie chuckled softly as she moved his hand to her right side. "Try here."

Sapphie proved she wasn't put off by his fumbling by loosening his tie, removing it and tossing it aside. Then she undid the top button of his shirt. And the next.

His fingers curved tightly against her side as she pressed a hot openmouthed kiss to the pulse at the base of his throat. Then went lower.

And lower. Unbutton, kiss. Unbutton, kiss.

He almost protested aloud when she halted with his shirt only halfway undone. *Don't stop now!*

She didn't. Scott couldn't hold back his groan as she separated the two sides and licked across his right pec, circling his nipple, then returning to repeat on the other side.

This time, when she arrived at the center of his chest, she started to trail downward. His stomach clenched with anticipation.

Uh, no. If she continued along that route, he'd embarrass himself in the worst way possible.

"My turn." He slid a finger under her chin and tilted her face to his.

Her sassy smile did crazy things to his insides. "Be my guest."

He nibbled her bottom lip, then licked it, relishing the taste of her. Sweet yet spicy. Champagne and chocolate.

Scott took her mouth fully, then deepened the kiss. This time, his hand moved aside the fabric that did such a good job of covering the damn zipper and slowly pulled the tab down. Then he slipped his fingers inside.

And found nothing but soft, bare skin.

That made his task much simpler. No more barriers to exploring to his heart's content. And he did.

First her back. Her skin was as smooth as the silk that had covered it. He trailed his fingertips lightly down the ridge of her spine.

He smiled as she arched her back, gasping slightly. So she was ticklish. Or very sensitive. Either way, he'd return shortly to investigate further. In the meantime, he wanted to move to other, uncharted territory.

His thumb slid under the front of her dress and traced the curve of her breast. First the underside, then up over the top. Then around the other way. When he tried to part the fabric, he noticed there was a hook at the top of the zipper, holding the bodice in place. He undid it and the front of the dress fell open.

Her breasts were as beautiful as the rest of her. Perfectly sized, perfectly shaped. A tan line from a bikini framed the creamy mounds, which were topped by taut, pink nipples. As tantalizing and mouthwatering as the most decadent dessert.

He dipped his head and circled one bud with his tongue.

The sound of laughter close by was like a plunge into an ice bath, shocking him out of the haze of desire.

Scott straightened. What the hell was he doing? He shouldn't have put Sapphie in such a potentially embarrassing situation. It was his responsibility to protect her from such exposure.

"I'm sorry." Carefully, he drew the dress back over her breasts, covering them. He tried to refasten the hook, but his fingers were too clumsy to manage the fiddly device.

Sapphie pushed his hands aside and neatly slotted the hook into its eye, then pulled up the zipper. The rasp of the slider against the teeth seemed harsh and discordant in the still night air. She then stood and wiggled, to rearrange the dress so that it fell properly into place.

Damn it if that wiggle didn't turn him on. Made him want to mess her up again.

"No harm done." Smoothing her tousled hair, she smiled.

He jammed his hands in his pockets. "I guess we should head inside, to the party." He looked at his shoes and socks. Probably ought to put them on.

Sapphie picked up his jacket and dusted off the

back before handing it to him. "If you insist. Or we could continue what we were doing in a more private setting."

Her steady gaze met his. "I have a room in the hotel. You're welcome to join me there."

OH MY GOD. Sapphie had asked *Scotty Matthews* to her room. She stifled a girlie squeal and tried to look like it was no big deal.

And it wasn't really. He was just a guy. Okay, a gorgeous, sexy—if a little serious—and utterly tempting guy. The thought of loosening him up, making him lose control, sent a shiver of delight through her.

Over the years, she'd slept with richer and more famous men. She'd even had a memorable night with one of her teenage Hollywood crushes. Sadly, it was memorable for the wrong reasons— one of which was particularly small. Her choice of man didn't depend on how famous he was, how much he had in his bank or whether he was on *People* magazine's list of sexy people.

Being in charge of her life meant that she chose who, when and for how long.

Scotty filled the bill very nicely.

Sapphie didn't want the night to end—and she would eliminate the possibility of another interruption. She wanted to investigate the unexpected fire that had erupted between them and see how hot it could burn. Given what he'd done to her with his kisses—holy moly, his mouth was lethal—she had no doubts they could shatter a thermometer. As for his touch, the man was as talented with his hands off the ice as he was on. Her skin still tingled from his caresses.

But still…this was Scotty Matthews.

She'd never been in such a dizzy whirl about a man.

Sapphie became uncomfortably aware of the silence. Scotty hadn't responded to her offer. He hadn't even blinked. The way he was looking at her made her nervous.

Had she misunderstood the signals? No. He wanted her. He'd been as turned on as she had. She'd felt his erection pressing against her. The slight tremble in his heated touch. Tasted the passion in his kiss.

Maybe a kiss was as far as he'd wanted to go. Was it too soon after his divorce?

"Won't we be missed?" His gravelly words cut through the maelstrom of her thoughts.

"Possibly." Her uncertainty made it sound like a question.

He cleared his throat. "You're Issy's bridesmaid."

Did that mean he wanted to leave with her or not? His even tone gave her no clues.

If she were at work, she'd cut to the chase. "What do you want to do?"

"I'll be honest—this is something different for

me." He scrubbed a hand across his jaw. "Being with someone new. Wanting to be with that person. I'm out of touch with dating etiquette, if I ever knew what it was. I married my high-school sweetheart."

His apprehension touched her and calmed her jumbled thoughts. He was so strong and steady and solid she hadn't appreciated that ending his longtime marriage would affect him at such a basic level. She was amazed he hadn't turned tail and fled at her offer.

She zeroed in on the key phrase in his admission. It wasn't that he didn't want to; he did but didn't know how to go about it.

"As I see it, we have several possible courses of action. One, we go back to the reception and wait for people to start leaving before disappearing upstairs. That way no one will notice our exit. Two—" she enumerated the options on her fingers "—we go inside, say our goodbyes and skip out. Three, we assume everyone has their mind on other things than what we're up to and skip going back altogether."

Scotty frowned, seeming to give it serious thought.

"Would it bother you if we're seen leaving together?" she asked gently.

He shrugged. "We're both unattached adults. What about you?"

"Doesn't worry me at all."

"I don't want to go to the party and waste time with other people that could be spent alone with you."

His slow smile made her stomach drop. "I like the way you think. Very much."

"Decision made. Let's go." He knelt and picked up one of her shoes. He held out the pump.

Delighted by his chivalry, Sapphie balanced herself with a hand on his shoulder, then lifted her foot so he could slip the shoe on. As she repeated the process with her other foot, she wondered how a simple act could make her long for him to trail those magical fingers higher, much higher, up her leg.

Low in her belly, muscles tightened. "Thank you," she said huskily as she straightened.

"My pleasure." He shoved his socks in his pocket, then reached for his wingtips and put them on, stuffing the half-tied laces down the side. Then he held out his hand.

They linked fingers and hurried toward the hotel.

Once inside the door, she steered them to the right. "If we go this way, we can avoid the ballroom. There are elevators at the end that go to the guest floors."

Though it wasn't late, the corridor was deserted and the elevator came quickly. Unfortunately, the car didn't stay empty as it rose to the first floor. People crowded in, pushing Sapphie and Scotty to the back corner. They moved closer together as more people tried to squeeze into the already-packed car, until Scotty put his arm around her shoulders and tucked her into his side.

The man was a gentleman. Although the way he caressed her shoulder with one fingertip did wicked things to her insides.

She slipped her arm around his waist under his jacket. Then she dipped her fingers between the belted waistband of his pants and started inching the shirt free so she could play with his bare skin.

"We're still in public," he murmured against her ear before nipping the lobe.

Sapphie covered her sigh with a cough. "Damn it."

They didn't move apart as the elevator made its way upward and gradually emptied. The journey seemed to go quickly and yet too slowly. Anticipation filled Sapphie as the top floor was announced and the doors swished open.

Scotty's grip on her shoulder tightened fractionally before he released her. They walked side by side along the plush carpeting without speaking.

Sapphie was unusually nervous. She sensed if she said the wrong thing, she might spook Scotty, even though he'd made it clear that he was as desperate as she was to get behind the closed door and finally be able to explore this crazy attraction between them in private.

Outside her room, she pulled her key card out

of her little blue clutch and held it against the lock until it clicked. As she stepped into the dimly lit room, her nerves vanished.

She was in her domain. Somehow that gave her the feeling of control that she'd been lacking since she'd stepped onto the dance floor with Scotty. She took out her phone and, ignoring the texts and missed calls, switched it to silent, then put it and her clutch on the desk.

Turning to face Scotty, she found him standing in front of her. He'd discarded his jacket—hanging it over a chair—and removed his cuff links, so his sleeves hung open, revealing muscled forearms. There was something incredibly sexy about this man, slightly disheveled in his formal wear.

He trailed a finger along her shoulder, over the ridge of her collarbone, to the hollow at the base of her neck. There, he let his fingertip rest momentarily against her skittering pulse before heading unerringly downward to the valley between her breasts. Then he hooked the neckline of her dress and drew her toward him.

She lifted her arms to his shoulders, then wound them around his neck. His arms pulled her against his body so they were plastered together from chest to toe.

Their mouths met, hot and urgent. The time for playing and flirting and teasing was done.

And there were too many clothes. Sapphie wanted to feel him skin to skin.

She went to work on his shirt, tugging it out of his pants before quickly undoing his buttons. Her palms tingled as she slid them over the hard planes of his chest to his shoulders so she could remove the shirt. She then tossed it behind her and focused on exploring his chest more fully.

Scotty kept himself in great shape even though he was no longer playing. Smooth, tanned skin, with a sprinkling of crisp dark hair, covered well-defined muscles. Not an ounce of fat on his impressive six-pack. In fact, the only thing marring his upper body was a long-healed white scar across the line of his collarbone, where he'd had surgery to repair a broken clavicle early in his playing career.

Sapphie put her lips to the scar, then kissed her way along it to the middle of his chest, then headed down to his flat stomach. As her fingers busied themselves with his belt buckle, her tongue traced the ridges of that six-pack, taking a roundabout path to his belly button. And lower still.

Scotty moaned, then tunneled his fingers through her hair, halting her progress. "My turn. Please."

"Always the gentleman." She pressed an open-mouthed kiss to the bare skin just above his open belt, then slowly straightened. She held out her hands, palms up. "I'm all yours."

In two simple moves, her unhooked, unzipped

dress slid down her legs to form a puddle of silk on the floor.

She stepped out of the dress and stood before him naked, except for her turquoise lace panties and her shoes.

Scotty stared, mesmerized, for several seconds. "You are stunning," he said softly, fervently.

"Why, thank you." She bobbed a curtsy.

His gaze traveled admiringly over her body, making her glad she'd kept up her exercise routine despite her crazy work schedule. Then all thoughts of treadmills and weights flew out of her head as his gaze settled on her breasts. She felt the heat of his look almost as clearly as if he'd touched her.

Yearning tugged at her chest. She wanted his touch. Badly. Now.

"You don't just have to look, you know."

His smile made her stomach flip. "Patience. We have all night."

She reached out to gently scrape her fingernail down the middle of his chest. "Ah, but I can't wait all night for my turn to play again." She deliberately let her finger wander below his waistband, where his erection strained against the black fabric. "I don't think you want me to either."

His short laugh sounded a tad strained. "Stop that or this will be over before it's started."

"O-kay." She shrugged but removed her hand.

He ran his finger over her bottom lip, then

leaned forward and nipped it. "It'll be worth the wait."

"Bold words, Captain Matthews."

"Ex-captain. Still, you know you can always trust promises made by the captain."

She bit back a moan as he mimicked her action and trailed a finger over her chin, down her neck and into the valley between her breasts. His mouth followed, then circled the swell of her right breast. His hands, meanwhile, skimmed over her sides to her hips, then settled on her bottom.

"This isn't one of those 'win guarantees,' like Messier in '94, is it?"

"Much as I hate to be compared to the Rangers' former captain, he delivered. So will I."

The matter-of-fact statement, uttered in that smooth, deep voice, heightened the anticipation. "Feel free to continue."

Her airy words ended with a gasp as he took her nipple into his mouth.

The seriousness and single-minded focus that had both drawn her to him and intimidated her were a major plus when he used them to turn her on. As he continued to stroke and taste every inch of her, she swore she could hear the "Hallelujah Chorus" building to a crescendo.

Before her legs could give out, he swept her into his arms and deposited her on the bed. He removed her shoes, then began to trace a path up her legs, starting with her toes. He quickly found and then lingered over her more sensitive spots—the back of her knees, the inside of her thighs and the lower curve of her backside. Then he reached the most sensitive place of all.

He'd barely begun to give that delicate bud attention when her first orgasm rippled through her. He paused until the tremors had subsided, then continued to play with her until he'd made her come apart a second time. Then he propped himself up on one elbow and gently caressed her as she recovered.

Totally spent, she looked up at him. "You were right. It was worth the wait."

His smile spoke volumes. "We're not done yet."

That cocky grin reenergized her. "We certainly aren't." She rose and pushed him onto his back. "And you have too many clothes on."

Sapphie made quick work of removing his pants and his boxer shorts. Then she gave him a taste of his own medicine, using her fingers and mouth to explore every inch of his amazing body. Whenever he tried to intervene, she batted his hand away and carried on with her sensual journey to its tantalizing destination: his straining erection.

Knowing she had him on the brink, she straddled him and sank slowly onto his hard shaft until he was buried deep inside her. She savored the way he fit her perfectly. Filled her completely.

His guttural moan resonated within her, rekindling the burning need she'd thought he'd sated. Suddenly, the time for playing was past.

Urgency overtook them. They moved together in perfect harmony, their bodies as attuned to each other as they'd been on the dance floor. Slowly at first, then with gathering speed, they raced toward completion. Harder, faster. Until, as one, they reached the crest and flew over the edge.

CHAPTER THREE

SCOTT AWOKE TO bright sunshine, the smell of coffee and the clacking of computer keys. He ran his hand over the sheet beside him.

Cold.

The bed had been empty for a while. He squinted at the clock and almost did a double take. He never slept this late. Then again, given how little actual sleeping he'd done over the past thirty-six hours, it wasn't really surprising.

What an incredible weekend. He and Sapphie had barely left the bed, except to sit on the balcony in the moonlight, sipping champagne and nibbling on snacks. And each other. They'd ordered room service whenever they'd needed sustenance, creating impromptu picnics, which had invariably ended with them burning off the calories they'd just eaten.

Scott grinned and rolled onto his back, propped himself on a pillow that still smelled of Sapphie and laced his fingers behind his head.

Their lovemaking had been out of this world. He'd never responded to a woman as he had to her. For the first time in a long while he felt alive and invigorated. Optimistic. Ready to take on the world.

For a moment, he was a little embarrassed. He was in his forties, with grown kids, not fourteen and sweaty palmed because the prettiest girl in the class had said hello to him.

He'd spent a lot of time since Sapphie approached him at the reception aware of his age and relative inexperience, conscious that he was finally getting around to doing things most people did when they were kids. Was he a cliché—lusting over a woman ten years younger than him?

Nah. He'd already had the fast car and he wasn't into ear piercing or low-slung jeans that showed his underwear. If this was his midlife crisis, so what? His life had been turned completely upside down since he'd retired. Why shouldn't he enjoy himself? More to the point, why shouldn't he enjoy himself with Sapphie? They were both adults who were free and single.

Scott smiled indulgently when he saw her on the balcony, seated at the little round table, tapping away intently at her laptop. One foot was tucked under her. She seemed to be speaking with someone via her Bluetooth earpiece.

Her long blond hair was wet. He wished she'd woken him up so they could have shared the shower, like they had yesterday. Man, was he glad he'd retained his strength and stamina.

Sapphie wore a white short-sleeved blouse and

tailored navy shorts, instead of the hotel's robes that they'd lived in since entering her room.

A tiny chill whispered down the back of his neck.

He propped himself up on one elbow and looked around the room. The chill spread to his chest. The remnants of their late-night snacks had been cleared away. The candles they'd ordered from housekeeping tossed in the trash. The closet was empty and the surfaces clear. Her suitcase was packed. The dress was in a dry cleaner's bag and draped over the case.

Other than the fact that he was lying in a rumpled bed, there was no sign of how they'd spent the weekend.

A memory of Celine, greeting him after his first commentating gig, her packed bags by the door, flashed through his mind.

He was about to toss the sheet aside and go to her, strangely needing the reassurance of touching her, when the door to the balcony slid open and Sapphie walked in, carrying her mug.

"Hey, sleepyhead." She put her mug next to the coffeemaker, then approached and leaned over to kiss him. She tasted of coffee, with a hint of mint.

When she would have straightened, he caught her around the waist and tumbled her to the bed. "How about a proper good morning?"

Sapphie laughed and twined her arms around his neck. "Good morning."

All too soon, she pulled out of his embrace and walked to the coffeemaker. "Would you like one?" She held up a mug.

"Sure. Thanks."

"I held off ordering breakfast until you were awake. Are you hungry?"

"Starving." He scraped his hand over his stubbled jaw. "I guess I should get cleaned up and put some clothes on."

"I'll call room service and breakfast should be here when you're done."

Scott hid a frown. Their previously easy conversation had suddenly grown stilted. Awkward.

"Great." He threw back the covers and grabbed a robe. He padded to the bathroom, mug in hand. Before he was halfway there, Sapphie's phone rang. With an apologetic smile, she answered the call and headed back out to her laptop.

The bathroom looked bare without her toiletries. Nothing personal remained. Talk about a reality check.

He understood she was an independent woman, with a successful business that was incredibly demanding. Efficiency and organization would be critical. He got that she needed to get her head in the game after a break; he'd always been the same. And he appreciated the lack of fuss. He'd seen enough of clinging women from being around his single teammates.

But he'd expected...more. Some recognition that

what they'd shared wasn't just another wedding-reception hookup. Not that it had meant everything, but that it had at least meant something.

Scott toweled off and, because he didn't have an alternative, dressed in his formal pants and white shirt. It felt weird to be wearing clothes again. He shook his head. Man, he had to get his brain in gear.

Sapphie was still on the phone when he came out of the bathroom. Breakfast was laid out on the table on the balcony. Her laptop was on the desk inside and she was typing quickly.

"All right, Marty. I've rearranged my other meeting. I've checked flights and I can be in LA late tonight, to see you tomorrow morning. I'll do a quick turnaround in Chicago. But I'll need to head there for Wednesday." She laughed. "Just remember my angelic status when it comes to my next contract."

She ended the call, then closed her laptop and slipped it into her briefcase.

The chill was back. "Sounds like you have a busy time ahead."

Sapphie looked up at him, grimacing. "I'm sorry. I have to catch an earlier flight. Which means skipping out on breakfast." As she spoke, she put her dress in the suitcase and zipped the bag closed. "I have the room until early afternoon, so you can stay and eat."

Damn. Not how he'd expected their time to-gether to end. "I should head home myself."

She went to lift her case from the luggage stand, but he did it for her and set the bag by the door.

"Thanks." Sapphie slung her purse over her shoulder, put her briefcase on top of her suitcase, then checked her watch. "It's been a lovely week-end. I hate to rush off, but you know how it goes."

"Yeah." His tone was more reasonable than he felt, but he couldn't match her smile. "Slow down." He put his arm around her waist and pulled her to him. "Have a safe trip and a successful meeting. I'll see you when you return to Jersey."

He went to kiss her, but she pecked him on the lips, then disentangled herself. Alarm bells started to ring.

"I'm not sure when I'll be back," she said airily. "It all depends on what my client's important news is and how it affects me. Certainly my plans over the next few weeks don't involve anything here."

That definitely sounded like a brush-off. How was that possible after what they'd shared and done?

Obviously, she hadn't found the experience as special as he had. Embarrassment twisted his stomach.

"Okay," he said carefully. He felt like he was tiptoeing through a minefield.

"I can let you know when I'm next around, if you'd like. We could grab a drink or have dinner."

She picked up her cell. "Do I have your contact details?"

"Would you like them?" he said coolly.

"Sure."

Her half shrug irritated him. He snapped out his cell number, like a soldier giving his serial number to an enemy interrogator.

She tapped it into her phone, then looked up at him, frowning. "Is there a problem?"

Scott tamped down his frustration. "I thought you enjoyed this weekend."

"I did. It was wonderful. You were unbelievable."

"Then why the brush-off?"

"Uh, I'm not sure what you mean." She looked confused. "I'm busy for the next month and will be traveling a lot. This is me. This is what I do. What did you expect?"

"A little more enthusiasm for seeing me again." Crap. He sounded like a whiny adolescent. "I thought we had something more than a roll in the hay."

Her eyes widened. "Trust me, you wouldn't have lasted more than a few hours if it hadn't been exceptional. I never allow men to stay the night, let alone a whole weekend."

He threw up his arms in frustration. He was clearly missing something. "Then what's with the 'so long and don't let the door hit your backside on your way out' attitude?"

"Instead of what—a teary goodbye? We're not 'going steady.'"

Her use of air quotes really chapped his ass. "No, but I didn't expect to be treated like a gigolo either."

"I didn't leave a tip on the bedside table."

"Good to know I'm a cheap date." He took some bills out of his pocket and laid them on her case. "My share of the room-service tab."

"Don't be ridiculous." She gathered the money and held it out to him.

He arched an eyebrow at her. "Just want to be sure you got your money's worth."

Sapphie tossed the money on the bed and sighed. "I don't know how this got out of hand," she said quietly. "I didn't mean to offend you by being honest about the future. I'm sorry if you thought otherwise, but at no point did I suggest this was anything more than a fun time shared by two consenting adults."

Her earnest apology made him feel like a petulant jerk.

She continued, "Aside from the fact that I don't have the working life to date anyone seriously, I'm not interested in a relationship or getting married. I don't have to answer to anyone and I do as I please, without feeling guilty."

"I'm sorry, too. I didn't mean to be a jackass. I don't know why I'm ticked. I'm not looking for a steady relationship right now either." He gave her a chagrined smile. "I told you I didn't know the etiquette for sleeping with someone these days. I guess I expected…more than this." He waved a hand to encompass the room.

Sapphie touched his arm. "You're a great guy and *this* was fabulous. But that doesn't change a thing. I'd be happy to see you when I'm in town. But if you can't go with the flow and accept how it will be, then there's no point in us getting together again."

He wanted to tell her he could handle things this way—especially for another weekend like the one they'd just spent. But he'd be lying to himself, as well as her. He might not know what he wanted from dating, or whatever the hell this situation was called, but he knew he wanted to be more than an itch to be scratched whenever she was in town. However much fun that might be.

Still, he hesitated. Maybe over time he could convince her to change her mind.

No. He cut off that idea ruthlessly. He wouldn't make the mistake of being led into something he didn't want because of great sex again. Better to make a clean break. Pull off the bandage and take the hit.

Scott shoved his fingers through his hair. "Then I guess this is goodbye."

Disappointment flashed in her blue eyes, making him want to snatch back his words. But he held firm.

She nodded once. "Your breakfast will be getting cold."

"Can't let good food go to waste." He leaned down and pressed a hot, hard kiss to her lips, stealing one last taste. Then he turned and sauntered to the balcony. "Safe travels."

He lifted one of the covers and breathed in the smell of bacon, hoping to replace her scent, which lingered in his nostrils. It didn't work.

"Thanks. Good luck, Scotty."

He didn't watch her leave, choosing instead to focus on pouring maple syrup on a stack of pancakes.

When the door snicked shut, he set down the bottle and slumped onto a chair.

Scott sat for a long time, wondering how something so wonderful had gone so wrong. When he finally shook off the introspective mood, his stomach turned at the sight of the congealing breakfast. Like the arena horn sounding the end of a game, it signaled the end of the weekend.

Time to move on. Tomorrow was another day… and all the other crap he'd cited to himself after tough losses.

He rose, grabbed his jacket and, with one final look around the room, strode out the door.

"So who was the lucky guy and did you have a fabulous time?"

Sapphie hesitated before answering Issy's question. She wasn't sure what to say about the weekend with Scotty—especially the awkward, unsatisfactory way it had ended—and she knew her best friend wouldn't settle for anything glib.

Thankfully, the waitress in the airline's first-class lounge stopped to ask if Sapphie would like anything to eat.

"Hold on a sec, Issy." She smiled at the waitress. "I'd love a club sandwich and a glass of Pinot Grigio. Thank you." She returned to the phone conversation. "Sorry, but I've been on the go since Marty called this morning and this is the first chance I've had to eat something other than an in-flight packet of pretzels."

"No wonder you stay slim," Issy said. "I'd have gnawed the seat in front of me."

"Trust me, you wouldn't have if you'd seen the man in that seat. He was the epitome of an aging lothario, from his coiffed hair to his shiny suit and patent shoes, with lifts. Not to mention the eye-watering cologne."

"Eww. Even your description of him is enough to put me off my food."

Sapphie laughed. "This life isn't as glamorous as you think."

"You sat a couple of seats away from Aidan Turner last month."

"And he was very charming."

"Speaking of charming, you never said who

whisked you away from the reception. I know it wasn't Taylor. He left early, too, but he was alone."

"What happened? He sent a text saying the night was a disaster, but I haven't had the chance to catch up with him." After arriving from New Jersey, she'd rushed to her apartment in Chicago to switch suitcases before heading back to O'Hare for her flight to LA.

"From what I understand, there was some macho male posturing between Taylor and Lizzie's date, which turned into shoving. One of them knocked into a waiter carrying a tray of drinks—which the date ended up wearing."

Sapphie winced. "Poor Mad Dog." That hadn't worked out quite as he'd planned.

"Lizzie was embarrassed and gave him a piece of her mind. He stormed out of the party. You missed all the fun. But then, I'm guessing you were having your own fun."

She might as well tell her, before Issy applied the thumbscrews. "I was." Sapphie paused, then said in a rush, "With Scotty Matthews."

There was a moment of stunned silence. "As in the recently retired Ice Cats captain?"

"The very same."

Issy giggled. "If I wasn't a happily married woman, I'd be so jealous. That's even better than your Aidan Turner story. Scotty Matthews is totally and utterly H-O-T."

Sapphie rolled her eyes. "I don't think my goddaughter is old enough to understand *hot*, let alone in that context."

"I'm not so sure. The way she batted her eyelashes at all the Ice Cats at our reception has J.B. threatening to lock her up until she's fifty."

"To protect her from guys like him. Or rather, how he used to be." The hotshot hockey star had been a real ladies' man before he'd fallen in love with Issy. "No wonder he's concerned. She's inherited his charm, as well as his good looks."

"Excuse me. Her good looks came from my side of the family."

"Of course they did."

"Speaking of gorgeous, Scotty has that whole handsome, brooding, hidden-depths thing going on. I bet he's intense in bed."

Desire tugged deep in her belly. "He's very… focused. Single-minded."

"Ooh, that's a delicious thought."

The memory was making Sapphie's body hum with need. She tamped it down, then changed the subject. "Anyway, Marty wants me in LA for a meeting. Apparently, something big is going down. If it's another acquisition, it could result in a major new contract."

"That's great. I'm so proud of you. We'll have to celebrate when you're next in Jersey." Issy paused. "But what aren't you telling me about Scotty?"

Damn it. Sapphie should have known Issy wouldn't let the subject drop so easily. "Nothing."

"Uh-huh. What's the opposite of 'the lady doth protest too much'? You're not normally so close lipped about your dates. Did he turn into a jerk when the weekend was over?"

"Of course not." Sapphie couldn't blame Scotty for how he'd reacted. She'd gone about the good-bye all wrong.

It hadn't been deliberate. She'd been swimming in unfamiliar waters and gotten scared. Instead of being cool, calm and collected, she'd blustered her way through it. And screwed up royally.

It had started going belly-up when she'd awoken, wrapped in Scotty's arms—his body curved around hers, her butt cradled in his groin, their legs entwined and his hand cupping her breast. The heat from his bare skin had seared the length of her body. And she'd loved it. She'd snuggled closer and savored the sensation of being co-cooned with him.

Until she'd panicked. *Because* she'd loved it. Because she hadn't pulled away, as she would normally have done.

Sapphie wasn't a cuddler in bed. Sex was one thing, but sleep required space. Which was why either she left or she asked her partner to. Perhaps her habit was a leftover from sharing a bed with her sister, Emerald, for years until she'd figured out a better situation—a discarded bunk bed that she'd rescued from the side of the road and re-painted. Since leaving home, she'd always had her own space and guarded it ruthlessly. Any invasion of that space was by invitation and never permanent.

The realization that Scotty had made her react differently had set off alarm bells. And the downward spiral had begun. She hated that instead of exiting gracefully, she'd blown it all up.

But she didn't want to explain that to Issy. At least, not right now. "I can't tell you anything more. I'm in an airline lounge, surrounded by business travelers."

"Hmm." Issy clearly wasn't fooled by her excuse. "Tell me one thing—are you okay?"

Sapphie cursed the hesitation before she answered. "I'm fine." She added hurriedly, "Just got a lot on my mind, preparing for tomorrow."

"Are you planning to see each other again?" Concern edged Issy's tone.

"I thought you said *one thing*." Sapphie's light laugh sounded forced.

"It's a clarification."

She sighed. "No. The weekend with Scotty was a one-and-done."

"For both of you?"

Another damn hesitation. "Yes."

"I'm sorry."

"That's the way it goes sometimes." She cleared her throat to mask the sudden tightness. Thankfully, the attendant brought her dinner. "I should go. My food has arrived and I need to eat before they call my flight."

"All right. But you know where I am, if you need to talk."

"Thanks." She couldn't bring herself to say there was nothing to talk about. "Kiss my goddaughter good-night."

Once she'd hung up, Sapphie ate and went over the weekend with Scotty. Even though it was for the best, she couldn't help wishing that their goodbye hadn't been so fraught. So final.

The problem was that they were bound to see each other again. It was almost impossible for their paths not to cross, given their mutual friends and her season ticket for the Ice Cats. It was hard to imagine bumping into him and not being able to spend time with him again. Maybe they could…

Sapphie cut herself off. Scotty had made it clear that he didn't do casual, and she didn't want anything else. So why was she tempted to break her own rules for him?

What was it about Scotty that turned everything upside down for her?

The announcement that her flight was boarding was almost a relief. Sapphie gathered her belongings and headed out of the lounge toward the departure gate at a brisk pace. She was able to get on the plane and into her assigned seat right away.

Though she worked on the flight, during the limo ride to her building and for an hour when she arrived at her apartment, Scotty hovered in the back of her mind. She gave up trying to read documents, because she wasn't able to concentrate enough to take in the information. Instead, she wrote and planned. Presentations, emails, anything to keep her brain active and on task.

Anything she could do without being affected by thoughts of the weekend and Scotty.

Sapphie hoped that exhaustion would lead to a deep, dreamless sleep. No such luck. Steamy, erotic dreams took over the minute her eyes closed. Frustrating dreams that ended with her jolting awake before she reached completion. That left her drenched with sweat, aching with need and desperate for relief. Restless, she tossed and turned until her sheets were a twisted mess.

She was awake before her alarm the following morning and had to press an icy washcloth to her eyes to soothe the puffy results of her disturbed night. After a long, pounding shower, artfully applied makeup and her favorite shoes, she finally felt ready to face the day's meeting. She reviewed the latest status of her projects for Marty Antonelli as she wolfed down juice and toast. By the time she headed out the door, briefcase in hand, to the waiting car, she was almost back to normal.

Which was critical; she had to be at her best for Marty. Not just because he was her biggest client, but because he constantly kept her on her toes. He gave the impression of being a genial, bumbling

Italian, but he was one of the sharpest business-
men she'd ever met.

The upside of rearranging her schedule for this
meeting was that he'd promised this would be
worth her while. Given that her current project
with the NBA team he owned was now in the
implementation stages and required less of her
oversight, that likely meant a new project for one
of his other businesses.

She wondered which one he wanted her to look
at next. His baseball team? His NASCAR team?
His movie complexes? All would be interesting
challenges. It was a shame he didn't own a hockey
franchise. Now *that*, she really would enjoy.

Arriving at the Antonelli headquarters, she
strode through the lobby toward the elevators,
greeting the security guards. On the executive
floor the receptionist told her that the meeting
was in the boardroom and gave her a heads-up
that it was a full house.

"Any clues as to what's going on, Sally?"

The elegant redhead shook her head but said in
a lowered voice, "The lawyers were here working with Mr. Antonelli over the weekend. Jenna
was also here, but you know she'd cut out her own
tongue before saying anything."

Marty's secretary was notoriously protective
of her boss's business.

Sally continued, "I've been asked to get A-1
fueled and ready for Thursday. The flight plan

is for Teterboro, via Chicago to pick you up. Mr. Antonelli wants the whole team to arrive on the corporate jet."

"I wonder why he's flying to New Jersey when he was in New York a week ago."

"I guess all will be revealed shortly." Sally smiled. "I got some of your favorite pastries, so don't let the vultures in the boardroom grab them all."

"Thank you." Sapphie waggled her fingers. "I'll catch up with you later."

Entering the packed boardroom, she noted that all the department directors were seated alongside the legal team. There was definitely about to be a major announcement. Excitement bubbled through her.

Marty bounded over, his dark eyes alight with excitement. "Ah, good, you're here, Bella Sapphire. Before I forget, Gloria said to tell you that you're to come to dinner tonight. No excuses or I'll be in big trouble."

Sapphie smiled. He might act as if Gloria was a scary harridan, but Sapphie knew better. His sweet, diminutive wife adored him. And while he might be a ruthless Rottweiler in business, Marty was like a spaniel puppy when it came to Gloria. "I wouldn't want you to get into trouble. Besides, it'll be lovely to see her again and catch up."

"Excellent. I'll let her know. Now, grab a coffee and we can get started."

She'd barely settled in her chair, midway down the long mahogany table, when Marty took center stage in front of the enormous plasma screen showing his corporate logo. The room quieted instantly.

Rocking on his feet, he brought up his first slide. "We've had a successful year. Our current portfolio is strong, profitable and growing ahead of market projections. It would have been nice to have done better in the NBA play-offs, but we made it to the party for the first time in five years."

Around the table, everyone smiled and nodded. As Marty went on to praise the management team, highlighting the roles key departments had played—which included a generous acknowledgment of Sapphie's work—a sense of anticipation built.

He didn't keep them in suspense too long. "I'm not one to rest on my laurels and I'm always seeking new opportunities. I like to acquire businesses where I see great synergy, as well as potential for growth and improved profitability. I also kinda like sports."

Everyone laughed on cue; Marty's desire to own a full complement of sports franchises—major and minor—was well-known.

"So, I'm pleased to tell you that on Friday we will be in New Jersey announcing to the media that I have bought the Ice Cats. Ladies and gentlemen, we have ourselves a hockey team. And not just any team, but the current Stanley Cup champions." Marty rubbed his hands together. "This is going to be fun."

There was a moment of shocked silence as the news sank in. Then the room erupted with applause and chatter.

Sapphie was stunned. Although he'd asked her to assess the viability of owning one of the NHL's expansion teams versus acquiring an existing franchise, the Ice Cats hadn't been mentioned—other than as a pipe dream. Marty had grown up supporting the Ice Cats, but as far as she'd known, they weren't for sale.

Sure, there had been rumors of the Scartelli brothers' financial trouble following some unwise investments, but they'd always managed to brush the speculation aside. Obviously, their most recent highly publicized refinancing deal wasn't as sound as they'd led everyone to believe.

Marty waved his hands, silencing the room. "I'm glad you're as enthusiastic about this new venture as I am, but we have a lot to do before we leave on Thursday. So let's get down to the nuts and bolts."

For the next couple hours, he and his vice president of business development took them through the acquisition. What soon became clear was that although the franchise was highly successful on the ice, it wasn't making nearly enough money.

Its profitability had declined considerably during the Scartellis' ownership, driven largely by the brothers' whims. Splashy promotional initiatives with poor returns, which at the time Sapphie, as a fan, had thought were unwise, had left the business in a weak financial condition.

The Scartelli brothers, realizing they were in trouble and unwilling to let the National Hockey League take over the team, had approached Marty, who'd been only too willing to buy his favorite team—for a knockdown price, naturally.

When they finally broke for lunch, Sapphie approached Marty. "Congratulations. That's one heck of a move."

"I told you this would be worth rearranging your schedule." Marty grinned. "I want you to be my right-hand woman with the Ice Cats. Given what you've helped me achieve with my basketball team, I know you can do the same with this team. And you'll be happier advising me on a sport you like, yes?"

"Of course. But I warn you, I'll be adding a pair of season tickets to the terms and conditions of the new contract, and they won't be in the nosebleeds."

He laughed. "Taken as read. Now eat. We have a long afternoon ahead of us. I want as much out of you as I can get before you have to head to Chicago."

"Yes, boss." She gave him a smart salute, then

headed over to the trays of food on the mahogany credenzas.

As she filled her plate, Sapphie's mind whirred with all that she'd have to do. Not least, alert her team, in the Chicago office, that they were about to get doubly busy. In fact, she should look into hiring more staff. She could afford the added expense because this new contract would cement her business's success.

Looked like she'd be spending more time in New Jersey after all. That would be great for seeing Issy and Sophia. And, of course, watching games.

She'd just bitten into a sandwich when it occurred to her that it also increased the possibility of seeing Scotty again. Sapphie chewed determinedly, even though she might have been eating one of the handouts for all that she could taste the food. She swallowed hard, then drained a small bottle of water.

What was she worried about? Scotty wasn't with the team any longer. Not that she'd deal with the players on a daily basis anyway, but she always believed in talking to the whole organization as part of her evaluation process. Besides, although it was inevitable that she'd run into him, it wouldn't be on this initial trip or even for a while.

She'd cross that bridge when she came to it.

"DRUMMER FOR A BAND?" Scott stopped lacing his skate and took his cell from where he'd lodged it between his ear and his shoulder. "Maybe I should come and check this new boyfriend out."

He was only half teasing. He didn't like the thought of some long-haired, drugged-out musician putting his hands on Angela.

"Da-ad." His daughter gave a loud, put-upon sigh. "I'm twenty-one and can take care of myself. I don't need you vetting my dates anymore."

"Maybe not, but it wouldn't hurt for Sean to know what will happen to him if he doesn't treat you right."

"I'll give him a taste of the business end of your hockey stick, like you showed me."

Scott grinned. "That's my girl."

"Got to go, or I'll be late for class. Love you."

"Love you, too. And if you see your brother, tell him the occasional text would be good so that I know he's okay."

"Will do." Angela laughed, then hung up.

Scott tossed his cell into his bag, then tightened his laces and tied them off. He grabbed his stick, then headed out of the locker room. Three of his friends who still played for the Cats would be joining him shortly for a prearranged practice, but he enjoyed this time with the rink to himself.

Relishing the crisp air and the fresh ice beneath his blades, Scott began to warm up by skating laps. He picked up speed and switched directions, doing crossovers forward and backward in time to the pounding rock beat blaring from the speakers. Then he switched to sprints between the blue lines.

"Looking good, old man," Rick "Ice Man" Kasanski called as he stepped out of the penalty box carrying a bucket of pucks. "Having your butt planted in a commentator's chair all season hasn't dulled your skills much."

Scott stopped sharply, sending a spray of ice over his friend. "I can still skate your candy ass into the ground, Ice Man."

"Please. You've never been faster than me." Kasanski brushed aside Scott's comment with a wave of his gloved hand. "At least, not going forward. I'll admit you might have the edge going backward, D-man."

"You can take that to the bank. It's all the racing to protect the net when you cocky forwards cough up the puck."

Ice Man swiped his stick at Scott's legs, trying to hook his skates from under him, but Scott managed to avoid him. He gave a colorful analysis of Kasanski's parentage in reply.

"Come on, ladies." Chance Rivera joined them, lining up water bottles on the dasher boards. "Put those handbags away."

"Yeah. We have work to do." The Cats' backup goaltender, Chaz "Monty" Montgomery, skated up, trailing a practice net behind him. "Chance and I have a small wager on how many he can get past me. He's buying me lunch when we're done."

Rivera snorted. "Have your wallet ready, Net-Boy. I've got moves that'll earn me a steak with all the works."

Monty pulled on his mask. "Winning at back-yard hockey with your toddler twins doesn't mean you can beat the master of the twine."

"Behold, the Master of the Twine," Scott in-toned in a Hollywood-trailer voice. "Fends off pucks with his mighty twig."

"More like the Knave of the Basket. Because of the biscuits he collects in there." Kasanski cracked up at his own joke. He only laughed harder when Monty flipped him the bird and told him where he could stick those biscuits.

Before anyone could drop the gloves, Scott cor-ralled his friends and got them skating warm-up drills.

After a decent workout, which had them all pretty gassed, they headed to the locker room. As they showered and dressed, Chance and Monty continued their debate about whether the goalten-der would still have won their contest if they hadn't been chased off the rink by a figure-skating class. Naturally, Kasanski did his best to wind up both sides, while Scott declared himself Switzerland.

Scott was zipping up his sports bag when his cell chirped with a missed call. Picking it up, he was surprised to see the name of his former gen-eral manager.

He looked at his friends. "Any reason Callum Hardshaw would be calling me?"

Kasanski shook his head. "Not that I can think of."

Rivera shrugged. "Maybe he wants to offer you a job."

"He knows I don't want to coach." Though even that would be better than sitting on his ass at home, doing nothing.

"What about scouting?" Monty offered.

"Definitely not. I'm done with traveling the whole time. Scouting would be worse. Heading to all those junior and college teams to check out prospects—I'd never be home."

"Team ambassador?" Chance pulled on a black T-shirt with the team's snow-leopard logo. "You know, schmooze the sponsors and the season-ticket holders at Ice Cats events."

"Not my scene either." A job where he had to spend his time making small talk? No way.

"I bet Hardshaw wants you for some PR stuff," Ice Man said, combing his wet dark hair. "Some fancy, high-dollar-a-plate dinner where you're the big-bucks draw."

"Why would the GM call me for that? Usually I hear from the marketing guy when they want my face or name."

"Didn't he move on?" Monty frowned. "To that soccer team, the Bridgers. He got pissed about the way the Scartellis kept nixing his proposals while spending crazy amounts of money on weird promotions the fans hated."

"There were changes in the front office over the summer," Scott said. "But I thought it was because of budget cuts. Either way, it's a shame. The kid was pretty switched on."

"If you ask me, those kinds of people—advertising, marketing, PR—are a dime a dozen," Rivera said.

"None of which tells me why Hardshaw called." Scott tapped his cell against his chin.

"You could do the obvious thing and phone him back."

He cuffed the back of Kasanski's head. "I know that, numbnuts." He hit Call Back.

Hardshaw answered on the first ring. "Hey, Scotty, how's it going?"

"Not bad. You?"

"Yeah, good. Busy. You know how it is."

He didn't but played along. "For sure. So, what can I do for you?"

"Any chance you could stop by sometime today? I have a couple ideas I'd like to bounce off you."

Scott tried to read the GM's voice but couldn't. "I have an hour this afternoon, at three, if that works for you." He had the whole freaking afternoon free, but he wasn't about to let Hardshaw know that.

"Great. See you then."

Once he'd hung up, Scott turned to his friends. "He wants to see me." He relayed the brief conversation. "I've got nothing to lose by hearing what he has to say. It's not like I have anything else on the horizon."

Monty clapped him on the shoulder. "They say the second year of retirement is the hardest. When reality sets in. If you can get through that, you'll be fine."

"Thanks for that."

"Good thing you have us around to keep you from turning into an old man—pipe and slippers and reading the paper by the fire." Kasanski smacked Scott's stomach with the back of his hand. "We'll keep you from getting fat and flabby, too."

Scott slung his bag over his shoulder. "Look who's talking, Ice Man. You were puffing like a steam train in those last sprints. Too much fun in the sun over the summer?"

"Too much junk food and too many margaritas in Cancún," Rivera said. "With that and J.B.'s wedding bash on the weekend, I don't think Kasanski has stopped partying since we raised the Cup."

"Like you're any better," Ice Man scoffed. "None of us are."

"You forget, I have the twins to keep me on my toes. Running around after them is a full-time job." Chance's wife had suffered badly from postpartum depression and walked out on him and their babies eighteen months ago. "Especially now they're walking, talking and into everything. It's the terrible twos times two."

"No joy finding another nanny?"

"The agency sent a woman who seems to be working out okay. Still, I want to spend as much time with them as I can. Especially in the off-season."

The three friends understood how hard it had been for Chance. They'd stood by him and seen him through the worst of it.

Always the smart-ass, Kasanski lightened the tone as they walked out of the rink. "Whatever you say, you were puffing as much as me, Net-Boy and the old guy here, Rivera."

"In your dreams, Ice Cube."

"You wish you had my dreams." Kasanski grinned. "Anyway, the hard work starts now and I'll be in prime condition for training camp. If only it didn't take so much longer to get in shape than it did when we were in our twenties."

"Amen to that," Scott said fervently. "That's why I had to hang 'em up in the end."

"Gone are the days when players used to have a drink and a smoke between periods," Monty said sadly, even though he was too young to remember that.

"The speed some of the old guys skated at, you could have a drink and a smoke between plays,"

Ice Man added, tossing his bag into the back of his SUV. "Now we have to watch calories and monitor food intake like Miss freaking America."

"Which brings us to lunch. Good thing, because I'm starving." Monty opened his car door. "Usual place?"

The four men agreed and headed off to the local bistro they'd been frequenting for many years. After lunch they agreed to meet up again the following day at the gym and then went their separate ways.

Scott drove to the Cats' head office. Though he was a little early, Hardshaw's assistant took him straight to the GM's office.

"Can I get you a drink, Scotty?" Doreen asked.

"Ice water would be great, thanks."

"Make that two, please." Callum came around his desk to shake Scott's hand. "Thanks for stopping by."

"Your call intrigued me." Scott took the seat his former GM indicated, while Callum leaned against the front of his desk.

"These are interesting times for the Cats. People outside the business don't understand that the summer after winning the Cup is actually more difficult than one when you've lost it. Riding high on the win creates its own set of problems."

Scott nodded. "I know you have some tough decisions to make, especially with the salary cap not going up as much as it has in the past." Plus he'd heard the rumors about the Scartellis' financial problems.

"Right. We have some big contracts up for renewal over the next twelve to twenty-four months. We also need to think about how to leverage our success into future strength. It's hard to repeat a Cup win the following year, no matter how much we want to."

It was true. Since the powerhouse teams of the '70s and '80s, few teams had managed back-to-back Cup wins.

"I want the Cats to be positioned to win in alternate years like Chicago and LA have done. But as an organization, we need to make sure we're delivering for our fans, our sponsors and our owners, too."

"For sure." Scott still wasn't sure where this was leading. "Having retired, I'm far enough removed to get that this is a business and the team's performance on the ice is only one aspect—albeit the most important one—of how success is measured."

"Exactly." Hardshaw snapped his fingers. "I knew you'd see the bigger picture."

"So, what can I do for you?"

"I understand that the commentating gig isn't working out for you."

"Yeah."

"Frankly, that was a waste of your skills. There are plenty of other guys who can do the talking-heads thing."

"That was the network's view, too." Scott made a dismissive gesture. "Can't say I'll miss it."

"Their loss is my gain, I hope."

"In what way?"

"I'm looking for a new right-hand man. One who can complement my strengths and weaknesses. Who can bring fresh insights to the organization. Who is close enough to the game to provide a player's perspective but still understand the financial needs of a business. I think you fit that bill perfectly."

Join the team's management? For the first time since he retired, Scott felt a genuine stirring of interest. The sports-bar idea was a bit of fun, but this was something he could get his teeth into. "What about Brendan?"

The current assistant general manager had been with the Cats since Scott was a rookie. He was also the only one left from the previous GM's era. Brendan was a nice-enough guy but, in Scott's opinion, resistant to change and lacking in vision.

Callum crossed his arms. "We both agreed it was time for fresh blood. He'll transition into one of our ambassadors, so he can still be part of the organization and we can tap into his knowledge base whenever we need it. The man has a phenomenal memory of the Cats' history and players."

"That's a good role for him."

"A win-win. So, what do you think? Are you up for a new challenge?"

Although it seemed like an interesting solution, Scott didn't want to leap into the job without knowing more. "I'd definitely like to hear what would be involved."

"I'M GLAD YOU'LL be part of my team. Welcome aboard."

Callum's simple words, when Scott signed his contract two days later, summed up what had really appealed to him. What Scott had missed since he'd retired. Being part of a team. And not just any team, but his beloved Ice Cats.

He'd discussed the job with Andy, his friends and his kids before accepting Callum's offer. Andy had reiterated his view that Scott would do well in a business role. Angela had teased him about finding another position where he could boss people around, and Wayne had thought it was cool that his dad would be in management. Kasanski had put in a bid for a mega-millions mega-year contract, which Scott had treated with the respect it deserved—he'd ignored it.

As for Scott, he was psyched. For the first time in a year, he was eager to get started. "Glad to be here."

Callum wasted no time throwing Scott in the deep end. After a quick introduction to the front-office staff—most of whom Scott knew from his time as a player—and a review of his induction schedule, the pair went through the issues that needed to be dealt with before training camp began.

They were about to break for lunch when Callum's cell rang.

He glanced at the caller ID. "I'm sorry, I have to take this. It's Jim Scartelli."

As Callum exchanged pleasantries with the owner, that familiar chill slithered down Scott's neck. The presentiment worsened when Hardshaw's face paled.

"I see. Thank you for letting me know. Yes, I'll be there." Callum ended the call and stared at his cell for several moments before looking at Scott, his expression a little bleak.

"Is something wrong?" Even though it was obvious, Scott sensed his boss needed prodding to be able to speak.

"The team has been sold. There will be an announcement tomorrow, but the Scartellis wanted to give me a heads-up." Callum swore. "I knew they were considering a sale—I helped with due diligence for potential buyers—but I had no idea things had moved so quickly. I thought we had more time."

"How will that affect us?"

"That's up to our new owner. Mr. Antonelli may want his own people in charge. I'll have my work cut out convincing him I'm the right man for the job."

And if Antonelli didn't want Callum, he

wouldn't want his management team either. "You built the Cats into a Cup-winning team, despite a bargain-basement budget. Our new owner has to respect that."

"I hope so, but the Scartellis' lack of investment has tied my hands with marketing and business development for a long time and it shows. I could be the easy sacrifice." Hardshaw sighed heavily. "Anyway, we'll find out more soon enough. Antonelli and his posse are flying in this evening and they expect to meet us right away." He gave Scott an apologetic look. "Looks like you're going to have a trial by fire."

What could he say? "It's an interesting first day, for sure." Scott shrugged, as if it was no problem to him. But he couldn't shake that sense of foreboding.

CHAPTER FOUR

WITH THE PRECISION of the Secret Service escorting the president, the three limos that had ferried Marty Antonelli's people from Teterboro Airport pulled up outside the Ice Cats headquarters.

Scott smiled when several of the well-dressed men emerging from the cars appeared to wilt as they encountered the notorious New Jersey humidity. He'd take any edge he could get for the upcoming meeting. Not that he expected to play anything but a minor part. Still, he was damned if he'd let them mess with his team.

"They look set for action," he said as Callum joined him by his office window.

"We will be, too. How free are you this weekend?"

"No plans. Why?" Glancing at his boss, Scott was intrigued by his buoyant expression.

"Good." Callum slapped him on the back. "I've decided to be proactive. I figure with all the media hoopla, we have until Monday before Mr. Antonelli gets down to serious business and I plan to use that time wisely. We're meeting with the department heads at my place so we can pull together our vision for how the organization should move forward. I want us to walk into Monday's meeting prepared to knock them on their asses."

"You're talking my language. I've always preferred to take the battle to my opponents."

Scott turned to the window. His smile faded as a pair of gorgeous, tanned legs in beige spiked-heel shoes emerged from the middle limo.

His body reacted instantly, recognizing who the legs belonged to even before Sapphie straightened and his brain caught up.

What's she... The question had barely begun to form before memories of their last morning together flashed and things clicked into place. He remembered the client she'd had to rush away for had been called Marty, but Scott hadn't made the connection with the new owner. Guess he now knew why it had been so urgent.

He couldn't take his eyes off Sapphie as she shrugged a red jacket over her red-and-white dress. She stood out like a colorful flower in the midst of the dark suits of her colleagues. His gaze followed her hungrily as she led the others toward the building, where she disappeared from his sight.

She'd be coming up here. She'd be in all the meetings.

Crap. This wasn't how he'd expected to run into her again. He wasn't ready.

Scott had hardly gotten his mind around that

uncomfortable fact when Callum's assistant informed them that their guests were waiting in Reception.

"Please get the management team to the boardroom. Scott and I will go greet Mr. Antonelli and his people." Callum turned to him. "Ready to face the enemy?"

No wasn't an acceptable response. Especially when driven by purely personal reasons. But Scott had never backed down from a challenge and he wasn't about to start now. Just as he had on so many nights before a clash with a tough opponent, Scott put on his game face. "Always."

"OF COURSE I KNOW our former captain."

Sapphie's smile felt overbright as she shook Scotty's hand. "Nice to see you again."

There—the perfect mix of good manners and enthusiasm. If anyone noticed an edge to her words or the color that crept into her cheeks from the touch of his skin against hers, they'd assume it was fan-girl awkwardness. Not that she was shocked at coming face-to-face with the man with whom she'd spent a glorious weekend burning up the sheets. God, was that really less than a week ago?

They certainly wouldn't see her frustration, that she was so jittery, while Scotty looked calm. But then, he was probably used to dealing with starstruck fans.

"Nice to see you, too." His deep voice sent a tremor through her, reminding her body of the sexy things he'd murmured in her ear.

Despite all the hard work preparing for this trip, she hadn't been able to get Scotty out of her head. If she was honest, she'd admit that she'd hoped they'd bump into each other at some point. At a fund-raiser or a meet and greet. In a few weeks, maybe a month or two.

Not now. Not today.

What was he doing here? Thankfully, before she could find a way to ask without giving herself away, Marty did it for her.

"As nice as it is to meet one of my all-time favorite players, we weren't expecting any media at this meeting."

"Scotty isn't with the network any longer." Callum explained the former captain's new role as AGM. "We're excited to have him."

Her gaze shot up to meet Scotty's.

The serious, steady look in those blue eyes confirmed the news. "This is my first day on the job."

"Excellent." Marty laughed and clapped Scotty on the back. "Smart move. I always thought you were wasted in the booth."

As her boss and the Cats' GM talked about how good it would be to have someone of Scotty's experience, Sapphie managed to clear her throat and force out some words.

"Congratulations. Welcome aboard."

"Thanks." The corner of his mouth quirked. "It's been…interesting, so far."

"For sure." Cursing herself for not being able to come up with a better response, Sapphie dropped her gaze to her jacket and picked off an imaginary thread.

"Shall we head upstairs so you can meet the rest of the team?" Callum suggested, holding the elevator door open.

Sapphie held back, waiting for the second car, thinking Scotty might go with the first group. Unfortunately, he had the same idea and they ended up standing next to each other. Although there was plenty of space between them, she was ridiculously aware of how close he was.

In the boardroom it was easy to move away from Scotty as she was introduced to the other members of the Cats' senior management group. While people took their seats, her stomach tightened as she waited to see where Scotty would end up.

"Sapphire, come and sit beside me." Marty stood at the head of the table and indicated her place at his right hand. He put Callum on his left with Scotty alongside him.

Which meant she and Scotty were practically opposite each other. Wishing she had some papers to fiddle with, she busied herself pouring glasses of sparkling water for those close to her.

Once everyone was seated—Marty's people on

the right, the Ice Cats' on the left—Hardshaw stood. "Welcome, Mr. Antonelli and your team, to New Jersey." He pointed to the painting of the famous hockey trophy on the far wall. "And to the headquarters of the reigning Stanley Cup champions."

Everyone whooped and clapped.

"We look forward to a bright and prosperous future for our organization as part of your group. We—" Callum waved his hand toward the Ice Cats' management "—and all the hardworking people in our departments are committed one hundred percent to giving you our best."

Once the applause had quieted, Marty rose, thanked Callum, then gave his usual spiel, reassuring the people around the table that he wasn't there to do a hatchet job. He emphasized that he was a fan and wanted continued success for the team. "I want the Ice Cats to be a dynasty. Winning the Cup every year is almost impossible, but alternate years would be perfectly acceptable."

Everyone laughed.

Marty grew serious. "I also want my teams to be well run and profitable. We all know, I'm sure, there is plenty of room for improvement on that score."

Nods and murmurs of agreement came from across the table.

"However, I assure you that it will be business as usual until I have a complete picture of what is required for this organization. I'm a great believer in talking to people at all levels and in all departments before making any decisions." He indicated the men and women on his left. "You know the strengths and weaknesses of this business better than anybody. My team has a lot of experience in making businesses perform at the level I want them to. Together, we will fix what doesn't work and, more important, leave alone what does. Together, we will create a winning team in the front office as well as on the ice."

As Marty continued with his speech, Sapphie sneaked a peek at Scotty. Though his body was angled to appear as though he was listening to Marty, his gaze clashed with hers.

For a moment, she was startled to see a flash of heat in his unguarded eyes. Maybe he wasn't as unmoved by their meeting as he seemed. That gave her a boost of confidence, and for the first time since setting foot in the Ice Cats' building, her tension eased. She sent him a half smile before turning her attention to Marty.

"Let's go around the table and introduce ourselves. Then we'll break and head to my club for drinks and dinner so that we can get to know each other. Tomorrow we'll have a press conference and announce the sale to the media. Beginning Monday, we roll up our sleeves and the hard work starts." He paused, then grinned. "Well, it will for you. I'm afraid my attention is required elsewhere.

There are definite perks to being the owner, other than the best seats for a home game."

This time, the laughter had a definite edge. Everyone in the room was aware of how important the coming weeks would be and what was at stake. No matter how jovial and avuncular Marty Antonelli seemed, his reputation preceded him. His standards were exacting. He did not suffer fools or incompetence. His decision, once made, was final.

Marty laid his hand on her shoulder. "You all know who I am, so I'll hand you over to my right-hand gal. Sapphire will keep you on your toes. She certainly keeps me on mine."

Sapphie was conscious of all the eyes on her. Not exactly true. Just one pair of blue eyes. A pair of serious, slightly damning but oh-so-sexy blue eyes.

She licked her dry lips and explained who she was. "Like Marty, I'm a longtime fan." She smiled. "Back-to-back Cups works for me."

Most in the room smiled, too. She wouldn't let the one man who didn't get to her.

"However, I also want the organization to be financially sound." She kept her tone upbeat. "I'm aware that those two objectives can seem at odds. My role is to facilitate and to challenge *all* of you so that you can achieve what is required on both fronts."

It was gratifying to see the positive response to her words. Callum and Scotty remained unmoved, but she was determined to win at least one of them over before she was done.

"Although I'm contracted by Antonelli Holdings, I am independent. I have no hidden agenda and my job is to ensure the Ice Cats continue to run smoothly while profitability improves. The next few months are your chance to have input into the plans for the future. Speak up. Negotiate and fight for what you believe in. I promise to make sure Antonelli Holdings listens."

Callum touched his steepled fingers to his lips and nodded.

She took the small victory, despite the inscrutable expression of the man next to him, and handed the meeting over to Marty's chief financial officer.

As the introductions continued, she kept glancing at Scotty. He listened intently to what everyone had to say but didn't relax. When it was his turn to speak, he kept it short.

"You all know my playing bio. And this Cup ring—" he held up his right hand to show off the knuckle-duster bearing the diamond-encrusted Ice Cats logo "—says everything about my commitment to the team."

Sapphie squeezed her knees together to stop the tingling feeling that his grin induced.

"What you may not know is that I have a business degree, which I intend to put to good use. If I didn't believe in our general manager, I wouldn't have signed up to work with him. Just as I did on the ice, I intend to defend this team and make sure we're a force to be reckoned with."

It sounded like the battle lines had been drawn. As his gaze met hers, she got the feeling the line in the sand was at her feet.

The meeting broke up a short time later. She didn't have another opportunity to interact with Scotty, as Marty wanted to leave. In the limo on the way to their hotel he was busy making phone calls—to his wife, then his personal assistant in LA—so Sapphie was able to think about what had happened and try to figure out how she felt about working with Scotty.

Ordinarily, she didn't face this kind of problem, because she deliberately kept her business and personal lives separate. This time, though, those two had collided in spectacular fashion.

Not quite true, she told herself. There wasn't a personal side to the situation. Nor would there be. She'd made it perfectly clear when she and Scotty had parted on the weekend, and his attitude toward her today said he'd moved on.

She had to admit she was a little disappointed there was no chance of rekindling anything with him—at least not in the foreseeable future.

Perhaps that was a good thing. Given her reaction to him during the meeting, she'd be smart to avoid breaking her self-imposed rule about relationships.

Still, she wouldn't have said no to another weekend.

Not to be. And that was fine. Really.

Yet, as she entered the function room in Marty's club a short while later, she was frustrated that her gaze searched the milling people by the bar and homed in on Scotty. She was only slightly mollified to see his eyes zero in on her. Their gazes met and held for a moment; then he looked away. Too damn easily.

Although Sapphie's attention shifted to Callum and Marty as they joined her, it didn't stop her from knowing where Scotty was as he moved around the room chatting. The sooner dinner was over, the better. At least she'd have the weekend to shore up her defenses before the meetings began on Monday.

Her relief when dinner was announced was short-lived. Marty practically dragged Scotty over to sit beside Sapphie. "I have a good feeling about you working together. It will be a marriage made in heaven."

Marty's enthusiasm for pushing them together mortified her. She hoped Scotty didn't think she was behind it.

Fortunately, the dapper little man on her other

side—apparently the Ice Cats' director of community projects—had some entertaining stories.

After Marty's champagne toast to a successful partnership, everyone settled down to their food.

Sapphie could hardly eat a bite. She was too aware of the man to her right. She could feel the heat emanating from his thigh so close to her leg. Her skin prickled when his elbow brushed against hers. The deep rumble of his voice as he talked with Antonelli's director of marketing resonated in her midriff, right below her ribs.

Scotty didn't seem to have the same problem. While she moved the salad around her plate, he ate heartily.

Her conversation with the director of community projects reached a natural conclusion by the time the entrées were served. As he engaged with the person on the other side of him, Sapphie had no choice but to turn to Scotty. Unfortunately, she couldn't think of a witty opening gambit.

"So it appears we'll be working together," he said.

Sapphie took a large sip of champagne, then said brightly, "It's a funny old world. Congratulations again on your new role. The Cats are lucky to have you in the front office. Your experience will be invaluable."

Stop jabbering at the man! She took another sip, to keep her mouth occupied.

"Thanks."

Silence stretched between them awkwardly, at least on her part.

She rushed to fill the gap. "What made you switch from color-commentating?" Stuffing a piece of shrimp into her mouth to prevent any inane babbling, she tried to make her expression politely interested.

"It switched away from me. Then this opportunity came up and it appealed, so here I am. Time will tell if I made the right choice. Especially under the circumstances."

"I'm sure it will turn out to be the perfect decision," she said, deliberately taking his words at face value. "This is a good time to join. You'll influence some important decisions and help determine the necessary organizational changes for the future."

"I'm not a huge fan of change for change's sake."

Sapphie refused to let her smile falter. "Neither am I. Equally, things can't continue as they are."

"I thought you didn't have a predetermined view. You've barely set foot in the building and you've already determined the front office has to change."

His attack surprised her. She was used to people being resentful and suspicious when she was called into a recently acquired business, so she didn't take it personally. She understood that they felt threatened.

Still, despite his mild tone, Scotty's jab felt pointed and distinctly personal. Would this be a feature in all their dealings from now on?

Sapphie wanted to tackle him on it but decided to hold back. Although everyone was involved in their own conversations, this wasn't the time or place for a private discussion that could quickly degenerate.

Matching her tone to his, she said, "To clarify, I'm not the one who determined that changes were needed. That came from Marty's people who evaluated the organization before he bought it. As it happens, I believe they're right. I thought you did, too. There is room for improvement and that's a good thing."

"As long as you don't throw out the baby with the bathwater."

"That's why I'm here. To make sure that doesn't happen." She gritted her teeth at his look of skepticism. "You'll have to give me the benefit of the doubt."

He gave a reluctant nod, which only irritated her more.

She tried another tack. "Antonelli Holdings will do more for the long-term health and prosperity of the franchise than the Scartellis. Marty certainly won't follow a personal agenda when it comes to investment."

"I guess time will tell." He paused, then seemed to think better of what he'd been about to say. "To be fair to the Scartelli brothers, hockey was their passion. They may not have been good with the money, but their ownership enabled us to win two Cups."

"Hopefully, you'll see that with Marty you get the best of both worlds."

"He seems like a decent guy and has a tough-but-fair reputation."

So it wasn't Marty he had the problem with. "I don't know what you've heard about *my* reputation, but I can promise you I've had many satisfied clients."

"I'm sure." His bland tone annoyed her.

"What's that supposed to mean."

"I have no doubt you talk a good talk. But in my experience, a pretty plan with lots of tweaks and twizzles keeps management happy but doesn't deliver anything of real value."

That stung. "My success is not based on the *number* of changes I recommend." She was about to add that her bonuses *were* based on results, but it was none of his damn business. "I don't believe in rearranging the deck chairs on the *Titanic*, nor do I believe in sticking a bow on a sow's head and calling her a supermodel."

"Even so, you're paid to give opinions and you won't be sticking around long enough to be judged on the outcomes."

"That was a cheap shot," she snapped.

"Just calling it as I see it."

"Really?" She lowered her voice. "And is that a dig at all consultants or just ones you've slept with."

"Now who's making cheap shots?"

She tossed his words back at him. "Just calling it as I see it."

Their server appeared to clear their plates, preventing the conversation from deteriorating further. If that was possible.

Disappointed by his sniping, Sapphie excused herself and headed for the ladies' room. She ran cold water over her wrists, hoping it would cool the anger and hurt. She patted her damp hands against her flushed cheeks and tried to regain her poise.

What was his problem? Did rejecting a relationship with him deserve a personal attack?

He gave her no credit for being honest. She could have strung him along. Used him to satisfy her needs, then dumped him when she'd seen that he was getting serious. But no. She'd treated him fairly and was now paying the price.

Fine. Two could play that game. She'd treat him like any other client. Politely, professionally and with minimal, strictly essential contact. She nodded her head firmly at her reflection, then freshened her lipstick and strode out of the bathroom.

She almost stumbled when she saw Scotty leaning against the wall, arms crossed. Her stomach sank at his intense expression. She did not need round two.

"Can we talk?" he asked quietly.

"I think you've said plenty." She kept her tone even. "I've certainly said all I plan to. Besides, I'm looking forward to the raspberry crème brûlée—apparently, it's to die for."

She spun on her heel, but before she could escape, he touched her arm. "Please. Just a couple of minutes. I'll even give you my dessert."

Sapphie would not be charmed. Still, there was no harm in listening to what he had to say. "You have two minutes."

"I know you won't believe it, but I'm normally a nice guy. Being around you turns me into a jack-ass." He sighed. "That didn't come out right either. It was meant to be an apology." He scrubbed his hand over his jaw. "Can we pretend that I didn't say any of that and start again?"

So much for not being charmed. "Sure."

"I'm sorry. I know you're not the villain. I don't like change or surprises. The past twelve months have been full of one after another. None of them nice." He dropped his head back and swore. "Apart from our weekend. Which was an unexpected pleasure. Of course."

"Of course." She understood some of his frustration—his divorce, coming so soon after his retirement, couldn't have been easy. "It's been a lot to take in. You signed up for a job and almost immediately the parameters changed. But this doesn't have to be bad. Think of it as an opportunity to make a good thing even better."

"Yeah." He made a face. "Problems. Opportunities. Those rah-rah team-building talks never did much for me as a player. I doubt they'll help now."

She held up her hands. "Okay, but this is how it's going to be. You can either work with us to influence those changes, or you can throw your toys out of the playpen and whine about it not being fair."

Those serious blue eyes speared her like a laser beam. Even though it did funny things to her knees, she held her ground.

Scotty laughed. "When you put it like that... I've never been a whiner and I don't intend to start now."

"Excellent." She patted him on the shoulder. "That wasn't so hard, was it?"

"I suspect the tough stuff starts Monday."

"As long as your arguments are reasoned, they'll be listened to. Like I said earlier, my role is to—"

"Facilitate and challenge. You'll forgive my cynicism, but after the Scartelli brothers bought the Cats, they promised their changes would be for the better. Their initiatives were disastrous to the feel of the franchise." He met her gaze squarely. "I won't let us become the laughingstock of the league again."

"You may not like everything Marty decides to do, but I promise he won't harm his favorite hockey team. No ugly third jerseys or dumb pink-kitty promotions." She gave an exaggerated shudder.

"Okay. I'll give Mr. Antonelli and…his team the benefit of the doubt. For now."

Sapphie knew he'd been about to say *you*. She was on trial, too. Despite Scotty's apology, he hadn't changed his mind about her. This trial was as personal as it was professional. But if he thought she was afraid of a little challenge, he was seriously mistaken.

Bring it on.

CHAPTER FIVE

SCOTT WAS READY to roll up his sleeves and get started.

After the weekend he'd spent with Callum and the Cats' management team, brainstorming solutions to the issues facing the organization, Scott was pumped. He hadn't been this motivated to go into work since he'd hung up his skates.

He'd discovered that some of the reasons why he'd been a good captain translated well to running the franchise. His knack for strategic thinking and tactical planning. His ability to see the whole picture, not just the individual details. More important, Scott had begun to understand how he could still contribute to the team.

Sure, it was torture not to be able to hit the ice with the guys. He wished he could play one more game. One more period. Hell, one more shift. But with this job, he could make a difference in a different way. What's more, he'd enjoyed himself. It had felt good. Right.

Shades on, hard rock blaring, Scott drove into the Cats' parking lot and found an empty space in the shade. Yeah, he was definitely ready to rumble.

As he strode through the glass doors etched with the snow-leopard's-head logo, he admitted he was apprehensive about working with Sapphie, who he hadn't seen since the press conference on Friday. Even then, they hadn't had the chance to speak. He wasn't sure how the next few weeks would pan out, but he suspected they'd clash more often than they'd agree. He didn't have a problem with arguing with her as long as he didn't say something stupid. He'd done enough of that already.

"All you can do is play it by ear," he muttered to himself as he jabbed the elevator call button. "And think twice before you open your mouth."

Though office hours didn't start for another hour, the building was humming with activity when Scott arrived on the top floor. Boxes and electronic equipment were being wheeled into the boardroom, which Antonelli's team had taken over temporarily as their base of operations. Through the smoke-gray glass, men and women were clustered in small groups, chatting with each other or talking on cells.

Scott mentally smacked himself for scanning the room to see if Sapphie was there. She wasn't.

He snapped his head forward and headed to his office. He'd barely had a moment to appreciate the spectacular view of the Manhattan skyscrapers, glittering in the morning heat over the top of the Cats' arena next door, when Doreen bustled in holding a sheaf of papers. Until he hired his own assistant, she was covering for him, too.

"Callum asked me to set up meetings for you with Marketing, Community Outreach, Sales and Corporate Sponsorship as soon as possible. The times are on your digital planner, too." She handed him a blue folder. "An electronic copy of the charts from the weekend is in your inbox, but I've printed them, too, in case you prefer paper, like he does." She tapped a yellow sticky note on the folder. "That's your log-in information. Keep it safe."

"I appreciate you setting everything up. Looks like it'll be a very busy day." He smiled. "Good job I like to hit the ground running."

She nodded approvingly. "Do what you always did when you were captain—put the needs of the badge on the front of the jersey ahead of the needs of the name on the back—and you'll be fine."

Doreen had been with the organization since it had relocated from Colorado in the early '80s. Despite the changes in ownership and management, she'd been a steady presence in the front office and her support was a major coup. "I'll do my best. Can I get you a coffee?"

"The way to my heart is a white coffee, no sugar. Chocolate also works." She patted his cheek before returning to her workstation.

It didn't take long for Scott to settle in and familiarize himself with the setup of his computer. Thankfully, the majority of the programs were standard and ones he was familiar using. By the time he'd figured out how to access the relevant data for his meetings, not to mention his calendar and email, it was time to head to Marketing. Lyle's office was two floors down and along the same wall as Scott's, so it was easy to find.

Scott almost faltered when he saw a familiar blonde seated at the round meeting table.

What was Sapphie doing there?

He gripped his tablet tighter as he paused at the threshold. "I'm not interrupting, am I? I'm a little early."

"Not at all. Come on in." Lyle shook his hand and indicated the empty seat beside Sapphie. "You two know each other."

"Sure. Hi." Damn, why did his voice suddenly have to drop an octave?

Sapphie looked lovely. Today's sleeveless dress was white with large brightly colored flowers and her spiked-heel shoes matched. For some reason, her outfit reminded Scott of the garden at Larocque's wedding celebration.

Her smile was friendly. "I hope you don't mind me crashing your meeting, but I thought we could kill two birds with one stone."

"I'm keen to have both your inputs on how we should overhaul the marketing program," Lyle said. "Our creativity was straitjacketed by the limited budgets and the previous owners' rules about the types of promotions we could run. My team is excited to have a new approach."

"No problem." He sat next to her, trying to look as though it didn't bother him in the least to spend the next hour with her. That the fresh, citrusy scent of her perfume didn't make him want to nibble on her bare shoulder. That he didn't want to run his fingers down those gorgeous legs and ease those shoes off her feet. *Focus!* "Seems silly to go through all this twice."

"Great." Lyle bounced on the balls of his feet. "I'll take you through the strategy behind the last couple of years' plans, how the execution turned out and also what impact the various activities had."

He flicked a switch and blinds lowered to dim the office. He then turned on the projector attached to his laptop and beamed the opening slide of his presentation onto the wall.

Sapphie sat forward, rested her elbows on the arms of her chair and laced her fingers. Scott went the opposite way, leaning back in his seat and stretching his legs in front of him. He noticed that she crossed her ankles and slipped her feet under her chair. A deliberate move to avoid touching him?

He didn't have time to ponder that, as Lyle began to speak.

"Feel free to jump in with questions."

As the team had discussed the marketing issues over the weekend, Scott was familiar with the information in the first few slides, so he was able to observe Sapphie in action for the first time.

He had to admit she surprised him. Whenever he'd had dealings with consultants before, they'd loved to hear themselves talk. Even when they'd asked for his opinion, they'd only half listened to his answer, and if they didn't like his responses, they were quick to rephrase his words to what they really wanted to hear.

Sapphie was different. She listened carefully, rarely interrupting. Her questions were mainly for clarification. When she spoke, she got straight to the point. She didn't offer an opinion, even when Lyle asked her directly.

"I don't want to get ahead of myself," she said. "Today is purely information gathering. Once I have everything I need, I'll evaluate it all so I can include the best ideas when we take our recommendations to Marty."

Though that reassured Lyle, Scott found it a little unnerving. Like a doctor's noncommittal *hmm* when he examined you.

As Lyle presented his proposals for how the marketing plans would need to change in the coming year, Scott's attention sharpened. The suggestions were solid and would certainly move things forward compared with previous years, but Scott was concerned that he couldn't see a real step change that would make fans spend more money.

He wondered what Sapphie thought. It was hard to tell; her expression was inscrutable.

When the meeting ended, Scott's mind was buzzing with ideas for how the program could be improved. The in-depth discussion had helped clarify further some of the points they'd discussed over the weekend, and he was keen to run his thoughts past Callum.

"That was great, Lyle—thanks." Scott took a leaf out of Sapphie's playbook and didn't say anything about the problem areas he'd identified. He didn't want to put Lyle on the spot with her around.

It might be silly to want to present a united front against the owner's people, but that was how he'd always managed himself and what he'd expected from his guys. Whatever the problems in the locker room, they weren't aired to anyone outside. Besides, he was conscious that Sapphie had a different agenda from him, no matter how conciliatory she appeared to be.

"Where are you headed next?" Sapphie asked as they walked to the elevator.

"Sales, followed by Community Outreach and then lunch with Corporate Sponsorship. What about you?"

"I was supposed to sit in on a meeting Marty has with the mayor." She rolled her eyes. "The man's got a list of demands as long as your arm. I'm sure he thought he could divide and conquer by collaring Marty separately. I suggested Callum should be there, too. The sooner the mayor realizes he can't play one off against the other, the sooner we'll get a sensible solution."

Her comments were unexpected and pleasing. Maybe his concerns were unfair. After all, both sides wanted the same thing: a strong Ice Cats franchise. The fact that Sapphie's side was more focused on profitability shouldn't mean they would be at loggerheads.

The thought cheered him. He held the elevator door open for her. "So, which floor?"

"Do you mind if I tag along with you?" Sapphie asked. "I'd really like to get an insider's view on those departments and it would save a lot of time if we joined forces. But I don't want to step on your toes."

He was torn. Pleased to spend more time with Sapphie but worried that the longer they were together, the higher the chance was of his saying or doing something that would put them at odds again.

"Sure," he said, trying to sound casual. "I'm all for expediency."

"Thanks. Maybe we could meet afterward to pool our thoughts and impressions." She leaned past him and pressed the button for the ground floor.

Her arm brushed against his stomach. Apart

from her touch searing him through the cotton of his shirt as if he were naked, he had a sudden urge to pull his already-flat stomach in. Damn it. She was keeping him off balance.

What was the question again? Meeting…later. "Uh, yeah. Good idea."

"Great. How about at the end of the day, once I've been debriefed by Marty on his meeting with the mayor?"

"I'm pretty sure that works, so come to my office when you're done."

"I'll look forward to it."

He blamed his sharp intake of breath on the blast of heat and humidity that slapped them in the face as they pushed through the doors for the short walk to the arena. That husky note in her voice didn't mean anything.

How the hell was he supposed to get through the next few meetings, without making an ass of himself, with her words echoing in his head?

MORGAN RASK WAS as sharp and aggressive as she was beautiful. She also clearly had a major problem with consultants, which had made the meeting with the director of sales rather like being the sidekick on the bull's-eye in a knife-throwing act from a Wild West show.

Which was frustrating, given Sapphie had earmarked Morgan as a future prospect within minutes. The woman needed to chill.

Although, if the skinny, green-eyed redhead stroked Scotty's arm one more time, Sapphie might be tempted to toss a glass of water in her face to really cool her down.

Sapphie wiped that thought from her head. It was none of her business who pawed Scotty. She ignored the cackling internal voice. She'd made her bed and she was fully prepared to lie in it.

"How are season-ticket and package sales compared with this time last year?" she asked.

Morgan's lips twisted. "They've been flat, although it's early days yet."

"Shouldn't you be benefiting from the Cup win?"

"We have, to a point. Renewals are strong and we'll get some interest from new purchasers early in the season. But that will be at the low end. It will be tough to sell the more expensive seats. We're in a market where the call on consumer pockets is dominated by the other major sports and the New York teams are all on a roll. We can only do so much without an innovative marketing package."

Sapphie arched an inquiring eyebrow. "You don't feel you have that?"

"Lyle has done his best in difficult circumstances, but we need a major overhaul if we're to make decent growth figures this season. The team's great performance helped produce strong sales in the second half of last season, as fans anticipated a play-off run. Matching those numbers will be challenging. People are doubtful of a repeat performance, especially since Scotty isn't there anymore."

Sapphie clenched her fist under the table, although Scotty seemed oblivious to the other woman's flirting.

"I wasn't playing last year when they won the Cup," he said. "The team is pretty much unchanged and the major contracts have been signed, so as long as injuries don't hammer us, chances are good that we'll make a deep run in the play-offs."

Morgan's smile was brittle. "That's obvious to the keen sports fan, but not to the more casual one. That's where the marketing package is crucial."

"Okay. So, what else would you like to see in terms of support for your team?" Sapphie smoothly shifted the onus back onto Sales.

Interestingly, Morgan became all business, dropping her antagonism as she outlined her vision and strategy.

Sapphie was pleased to note that Morgan's ideas were sound and her proposals well researched. They were exactly what had been missing from the marketing presentation Lyle had made. She asked Morgan to formalize her ideas in a document.

"Send it to me and I'll make sure it's seen at the highest level."

Scotty nodded. "Some great stuff in there, Morgan."

"Thanks. Our discussions over the weekend got me thinking."

Sapphie blinked. They'd spent the weekend together?

That was none of her business. Still, she watched Morgan and Scotty's behavior toward each other for the rest of the meeting. By the end of it, she was pretty sure that whatever they'd done together hadn't been personal.

Hiding her relief, she stood and shook Morgan's hand. "That's been really useful. I appreciate your time."

"No problem. Lovely shoes, by the way. Are they custom?"

Sapphie was startled by the girl talk. "No, but they're old. Like maybe five or six years."

"Darn it. Why is it every time I see something I like, it's not this season?"

"I know. It's so frustrating. I saw a Kate Spade purse that was to die for and the lady told me it was almost ten years old."

They chatted for a few more minutes. Then Scotty shook Morgan's hand and they left. Sapphie noted that he didn't react when Morgan held his hand a little longer than necessary.

That internal voice cackled again. Who was Sapphie kidding?

After what had happened on Thursday, it had

seemed sensible not to have too much to do with Scotty. She'd been careful to keep her distance whenever their paths had crossed. Even so, she'd noticed every time Scotty had been in the room. Over the weekend, she'd decided she needed a different approach and changed tactics based on the idea that familiarity would breed contempt. The more time she spent with him, the more they'd clash and the less appealing he'd be. The strong, quiet, brooding thing might be fun for a fling but on a daily basis would wear thin.

So, Sapphie had gotten a copy of his schedule and deliberately inserted herself into his meetings. She'd figured by the end of the day, they'd be fed up with each other.

How's that working out for you?

Not so good, she admitted. Not helped by the fact that every time those serious eyes looked at her, her pulse fluttered. No man had ever affected her this way.

Beside her, Scotty let out a heavy breath. "Man, Morgan is a shark. I'm glad I won't have to swim in her waters too often."

Ridiculously pleased, she teased, "Aw, did the big, bad sales lady scare you?"

"Hell yes. I'd rather face a team of enforcers with a grudge than have to work for her."

"She's very good at what she does. Sales have been stronger under her than for any of her predecessors."

"Don't get me wrong—I have nothing but admiration for her ability. She leads by example and has earned her people's respect. Still, she always makes me feel that I'm about to be trapped in her web and devoured for lunch."

Sapphie laughed. "You're mixing your metaphors, but I know what you mean."

"What do you think of what you've seen so far?"

"It's been fascinating to see what's behind all the facts and figures," she said carefully. "Every business is different, and while you can have an idea about what it's like on the inside, you can't know for sure until you meet the people who make it tick."

"That's a nice nothing answer. Kind of like the stuff they trained us to say when we were interviewed by the media." He smiled wryly. "I'm not asking you to give away any secrets. I'm genuinely interested in your impressions. This organization is important to me and I want everyone to love it as much as I do."

"Don't worry. I'm not trying to find a polite way to say I think your baby's ugly."

"That's a relief."

She cursed herself for noticing how sexy he looked and the way his eyes crinkled as he laughed. "Honestly, at this point, it really is all about getting a feel for the people and processes."

"Okay."

He held the door open for her, then followed her into the main headquarters. Sapphie appreciated the cooler air as they got into a waiting elevator.

Once the doors closed, he asked, "So are you getting a good vibe?"

"I don't like to make snap judgments. I prefer to let my impressions percolate for a bit. Something I learned early in my career, when I made a couple of naive mistakes."

"You made mistakes? I find that hard to believe."

Delighted by the comment, she smiled. "I like to think they helped me to learn that in business what you see isn't always what you get."

"Yeah. Took me a while to learn that, too."

The edge to his voice intrigued her. But before she could ask him about it, the doors opened and a group of people piled in. As they were crowded closer together in the rear of the car, memories of Issy's reception came flooding in.

Heat filled Sapphie's cheeks. She sneaked a peek at Scotty through her lashes and wasn't sure whether to be pleased or disappointed by the rigid way he held himself so they didn't touch. It was only when she saw a muscle tic in his jaw that she knew he wasn't unaffected by her.

Community Outreach was light relief compared with the previous meeting. Vern was on the ball and had the local area, if not the whole tristate region, on board. His program had the usual player visits to sick children and equipment donations to youth teams, but Vern had also built interesting partnerships with schools, libraries, animal shelters and other local charities. Sapphie picked up some ideas that could be translated to others of Marty's businesses and made a point of telling Vern so.

Unfortunately, there was nothing light about the meeting with Corporate Sponsorship. The snappily dressed director, Darren, was overly full of himself and his capabilities. Though he ran the poorest-performing department, he behaved as if it were the best. He smoothly brushed off every question about lack of growth and managed to blame everyone but himself for the gaps in their program.

Darren's patronizing attitude toward Sapphie grated on her nerves. Unlike in the Sales meeting, she didn't hold back on her views. Her comments were pointed and direct, but he dismissed them. The few times he did respond, he directed his answers to Scotty, as if he were the only one who mattered.

She'd dealt with sexism before, especially working in male-dominated environments like professional sports teams. But it had never aggravated her as much as Darren's behavior did.

It didn't help that Scotty said little. When he did speak, it was to support elements of Darren's program that she'd challenged or to expand on issues she'd raised that the director was unwilling to explain. While Scotty didn't defend his colleague, he didn't take him to task either.

"If we're done here..." Darren got to his feet. "I'm afraid I'll have to skip lunch—a potential sponsor has invited me to be part of his four at Knickerbocker." Darren tapped the side of his nose. "The things we have to do to bring in the big bucks."

Given how few new sponsors he'd brought in over the past year, she suspected that playing at the prestigious golf club was more important than getting the man's money. Still, she was relieved to have the excuse to leave.

"Not a problem," she said coolly, gathering her things and rising.

"Hey, man." Darren slapped Scotty on the back. "We should talk about what we can do together. Some of my contacts would give their left nut to spend time with you. Might net us a few more deals."

"It'll have to be after the start of the season. I'm going to be tied up for a few months. New job, new owner. You know how that goes."

Sapphie ground her teeth. Surely, Scotty wasn't buying Darren's spiel? He must have seen through the slick presentation and glib answers. She understood Scotty's need to support the organization, but was he really prepared to accept incompetence for the sake of loyalty?

Since the men were talking schedules as if she

weren't there, she made her escape and headed to the boardroom via the stairs. Might as well burn off her frustration with a few flights of cardio.

She'd made it up two floors when she heard someone coming up behind her.

"Sapphie, wait up."

Though her heart gave an extra thump at Scotty's voice, she kept going.

It didn't take him long to catch up. "Since our lunch plans have changed, do you want to get together to compare notes on the meetings? We can grab something in the cafeteria."

"Thanks, but I'll have a sandwich at my desk and use the time to catch up with my people."

Scotty came around in front of her, forcing her to stop. "Is there a problem?"

Biting back a retort, she said carefully, "I'm busy and have a lot to do."

He frowned. "Not so busy that you couldn't change your schedule to sit in on my meetings this morning."

"I appreciate you letting me tag along, but I should take advantage of the free hour and check off some things on my to-do list. I do have other clients to take care of."

"Yeah, I know how important your business is to you."

She ignored the sarcastic undertone. "As yours is to you. Now, if you'll excuse me…"

When she tried to move past him, he sidestepped

to block her path. "Have I done something to tick you off?"

She should deny it and carry on her way, but she suspected Scotty wouldn't let it go. Besides, beating around the bush wasn't her style. "I'm disappointed that you supported Darren, when it's clear both he and his strategy are not delivering."

He crossed his arms. "Since I was there to fact-find, I didn't see the point in slamming him before I got the full picture. Especially when you were hell-bent on tearing strips off him."

"You mean you didn't want to upset the 'boys together' feeling." Her lip curled.

Understanding dawned in his expression. "I'd have thought you'd have plenty of experience of dealing with jerks like him."

"Of course I have. I just didn't expect you to effectively condone his behavior by saying nothing."

His gaze narrowed. "I may have ignored what he did, but I sure as hell didn't approve. I knew you were capable of handling him and I didn't see the point in winding him up further by joining in. Guys like him get their backs up when challenged by another man."

"For a guy who is determined to take sides, you picked a strange time to be neutral."

"I know how to pick my battles. What mattered more to me was that you didn't overlook the good points in the corporate sponsorship program because Darren was being a jackass."

He had a point, she allowed. Sapphie's irritation cooled. "If I let people likc him distract me, I'd be a useless consultant."

"True."

"Nonetheless," she warned. "There will have to be some big changes in that area. Things can't continue as they are."

He held up his hands. "You'll get no argument from me. The only reason he's lasted as long as he has is because he's our previous owners' nephew—their sister's son."

"That explains a lot." She jammed her hands on her hips. "Nepotism at its best."

"I doubt the brothers would have worried about Darren being fired, but they were probably scared of their mother's reaction. Mama Scartelli is a small but fearsome lady."

She arched an eyebrow at him. "A Jersey Italian mama?"

"Oh yeah. Tru Jelinek, Ike's brother, had dealings with her a few years ago and told us about her."

"Well, family ties won't protect Darren anymore."

"I'm with you." Scotty grinned. "Now that we've got that settled, and since you're busy for lunch, are we still getting together later?"

Startled by the change of tack, she couldn't think of a reason to say no without looking snippy. "Uh…sure."

"Good. How about we do it over a drink? There's a nice English-pub-style bar not far from here."

"Okay. Why not?"

"Sounds like a plan. Call me when you're done with Marty and we can head out together." He touched two fingers to his temple in a salute. "Later."

Sapphie watched him disappear up the stairs before continuing to the boardroom.

So much for keeping things on a professional footing. As she sat at the table and opened her laptop, she told herself to calm down. It was only drinks.

CHAPTER SIX

"I'M SORRY. MY MEETING is running over and it'll be closer to seven thirty before we're done. There's no point in you hanging around waiting for me."

Scott had been half expecting this call from Sapphie all afternoon. She probably regretted accepting his impromptu invitation. When his office phone hadn't rung by six o'clock, he'd thought his pessimism had been unjustified. No sooner had the thought crossed his mind than his extension lit up.

"No problem," he said lightly. "Shi— Stuff happens. Another time."

"Oh, I don't want to cancel."

He almost dropped the phone. She didn't?

"You should go ahead to the bar," she said. "I'll meet you there once the meeting's finished."

"Sure. That'll work."

"Great. Thanks for understanding."

"Same thing could have happened to me. We could—" He cut himself off before he suggested they turn drinks into dinner. "Do you know how to get there?"

"If you give me the bar's address, I can plug it into the GPS."

"It's called Ye Olde Englishe Pubbe and it's across the arena plaza. Because the plaza is pedestrian only, you'll have to take the side streets around the arena."

"You'd better give me your cell number, in case I'm delayed further. Here's mine." She reeled off her number, which he scrambled to write down.

"I already gave you mine, but clearly that weekend wasn't memorable to you." Then he took a deep breath and added, "No rush. I'll see you when I see you."

After he'd hung up, Scott entered Sapphie's details into his phone. He then swiveled back and forth in his chair, debating whether to head out now or hang around a little longer. He had plenty to do, but his head wasn't in it. All he could think about was seeing Sapphie again.

He stopped his chair sharply. This wasn't a social event. It was business.

He had to do better than this. He was a professional with a job to do. Anyone would think he'd never been around a woman before. He'd been married, for crying out loud. The fact that Celine had never once derailed him from anything—not even when they'd first met—was irrelevant. That had been a long time ago and his mind had been firmly fixed on hockey.

Celine had never challenged him. She'd made

it all easy. She'd asked him out. She'd practically proposed to him. She'd taken care of their wedding, each of their homes, all their moves and, of course, their kids. It shouldn't have been a surprise really that she'd also taken care of their divorce.

Since his mind clearly wasn't on work, he should get out of there. He shoved some files into his case, shut down his computer and headed out.

Scott decided to walk to the bar. Unlike on game night, when the area was packed with fans, tonight it was quiet. Several runners and dog walkers passed him as he strolled past the central fountain, making his way toward the low brick building with the blinking neon sign.

The cool, dim interior of the tavern was a blessing after the late-summer heat. He chose a booth in the back, with a view of the TV playing the Yankees pregame show. The Angels were in town and he'd be able to catch an inning or two before Sapphie arrived.

At the bottom of the second, his cell pinged with a text. It was Sapphie.

On my way.

Good thing he'd decided against the tie this morning, because it would have been strangling him. He drained his glass of ice water and tried to focus on the pitcher, who was on a full count with a man on first. Scott groaned with the rest of the bar when the pin-striped batter hit a pop fly that resulted in a double play.

Even though he knew it would take at least fifteen minutes for Sapphie to get to the tavern, he looked up every time the heavy door opened. He felt like a fool.

He felt an even bigger fool for the way he deflated each time it wasn't her.

When Sapphie breezed into the tavern, instantly she brightened the place. A colorful bloom amid the dark wood and leather. She spotted Scott and waggled her fingers, then walked toward him. Every male head in the place turned to watch as she passed by.

Scott pretended he didn't feel her leg brush his as she slid into the booth opposite him. "No problems finding the place?"

"No, but I'm glad I had the sat nav. The one-way-street system is a killer."

"Your meeting must have finished up quicker than expected."

"It did. We'd done as much as we could for now." She sipped from the glass of ice water their server poured for her. "Sorry about keeping you waiting. That damn mayor has a lot to answer for. He has the concerned tone and the earnest expression down pat. A shame it hides him rubbing his hands all the way to the bank."

"What's he done?"

Before she could answer, their server reappeared and asked for their order. A mojito for Sapphie and a beer for him, plus a plate of chips and sour-cream dip.

"So you were telling me about the mayor," he prompted.

"It appears the Scartellis *forgot* to mention during due diligence that they had an agreement with the city regarding the arena and a local redevelopment plan. There are a bunch of payment clauses based on the Scartellis and the Ice Cats failing to deliver on key targets—which they have—that come into play in the next twelve months."

Scott nearly choked when she told him how much money was potentially involved. No wonder the Scartellis were so keen to sell. "Holy cow."

"Marty's spitting blood. So is Callum, who was also kept in the dark. Of course, there are failsafes built into acquisition contracts for such an eventuality, but it'll take a while to untangle the mess. Luckily, Marty's legal team is the best and they're already on the case. In the meantime, we need to operate on the basis that those payments will have to be made and take them into account in our financial projections. Which, in turn, will impact the budgets."

"Which won't be good for the Ice Cats." That was an understatement. Cash-strapped organizations had to cut back in all areas, including player salaries.

"I'll tell you now Marty won't rob Peter to pay

Paul. He keeps each business separate. So if he has to pay the city, it'll come out of the Ice Cats' coffers and not from any of his other teams."

"Which will make Callum's job—and mine—a lot tougher." So much for the new owner meaning things would be different.

"At least none of your plans are set in stone. There's time to adapt."

Your plans, *your* obligation, *your* problem. A stark reminder they were on opposite sides of the fence.

"Callum is experienced. He'll have come across this kind of situation before." At least, he hoped so. From where he sat, it looked bleak.

Their server returned with their order and menus. "Are you planning to have dinner with us?"

There was an awkward silence, as if neither of them wanted to be the first to speak.

To hell with it. He reached for a menu. "I'm starving. You're welcome to join me."

Sapphie hesitated, then nodded. "I'm hungry, too."

They perused the food options, then both settled on cottage pies. Once their server had gone, silence fell again.

"How was the rest of your day?" Sapphie asked brightly.

It was an innocent-enough question. No obvious hidden agenda. So why did Scott hesitate before answering?

"Pretty good. I spent most of the afternoon reviewing the information from this morning. It's interesting seeing things from the other side of the fence."

"I bet. Front-office issues probably never cross players' minds. I don't think that's a bad thing, by the way. They shouldn't have to worry about butts on seats or how many boxes have been sold for a game."

"We don't—unless they impact on us. Like when your barn is half-empty or full of too many opposing-team fans. Or when financial constraints lead to player trades and problems with contract renewals." He hoped that wouldn't happen as a result of the mayor's little bombshell. He damn well wouldn't let it.

"Marty's fair. He'll give you a chance to figure out how to fix the problems."

But would he give them long enough to turn things around before heads started to roll? "That's good to know. I still feel like I've been tossed in the deep end."

"If it helps, you didn't seem out of your depth at all."

Her unexpected praise made him feel like he'd been awarded the first star of a game. "Thanks. It's been a while since I did my degree, but it's coming back pretty quickly."

"Shows you have a natural bent for it." She

raised her drink and toasted him. "Here's to a relatively pain-free first day."

"I don't know." He clinked his beer bottle against her glass. "My backside aches from sitting too much."

She smiled and seemed about to say something, but their food arrived. They spent several minutes tucking in.

"What did you think of Lyle's marketing plan?" Sapphie asked.

Once again, Scott hesitated before answering. It wasn't that he didn't trust Sapphie, but he felt uncomfortable—even a little disloyal—talking about his colleagues with her. He said as much to her.

Disappointment clouded her expression. "I keep telling you, I'm not the enemy. My job is to get the best out of the organization, not pick people to fire. If there are areas of weakness, I need to identify them and look for ways to improve them."

"I get that. I just think I should discuss my impressions with Callum first."

"Fair enough. But I hope once you've spoken with your boss, we can share notes. Your perspective— as former team captain—will be invaluable. Too often we don't see the impact of our decisions on the players and you can provide that viewpoint."

"I don't know how much I can add. You guys are the experts. I'm the rookie."

"Sometimes fresh eyes provide the best insights."

He shrugged. "Okay."

Having exhausted the conversation about the business, they focused on their food again. Scott wasn't sure what to say next. He'd never been good at small talk.

Sapphie finished her meal and pushed her plate aside. "That was almost as good as home cooking. I'll have to remember this place. I eat far too much hotel food when I'm traveling."

Grateful for the opening, he asked, "Are you staying with J.B. and Issy?"

"No. I rent a serviced apartment in Edgewater. It's easier than a hotel and it means I don't have to impose on friends. Plus I can come and go as I please. My hours aren't very sociable and I hate to be a bad guest."

She really didn't like commitment. Other than her work, everything in her life was temporary. Disposable. Somehow that felt sad. But if she was happy, why did he care?

"But I did see my gorgeous goddaughter, Sophia, yesterday. We had a picnic in the park." She pulled her cell out of her purse, swiped the screen, then turned it to show him. "I got her that outfit, complete with the adorable sun hat."

The picture showed Sapphie with the grinning baby, decked out in a red T-shirt with a big daisy on her chest and red shorts, mugging for the camera. Sophia's red hat also had a big daisy on it.

"Very cute."

Sapphie sighed. "She's growing so fast. One of the benefits of this acquisition is that I'll get to spend more time with her than I would otherwise."

"Time passes quickly. It seems like only yesterday my kids were that age and now they're in college."

"Come on." She motioned with her hand to give her his phone. "I've shown you mine—well, Issy's. Show me yours."

He dutifully pulled up pictures of Angela and Wayne that he'd taken over the summer. "Luckily, they take after their mother and not their old man."

Sapphie studied the photos. "They've definitely both got your eyes. And your mouth."

He raised his eyebrows. "Really? No one's pointed that out before."

"Then no one's looked properly before." She glanced up.

Their gazes met and held. A fire bolt hit him in the chest with the force of a slap shot. Heat spread outward, filling his body. From the flush in her cheeks, it seemed she'd felt the connection, too.

Sapphie looked away first and reached for her purse. "I should probably go. I managed to speak with the staff in my office here, but I still need to touch base with my people in Chicago and LA, and I have another full day ahead of me tomorrow. Which has probably now become even fuller after that thing with the mayor."

"Yeah. Mine, too." Scott signaled for the check,

then pulled out some bills and tossed them onto the table.

Sapphie got out her wallet and extracted some money. "Here's my share."

He put his hand over hers. "I've got it."

"This wasn't a date."

He gritted his teeth at her terse tone. "I know."

"As your colleague, I can cover my food and drink."

He ignored the jab of irritation her words gave him. "I'd like to think we're more than colleagues. Aren't we friends, at least?"

"I split the tab with my friends all the time."

"Not this time. But you can pay next time. Deal?"

"Deal." She smiled, easing the tension.

As she went to put away her wallet, they both realized that his hand still covered hers. Her gaze snapped up to meet his. This time awareness shimmered in the clear blue depths, mirroring the feeling rippling through him.

He swallowed hard. This was dangerous territory. He hardly dared breathe in case he spoiled the moment.

Slowly, he leaned toward her. His gaze dropped to her mouth.

She licked her lips. For a moment, she seemed to move toward him.

Then, as if she'd realized what was happening, she sat back abruptly and slipped her hand out from under his.

"Thank you for dinner." She was suddenly very focused on her wallet.

Scott cleared his throat. "You're welcome."

He rose and gestured for Sapphie to precede him, then followed her out. Although the temperature had dropped a little once the sun had gone down, the evening was still hot and sultry.

"Where are you parked?"

"It's over there, under a light." Sapphie held up her keys. "You don't have to escort me. I'm always sensible about my safety."

"I'm sure you are, but I can't let a woman go to her car on her own at night. Call me old-fashioned, but I'd do this for any woman I know."

She looked like she might argue further but said, "Okay. In that case, thank you."

She strode off at a smart clip, so he had to move quickly to catch up.

When they reached her car, the moment became awkward again.

"Thanks again," she said stiffly. "I'll see you in the office tomorrow."

Suddenly, he was tired of her being tense and edgy with him. "I get it, you know. Last weekend isn't going to happen again. Especially now that we have to work together."

"Maybe you're not the one who needs to get it," she said softly.

Stunned, he didn't know how to respond.

Sapphie smiled ruefully. "I know all the reasons why it would be wrong, but I wonder if I was too hasty saying we shouldn't see each other."

He told himself not to get excited. That didn't mean she'd changed her mind.

"I see." This was another of those tricky moments. One wrong word or move and...game over.

"Ordinarily, I might say what the heck and give it a shot. But the Ice Cats acquisition is a major complication. And I don't mix business with pleasure. Plus I don't do serious and you don't do casual."

"What if I was prepared to ease up a little?" Where the hell had that come from?

"I can't see you ever settling for a sex buddy and that's the only arrangement that will work for me."

He tamped down the urge to disagree. That wasn't him, for sure. But the alternative was having no personal connection with Sapphie and he didn't want that either. There had to be some way to bridge the gap.

"Can't we just hang out together, as friends? Go for a drink, maybe the occasional meal, like tonight. At least until your time with the Ice Cats is done."

She tilted her head and studied him carefully. "I suppose we could. But we'd have to set up some rules in advance so we're both absolutely clear where we stand. What's acceptable and what's not."

"Sounds really formal." Scott frowned. "Can't we just play it by ear?"

She looked dubious. "There's a lot of chemistry between us. What if one of us decides to add benefits to that friendship?"

Though he was pleased she'd admitted that the attraction, the heat, was there, his gut tightened at her question. "We're adults, not teenagers. We can handle it."

At least, he hoped he could. If not, he could lose even her friendship and he couldn't stand the thought of that. It would be tough, but it was worth trying. "We don't need to worry about that until your contract is over. Until then, we simply enjoy each other's company."

"Okay," she said slowly. "I guess we could give it a shot."

"Great." He deliberately kept his arms at his sides to keep from reaching out for her. "In that case, good night. See you tomorrow."

"Safe trip home. Sleep well." She opened her car door and tossed her purse onto the passenger seat. Then she reached up, bussed his cheek and gave him what was meant to be a quick hug.

His hands had other ideas. Before she could pull away—and definitely without his permission— they drew Sapphie closer, until she was pressed against him. His arms wrapped around her, not too tightly, ready to let her go the minute she showed signs of wanting to be released from his embrace.

She stiffened but didn't move away. She tilted her head and met his gaze.

"DIDN'T WE JUST talk about this?" Sapphie tried to lighten the moment with a smile. Unfortunately, the husky words sounded anything but light.

"Uh-huh." Scotty nodded once, slowly.

She brought her hands up, ostensibly to push out of his embrace. Only, she didn't. She rested them on his chest. Her fingers fiddled with the lapels of his jacket until she registered what she was doing and stilled them.

"So...um...isn't this classed as benefits?"

"What do you think?" His palm rubbed her back gently, sending tingles through her.

"I suppose, technically, we weren't talking about hugs or kisses. Friends hug. But do they kiss? Obviously, they do on the cheek, but..." She was babbling again. "This is why we need rules."

"Tell me what you want and I'll abide by it."

She wanted to kiss him. For kisses to be allowed. But that would be a mistake. Wouldn't it? Kisses might—almost certainly *would*—lead to other things and... Now she was babbling in her head.

Sapphie narrowed her gaze. "You're not being much help."

He leaned his forehead against hers. "I'm sorry.

I shouldn't have put us…you…in an awkward situation." He eased away and released her.

Despite the hot night air, she felt chilled by the loss of his warmth. She rubbed her hands along her arms. "No need to apologize. It's that chemistry. Kind of hard to resist."

"Yeah." He ran his hand over his head. "But we've just got done agreeing we'd keep things cool, and I messed with that."

Sapphie laid her palm against his cheek. "Just so you know—while we're being open, honest adults—I do want to kiss you."

"I want to kiss you, too."

His crooked smile, that scar, were nearly her undoing. "We have to be sensible."

Scotty gave that slow nod again.

Damn him! She would not be tempted.

If she didn't make a definite stand right now, she knew she'd regret it. "Until my time with the Cats is over, we'll settle for being friends. No benefits. Period." She pecked him on the cheek, then got in her car before he could respond. "Good night."

She peeked at him in her rearview mirror as she drove away. He stood watching until she'd turned the corner. Once he was out of sight, she sighed heavily.

So much for familiarity breeding contempt. For avoiding anything that smacked of a relationship. In the past twenty-four hours, she'd flip-flopped as often as a politician. Spend time with Scotty.

Don't spend time with Scotty. Kiss him. Don't kiss him. Be friends. Don't be friends.

Who was she trying to kid? She wanted to sleep with him. Wanted another glorious weekend. Why couldn't she give in to it and go along for the ride, for as long as it lasted?

Because this wasn't about just her.

Sapphie could handle all that and keep her heart intact. She wouldn't suddenly start smelling orange blossoms or flipping through brides' magazines because she and Scotty had a few dates. Even the thought of getting serious would remind her of what responsibilities and commitments had stolen from her as a child, and she'd backpedal so fast she'd get whiplash.

That wouldn't be fair to Scotty. He wasn't a fling kind of guy. Even if he said he could handle it, she knew he couldn't. And sooner or later, his need to deepen their relationship would feel like a noose around her neck. Worse, because she genuinely liked him—admired and respected him— she'd want to let him down gently. So she'd let things drift on the surface, while inside she already had one foot out the door.

No matter how hard she tried not to, she'd end up hurting him. That was the last thing she'd ever want to do. He deserved better.

So did she.

What to do?

Sapphie continued to ponder the issue at her

apartment and late into the night. She was no closer to a solution as she drove to work the following morning. Nor by the end of a grueling day. She'd spent the morning trying to untangle the mess the previous owners had left and the afternoon on a Skype call resolving issues on a project in her Chicago office. She wasn't sure if it had been a help or hindrance that she hadn't seen Scotty, except in the distance.

On impulse, instead of going home, she decided to stop by Issy's. Her friend had always been able to give her perspective. The smell of grilling food greeted her as she pulled into a parking slot outside Issy's apartment.

Issy and J.B. were living here while they looked for their new home. As J.B. had been renting the town house where he'd lived—and he'd shared it with a couple teammates—it had made more sense for him to move in with his new wife.

"This is a nice surprise," Issy said when she opened the door. "I'm afraid you've missed Sophia. I put her down about half an hour ago."

As usual, Sapphie had lost track of the time at work. When Issy was single, it wouldn't have mattered, but Sapphie didn't want to cut into her friend's baby-free time with her husband.

"I'm sorry. I hadn't realized it was that late. I can come back another time."

"Don't be silly." Issy pulled her inside. "Join us for dinner. J.B. can toss another steak on the grill. You look like you could use a glass of wine. Tough day at the office?"

"No more than usual," Sapphie hedged.

J.B. greeted her warmly. "Great. In return for dinner, you can give me the inside scoop on what's happening in the front office."

"It's early days, so there isn't anything to tell. You probably know more than I do."

"Dam— Darn it. Oh well, I'll feed you anyway."

Sapphie laughed. "Thanks. First let me sneak in and see my goddaughter."

Sophia didn't stir when Sapphie leaned over the crib and pressed a kiss to her soft pink cheek. So precious. Sapphie's heart swelled with love for the baby. Yet she didn't feel the slightest urge to have one of her own. Perhaps because she knew all too well that babies were hard work. Then they became toddlers. Then children, then mini adults. The work never got easier. They took more and more out of you.

Never again.

Shaking her head sharply to get rid of the claustrophobic feeling, she cast one last look at Sophia.

While motherhood was not for her, Sapphie was a great doting godmother. "Sleep well, sweetheart," Sapphie murmured before joining her friends.

As J.B. served the steaks, Issy caught Sapphie up on what various members of the Ice Cats and their families had been up to following the wedding celebration. Over dinner the conversation shifted to the couple's search for their new house, which was going more slowly than they'd expected. They were thinking about building their own place if they couldn't find somewhere they liked.

After they'd eaten, J.B. excused himself. "I promised I'd stop by and see Mad Dog tonight. Kenny said he's still cut up about what happened with Lizzie."

Kenny Jelinek and Taylor were J.B.'s closest friends, as well as his teammates.

"He was pretty down when we spoke a couple days ago," Sapphie acknowledged.

"Give him a hug from me," Issy said as she kissed her husband goodbye.

J.B. shot her an exaggerated look of pain. "Can't I just slap him on the back?"

Issy rolled her eyes. "You'd hug him if he scored a goal."

"That's different."

"Use your imagination, then. He needs cheering up."

"A hug from me won't do the trick. Trust me."

"In that case, tell him I sent him a hug." Issy grinned at her husband. "And lots of love."

"Forget that," J.B. growled. "He gets your best regards. If he's real bad, a handshake."

Sapphie and Issy laughed as he stomped out.

Once he'd gone, Issy gave Sapphie a stern look. "All right, spill. Why are you really here on a work night?"

Sapphie considered pretending she had no idea what her friend was talking about, then told her about Scotty. "I don't know why I'm fretting so much. I agreed to drinks, food and the occasional social event. Nothing more. Why am I worrying about what-ifs and maybes?"

"I've never seen you this wound up about a guy before," Issy said thoughtfully. "Except for that jackass with stalker tendencies in LA. The appropriately named Randy."

"He was intense. And, to be clear, I never went out with him. He had an apartment in the same building and took my friendly hellos to mean that I *lurved* him as much as he *lurved* me." Sapphie made a face as she mimicked his emphasis.

"He was weird. He stole your dry cleaning and wore your sweater to bed."

Sapphie winced. "I don't need reminding. This situation is completely different."

Issy sipped her drink. "Honestly, I don't see what you're so worried about. Scotty's a grown man. More than capable of making his own decisions about dating. Why are you tying yourself in knots trying to protect him?"

"He's been through a difficult year. He seems… vulnerable."

Issy's eyebrows shot up. "We're talking about Scotty Matthews. He laid out opponents for a living. He had the hardest slap shot in the league and the deadliest hip check."

"Come on. You know Scotty's more than that clichéd image of a hockey player. He's a totally different man off the ice."

"That's true. But I still think you're not giving him enough credit. Vulnerable or not, he can hold his own—with you or with anyone else. Leaving aside the work issue, what have you got to lose?"

"His friendship." That mattered a lot. Even though in truth they barely knew each other. "If… When things end between us, he won't want anything to do with me."

"Sweetie, if you don't do this, you won't have a friendship anyway. This arrangement you've agreed to gives you both a chance to get to know each other better. And if things work out, more. Why worry about how it *might* end before it's even started?"

"Because it *will* end. It has to."

"Your friendship with Taylor didn't when you stopped sleeping together."

"That's different."

"How?"

"Because Mad Dog and I were on the same

page. Neither of us wanted more than what we had. Scotty and I aren't even in the same book."

"Except you just told me that you *are* for this dating-without-commitment deal."

Sapphie threw up her hands. "See, I'm going round in stupid circles."

"Stop overthinking this. If you like him, consider this a chance to start again. Put the weekend you spent together to one side. Imagine you've just met and go from there. One step at a time."

Put like that, Sapphie began to see that maybe it could work. The problem was that she and Scotty had gone about things back to front. If they hadn't slept together, would she be having any of these worries? "You're right. Sex was the complicating factor."

Issy smiled ruefully. "It usually is. Look at me and J.B."

Although it had worked out in the end, her friends' relationship had turned rocky when their no-strings vacation fling had resulted in Issy's pregnancy.

"Much as I love Sophia, she's the perfect cautionary tale. She'll remind me to take things slowly and carefully."

The key was not to sleep with Scotty again. Sapphie would just have to make sure they weren't in a situation where their chemistry could spiral out of control. No romantic evenings. No time alone, even at work. She could handle that.

Sapphie toasted her friend with her wineglass. "I think things will be okay after all."

CHAPTER SEVEN

WHAT A DIFFERENCE a couple weeks made.

Scott whistled as he sauntered around outside the Brew House. Grey had recommended the run-down tavern in the bustling riverfront district on the Jersey side of the Hudson as a possible investment opportunity. Given his friend's eye for a business with potential, Scott had come here to give it the once-over.

It had also given him the perfect excuse to invite Sapphie to join him again for after-work drinks. He hadn't seen much of her at the office over the past two weeks because they'd each had their own work commitments. Marty's team was busy evaluating the organization for their final report, which was due shortly. Meanwhile, Scott and Callum had had to not only pull their own proposals together but also manage team and player issues—training camp was less than two weeks away.

On the one hand, the lack of contact was fine, because it kept the lines clear between business and pleasure. On the other, it added to the awkwardness when they did get together, because they had to get over the tense initial few moments.

Maybe if they were around each other more, meeting up would be more comfortable from the outset.

Scouting the Brew House had given Scott the perfect way to change things up.

His cell rang as he was walking into the tavern. Half expecting it to be Sapphie phoning to say she was late, he was surprised when the caller ID showed Cam "Bullet" Lockhead, his old friend and former teammate.

Scott was lucky that he'd been able to stay with the Cats for his whole career, whereas Cam had moved from team to team, especially after he'd hit thirty. Often traded at the spring deadline to a franchise that needed grit for a play-off run, Cam would then be moved again in the off-season. His last few years before retirement he'd bounced back and forth between the minors and the NHL. A victim of the changing game, which didn't need enforcers anymore, Bullet had hung up his skates two years before Scott had.

Scott answered. "Hey, man, good to hear from you. What's going on?"

"Not much. You know how it is."

Scott winced at his friend's flat tone. Bullet had always been taciturn, but recently he'd sounded depressed. Scott knew Cam had struggled with retirement, initially going to his small hometown in Canada, intending to leave the game completely. But he'd missed the sport he loved and turned to scouting.

"Are you still with Seattle?" Scott asked.

"Yeah, but the travel's a bear. Too much time on my own, freezing my ass off in miserable rinks, watching too many kids with barely enough talent. And don't get me started on the parents. Plus Laurel says she sees less of me than when I was playing." Cam paused. "So, I'm thinking of reaching out to the Cats for an ambassador's role," he said casually.

"Didn't you say you'd rather lick your gloves than schmooze with the suits?"

"It can't be as bad as what I've been doing. I'd be in one place and Laurel might be happier. She enjoyed living in Jersey."

"But it would mean talking to, you know, people."

His friend's laugh sounded rusty. "I can manage some occasional small talk with the posh muckety-mucks."

"I could put in a good word for you with our GM. Callum's a stand-up guy. He'll give you a fair hearing."

"Okay. If you think it'd be worth it."

"For sure."

"Thanks, man." His friend sounded brighter. "I appreciate it."

Trying to keep Bullet positive, Scott asked about his kids, who were also in college. They exchanged family updates, and then he explained what he was doing at the tavern.

"I keep meaning to call Grey," Cam said. "We can compare notes on battered brains."

"Are you still getting headaches and dizziness?" Like Grey, Cam had suffered several concussions during his playing years.

"The medication keeps them under control most of the time, but you never know if it's going to be a good or a bad day. The doc says I'm doing all right, so I mostly ignore it and soldier on."

"I hear you." Some mornings his body was so stiff he felt like a tin man whose joints needed oiling. "You'll get there."

Scott's heart kicked as he saw Sapphie pull into the parking lot. "Sorry, I've got to go. The person I'm meeting has arrived."

"You're dating?" There was a smile in Cam's voice.

"We're just friends."

"Uh-huh. Hot blonde, spicy brunette or cool redhead?"

Scott grinned. "Hot blonde."

"On a scale of one to ten, is she a fifteen?"

"At least. More like a twenty." Well, a fifty, but he wasn't telling his old buddy that.

Cam whooped. "That's what I'm talking about." He sobered. "Laurel will be pleased you're not on your own anymore."

"Whoa. It's not like that."

"Then, bro, you ain't doing it right."

"What do you know? You've been married to the same lovely lady all your life."

"How do you think I've kept her with me? I'm not just a pretty face."

With a broken nose that hadn't fixed straight and several nasty scars, he wasn't even that. Scott laughed. "I'll let you know what Callum says, but don't be a stranger in the meantime."

He hung up as Sapphie walked toward him. Today's dress and heels were the same blue as her eyes. Despite the early-evening heat, she looked as fresh as a spring morning.

The hostess showed them to a booth in the back and slapped down two dog-eared menus. "Marge will be your waitress tonight. Enjoy."

He and Sapphie exchanged looks at her bored tone.

"A miserable front of house puts you off before you've even ordered." Sapphie shook her head. "Too many empty tables for a Friday night. Since it's the last weekend before Labor Day I know people are headed to the shore, but this place should be doing better."

"Grey said the price was much lower than he'd have expected given the prime location."

"Ryan Grey? As in the former Cats defenseman who runs that amazing steak house."

"The very same." He tamped down the jab of jealousy and explained that Grey was helping him look into investment opportunities. "Apparently, for the asking price, you can't find a better deal. The business is sound and there aren't any hidden nasties. But the sales figures are poor and getting worse. Plus there's a high staff turnover."

"Not a great reflection on the current management."

"What can I get you to drink?" Their waitress sloshed ice water into the plastic tumblers.

"A Miller Genuine, please." Sapphie's smile wasn't returned. "And some chili poppers."

"Same for me," Scott said. "But I'll try your buffalo wings."

"Sure thing. I'll be right back with your order."

Unfortunately, *right back* was twenty minutes. The beer was warm and the appetizers cold. Scott and Sapphie hoped as they placed their dinner orders—a loaded burger for him and meatball mac and cheese for her—that the simple fare would be edible.

It was, but the service was again painfully slow and their waitress disappeared, so they couldn't get another drink.

"What do you think?" Scott asked once they'd taken the edge off their hunger.

"This place needs a lot of work to improve it, but if you fixed it up right, you'd make a killing. It's in a prime riverfront spot with ample parking and space for an outdoor dining patio. Plenty of room inside to add a decent-sized bar." Sapphie swept her hand in a half circle to illustrate her point. "Give the place some atmosphere, add decent food and drinks, plus slick service, and people will flood here."

He agreed with her appraisal. "Obviously, I'm thinking about a sports bar. Large flat-screen TVs, memorabilia on the walls and in display cabinets." He grimaced as he ate his dinner. "Definitely a better chef, too."

"A change of name, look and management, and the added benefit of your name, should encourage people to give the place a try." Pushing aside her unfinished meal, Sapphie sipped her drink. "But how do you plan to make this work? You've never managed a restaurant and you have a full-time job with the Cats."

"Grey wants to be involved as a silent partner. He'll invest some money, oversee the menu and personnel, and help me hire a manager to run it, but it won't be overtly linked to him or his restaurant."

"That should work out nicely for both of you."

"So you think it's worth pursuing?"

"Bearing in mind I haven't checked out the books, and basing my opinion on what I've seen, I'd say go for it." She smiled. "If you'd like and you're serious, I can look at it in more depth and give you a better-informed opinion."

He was stunned by her unexpected offer. "That would be great, but I know you're really busy with your clients."

"If this has the potential I think it might, I

wouldn't mind investing myself. If you'd be open to another silent partner."

"Definitely." As pleased as he was by her enthusiasm, he was bemused that she would commit to a business venture with him but not a relationship. And why did she want in on a project based in New Jersey, when her main office was in Chicago? Did she have a hidden agenda—maybe one that involved seeing more of him?

"Are you planning on spending more time here?" he asked casually, searching for a clue to her thinking.

"No more than usual. Once I've finished with the Cats, I'll have to check in on my other clients, so I'll be traveling again. But I don't need to be here to invest, do I?"

"Nope." Hiding his disappointment, he said, "I'll discuss it with Grey and let you know."

"Sounds good. Now, I'm going to try their strawberry cheesecake."

Over dessert and coffee, Scott and Sapphie talked more about ideas for the sports bar. They bounced ideas off each other, then challenged and built on those ideas. Their debates were occasionally heated, but there wasn't the underlying tension their meetings at the office had. Their strengths—her ability to look strategically at the big picture and his ability to plan tactics and problem-solve—dovetailed nicely.

There were also more of those lingering looks

and sizzling touches. It was as if a bubble of intimacy had formed around them and the rest of the tavern didn't exist.

All too soon, it was time to leave.

"Would you like to walk along the riverfront?" he asked as they headed out into the night air, trying to delay the moment the evening would end.

"I'd love to, but I have a conference call with my people in LA about a client issue." She looked at her watch. "If I don't get moving, I'll be late. Thanks for dinner. Have a great weekend. See you on Monday."

It seemed like he barely blinked and she was in her car, heading out of the parking lot.

He ignored his frustration and tried to focus on the fact that they were making progress. Just not quickly enough. Especially as Sapphie's time with the Ice Cats would soon be over.

Of course, if she was involved in this sports-bar project, he'd still have a reason to contact her on a regular basis and he could continue his plan to win her over.

That thought lifted his spirits as he started for home.

Slow progress or not, things might be working out in his favor after all.

"HERE'S TO A long and fruitful partnership."

Sapphie clinked her flute against Ryan Grey's and Scotty's, then sipped her champagne. "I can't believe I'm at the same table with two of my favorite Ice Cats players, let alone embarking on a joint project with you."

"Would you like our waiter to take a picture of us for your scrapbook?" Ryan grinned.

He'd been teasing her like an older brother since they'd been introduced tonight. Sapphie caught herself. What was wrong with her? One of the best-looking players, retired or not, and the man whose tastefully naked picture from a famous sports magazine's body issue had been her computer wallpaper for years, and she thought of him as a brother?

Because he's not Scotty. The thought shocked her.

She looked at the two men seated with her in Grey's restaurant and couldn't help comparing them. Both were tall, with great bodies that said they continued to work out. Both had short dark hair flecked with silver. But Ryan's face was longer and thinner, with high Slavic cheekbones, and his silvery-gray eyes matched his name.

But when Ryan looked at her, his gaze was clear and friendly, while a banked fire smoldered in the depths of Scotty's blue eyes that made her feel far from sisterly.

They were formalizing their partnership for the proposed sports bar. There were still some reports pending and contracts to sign, but in principle they would be the new owners of the Brew House.

"Are you kidding? That photo will take pride of place on my desk." Sapphie gave her cell to their server and beckoned the men closer. "Smile big, boys."

Ryan slung his arm over her shoulders, while Scotty leaned against her. The press of Scotty's arm affected her more keenly than Ryan's. Where his shoulder touched her, her bare skin tingled, making her nerve endings pop like the bubbles in her champagne.

What's more, she liked the feeling.

When she got her phone back, she flipped through the pictures. "Very nice."

Ryan looked at the screen. "We don't look bad for two guys past their sell-by date."

"Speak for yourself, old man." Scotty smiled. "I'm still in my prime."

"Once you stop playing, it gets harder to keep those pounds at bay." Ryan patted his flat stomach. "Especially when you own a place that serves great food."

"Maybe I should keep the Brew House chef so I won't be tempted to chow down."

"Trust me, it's better to do the extra reps and enjoy what you eat. Your customers will thank you."

"Even if my waistline doesn't."

As Sapphie cut into her perfectly cooked steak, the two friends continued to rib each other. It was fun to see this lighter side of the normally serious

Scotty. He was more at ease in Ryan's company than he was with most other people.

He was even more relaxed with her. As lovely as their evenings together had been over the past couple weeks, she'd felt an underlying edginess in him. Like he wouldn't let himself loosen up fully. She had to admit, she'd held back, too. But in her case, it was because the more she'd gotten to know him, the more tempting he'd become.

Before she could examine that thought, a woman in a blue suit appeared at their table and murmured in Ryan's ear.

Grey rose. "I'm sorry, but a problem's come up in the kitchen that needs my attention. Carry on and enjoy your meal. I'll be back once it's sorted."

Once he'd gone, the easy atmosphere turned a little tense. Just a notch, but noticeable nonetheless. Sapphie and Scotty talked about the quality of the food, the weather and the latest Ice Cats trade rumors. As they ate, their glasses were topped up regularly. She was aware of her defensive barriers lowering. She noticed that Scotty's came down a little, too.

When Ryan still hadn't returned by the time they'd finished, they ordered dessert. The conversation turned to books, movies and TV shows. They shared their love of Nordic noir crime procedurals, imported period dramas and classic Westerns and their dislike for reality TV, popular guy comedies and miserable literary tomes.

Gradually, the last vestiges of tension dissipated. They exchanged warm smiles. Every time he laid his hand on hers, pleasure rippled through her. When she touched him, the banked fire in his eyes started to burn more brightly.

The spell was partially broken when Ryan returned as they were finishing their coffees. Disappointment nudged.

"Apologies. That took longer than I thought." He explained briefly about the piece of equipment that had failed. "These things always happen during service on our busier nights. This is why you don't want to be hands-on in the restaurant business."

"I'm happy to leave that to the experts." Scotty nodded. "When I was playing, I always trusted the equipment guys. I trust *you* to help me hire a great manager, Grey."

"Like you trusted me to keep the snipers away from our net."

"And you trusted me to steal the biscuit off their sticks."

Sapphie smiled at their banter. "I wouldn't trust either of you as far as I could throw you, but I figure you're too stubborn to let this venture fail."

"Especially since we've retired and the money we earned playing doesn't last forever." Ryan slapped his friend on the shoulder.

"You've got that right." Scotty pushed back his chair and stood. "I have early meetings tomorrow.

Callum and I are seeing a couple of agents who've gotten nervous about their clients postacquisition. Who knew general management involved so much hand-holding?"

Sapphie rose and hugged Ryan. "Thanks for a lovely evening and for the opportunity to join your project."

"My pleasure. Don't be a stranger, partner."

"If you serve that caramel trio dessert when I visit, I may move to Jersey permanently."

Ryan laughed. "Done deal."

"Come on, *partner*, let's get you a ride home." Scotty crooked his arm, but his tone was a little curt.

Could he be jealous? That thought went to her head faster than the champagne.

Sapphie slipped her arm through his. "I'm in your hands, Captain."

"Now, there's a thought," he murmured so only she could hear it.

As they strolled out of Grey's toward the valet stand, she realized she didn't want the evening to end. She didn't want to scoot off like she had previously. Nor pretend she couldn't feel the heat shimmering between them like the waves rising off the sunbaked tarmac.

Their time working together with the Cats was almost over. At the end of the week, Marty would return and both groups would present their recommendations. Then she'd be moving on—either to Marty's next project or one of her other clients'.

Her company was in such great shape, with new projects coming in all the time, she could be flexible about what she focused on next. A lot of her work was repeat business or recommendation and referral, so she never had to hunt for new clients. Her people were top-notch. Sharp, innovative and loyal, they could be trusted to deliver to her standards. That left her free to be involved in only the most important projects.

Strangely, she was loath to head to Chicago and wondered about choosing an East Coast project for her next challenge. Confused by that feeling, unsure whether she was being influenced by her growing desire for the enigmatic man standing beside her, she decided to test the water.

"Let's go for a walk along the river." She tugged on Scotty's arm, pulling him toward the walkway beside the Hudson.

"Okay. Sure." He tucked her arm more firmly in his. "Which way would you like to go?"

"Left takes us toward the Brew House." She wrinkled her nose. "Let's go right. I know there's a lot of condo construction that way, but at least the waterfront is being retained and they're trying to keep it parklike." Damn it, the babbling struck again.

"Sounds good."

They strolled for a while saying nothing. Darkness had fallen, but old-fashioned lamps lit the path. The bright lights of Manhattan sparkled across the water. Lapping waves, chirping crickets and the low rumble of traffic provided an almost musical backdrop.

Scotty was easy company and comfortable with the silence. She smiled to herself. He was probably glad she wasn't her usual chatterbox self.

"What's so funny?" Scotty's deep voice washed over her like a caress.

"I was thinking that you were likely relieved I can keep my mouth shut for five minutes."

His laugh startled her. She stopped and looked at him.

"It hadn't crossed my mind." His eyes twinkled in the moonlight. "I *was* amazed that it was this quiet so close to the city."

"Maybe those mega condos help absorb the noise."

"Think of all the potential new customers living in those buildings, eager for a place to chill, eat great food and watch a game."

"Suddenly, I feel like they should build even more." She sighed happily. "This time next year the Brew House will be named Scotty's—or whatever you call it—and we'll be sitting on the new patio, enjoying an after-dinner drink."

His eyebrows arched. "That's a whimsical thought from someone who usually worries about turnover, profitability and market share."

"I'm not all work, all the time." Her defensiveness surprised her. Since when did her focus on her business bother her?

"It wasn't a criticism," he said softly.

"I didn't take it as one." She hoped her smile didn't look as forced as it felt. "Shall we go farther or head back? I don't want to keep you out too late."

"We can go a bit longer."

Inordinately pleased that he hadn't opted to curtail their time together, she nodded and they resumed walking.

After a few hundred yards, the path began to break up near a construction site, so they turned and headed toward Grey's. By unspoken agreement, their pace slowed as they neared the restaurant.

"Do you know yet where you'll be working next?" Scotty asked.

She shook her head. "Marty's my biggest client, so he tends to get priority. I'll head to Chicago for a few days and touch base with my people." She didn't share her earlier thoughts about choosing a project closer by.

"So you won't be sticking around Jersey?"

Did he want her to stay? "Not initially." She added, "That doesn't mean I can't come back for nonwork reasons."

They stopped again. This time, Scotty slipped his arms around her. "I know this isn't what we agreed, but I feel like if I don't do it now, I may not get another chance."

She wanted to say something light, but her throat was so tight she couldn't get any words out.

He continued, "Once Friday's meeting is over, things will be different for us. We won't be working together anymore, so the rules will change."

"That doesn't have to be a bad thing." Her breathy words sounded like an invitation.

"I don't know about you, but I'm hoping it's the opposite."

Sapphie hesitated. If she took the next step, she'd be opening a door she'd always kept firmly closed. A relationship was not in the cards, no matter how much she liked Scotty. Nor how much her body wanted him. She would walk away the minute she felt the commitment noose tightening. But she didn't want to hurt him.

She looked into his face. Thanks to the moonlight, she could see the steady, determined look in those serious eyes as he watched her patiently, waiting for her response.

Her conversation with Issy came to her. Why was she worrying about the end before it had even started, again? If Scotty was prepared to take a chance on them having a no-strings relationship, then who was she to argue?

Assuming he was still interested. There was only one way to find out. "I've changed my mind about us."

He looked startled by her abrupt words. "In what way?"

"I think, once this week and this contract are done, we should date. With the understanding that there's no commitment on either side and that we can both walk away at any time."

"I see. So we get together whenever you're in town and enjoy each other's company."

"Right. Or you could fly to Chicago. Or we could meet somewhere halfway."

"Okay. Any other conditions I should know about?"

She couldn't tell from his tone how he felt about it. "I don't think so."

"All right. That works for me." He smoothed some strands of hair that had blown across her cheek. "Since Friday's only a few days away, we could get a head start."

Sapphie didn't want to wait either. She wanted him now. But she didn't want to upset a delicately balanced situation. Once again she heard Issy's admonishing voice. Sapphie needed to get over herself and let Scotty decide how he wanted to play this.

"It seems silly to waste a perfectly good evening," she said finally.

"So you wouldn't mind if I did this?" He ran his thumb over her bottom lip.

The tip of her tongue followed the path his thumb had taken. "Not at all."

"That's a relief. I wouldn't want to go too far."
Not far enough!

His chuckle made her realize she'd said the words aloud. Heat brushed her cheeks, but she didn't retreat.

"How about this?" He pressed his mouth to her forehead.

"That's better."

"And this?" He kissed the tip of her nose.

"That's okay, too." She wanted to tell him to speed it up, but she enjoyed this teasing side of him.

He skimmed his lips over her cheek, lingering for a moment, then moved lower and along her jaw to her chin. "Still all right?"

"Yes." Instead of boldly, the word came out on a breath.

"What about now?" He kissed the corner of her mouth.

She turned her head, wanting the full press of his lips against hers. But he wouldn't let her have her way and repeated the kiss on the other side of her mouth.

"Scott," she moaned softly with frustration.

"I'm taking a flier here and assuming you won't object to this." His mouth covered hers and the teasing stopped.

Her lips parted, turning the kiss fiery almost instantly. Her arms wound around his neck.

He crushed her against him, one hand anchoring her head.

Their tongues tangled, making the kiss burn hotter and brighter, until they broke apart, gasping for air. She dropped her cheek to his shoulder, trying to calm her heart rate. His chin rested on top of her head and they stood for several minutes, wrapped in each other's arms, chests heaving in unison.

Stunned by how quickly their kiss had threatened to spiral out of control, she knew it was time to stop. Reluctantly, she pulled out of his embrace. Unsure what to do with her arms, she crossed them over her stomach.

"It's probably not a good idea to take this any further tonight." Then, concerned that sounded cold, she added, "Not because I don't want to. It's just that…" Her voice trailed off as his finger pressed to her lips.

"I know. I agree."

"It's only a few more days, and then we are free to explore this any way we like and…" She puffed out a frustrated sigh. "What is it about you that makes me babble like a loon?"

He smiled. "If it makes you feel better, I've talked more to you than anyone else, ever."

Gratified, Sapphie stored that tidbit away.

They strolled to the restaurant, hand in hand. How was it that the walk out had taken almost half an hour, but the return seemed to take only a few minutes?

A yellow cab was discharging its passengers when they got to Grey's. The driver agreed to take Sapphie, as she was on his route into the city.

She got into the taxi. "I'll see you in the office tomorrow."

"Look forward to it." He pressed a quick, hard kiss to her lips, then stepped back and closed the door. Once again he watched until the cab turned the corner.

As it turned out, they didn't see much of each other over the next couple days. The pressure to finish the presentations before Marty arrived meant they were tied up in meetings with their respective teams.

But Scotty surprised her by texting. Short messages—some cute, some funny, some simply saying hi—to let her know he was thinking of her. She looked forward to those messages more than she wanted to admit. Each one warmed her heart and made her eager to finish this contract.

There were hints in the messages that they might get together on the weekend, but nothing was said outright. Anticipation built, until she knew that whatever happened on Friday, she wanted to be with Scotty on Saturday.

On Friday morning, she dressed carefully. This was an important day for professional and personal reasons, so she wanted to be at her best. She picked out a bright floral shift dress with a matching short-sleeved jacket and her lucky Louboutins. She slipped her favorite lipstick into her purse and headed for the Ice Cats' head office with a spring in her step.

Marty was already there when she arrived, having flown in late the previous night. Over coffee, they caught up on a couple of their other projects, which were running smoothly, then headed to the boardroom.

Her pulse skipped when she saw Scotty inside, talking to Callum. The look they exchanged was full of promise for later. Damn the man! He'd turned smoldering into an art form. From the half smile curving his lips, he knew it, too. Who knew Scotty had such a playful side? She deliberately moistened her lips, letting him know that two could play that game, and enjoyed seeing his pupils flare.

Marty called the meeting to order, and all too soon, it was her turn to speak.

She was surprised that, like the last time she stood before this group, she was uncharacteristically nervous. Unlike before, though, Scotty's eyes weren't accusatory.

This would be a piece of cake. They'd make their presentations, agree about the actions and move on to the next step. She couldn't wait.

Smiling at her audience, Sapphie pulled up her first slide.

CHAPTER EIGHT

"YOU CANNOT BE SERIOUS."

Thanks to one of those fateful split seconds of silence, Scott's muttered words boomed across the boardroom.

Ah, hell. He'd tried to keep his growing dismay under wraps as Sapphie's group went through their presentations. He'd reminded himself that their proposals were only recommendations and that he and Callum had yet to put forward their perspective. But when the cocky kid in the trendy suit had said what had been successful for Antonelli's basketball team would work for the hockey franchise, Scott had started to lose it.

Beside him, Callum shifted in his seat. Scott glanced at his boss and was relieved to see he was fighting a smile.

"Is there a problem, Scotty?" Cocky Kid curled his lip.

Scott had faced decades of chirping from better opponents without blinking, yet something about the puffed-up jackass got to him. Using the cool, reprimanding tone that had terrified many a rookie, he said, "It's Scott, unless you're a teammate. And yes, there's a problem. But I'll wait until a more appropriate time to air my concerns." He turned to Marty. "My apologies for the interruption."

The owner waved off his apology. "Passion is always welcome. I'll be interested to hear what you have to say."

Scott nodded and turned his attention to the dickwad presenting. "Please carry on."

Callum murmured, "One–zip to the Ice Cats."

As Cocky Kid began speaking again, Scott noticed Sapphie's frown. She'd obviously figured out, as he had, that the two groups were fundamentally at odds. And it could only get worse.

That he and Sapphie would be on opposite sides of a professional argument, just as things were finally beginning to improve for them personally, bothered him more than it should. It wasn't that he was worried about upsetting her, but he didn't want business to come between them outside the boardroom. Especially after that kiss at Grey's.

Even so, he wouldn't let anything damage his team. Unfortunately, if it came to pissing off the beautiful woman opposite him or protecting the Cats, there would be only one winner.

Celine's voice echoed in his head. "You've never cheated on me with another woman, but those damn Ice Cats are a demanding mistress."

As far as his marriage was concerned, it was probably true. His commitment to the Cats had become an easy excuse to avoid the tension at home once he and Celine had drifted apart, though he'd tried to be there for his kids whenever possible.

Pushing the memories aside, Scott focused on the meeting. Thankfully, Cocky Kid was winding up. Once he was done, Marty suggested they break for lunch.

As people stood, stretched and took advantage of the break, Scott noticed the room split into factions. Antonelli's people gathered around Sapphie, while the Cats' staff stood near the credenza, where lunch was being laid out. There were no overt signs of animosity, but the urgent conversations in both groups didn't look friendly.

"What makes you think we'll get a hostile reception when we speak?" Callum didn't sound fazed by the prospect.

"Yeah. Somehow I prefer the hostile reception I used to get on the ice. Battling with words isn't my strong suit."

"You can handle those people." Callum loaded his plate with sandwiches. "You did right. You made it clear that we won't be bullied into accepting things we don't agree with."

"As long as I haven't made things more difficult."

"It was never going to be easy. New ownership always wants to get a bunch of quick wins. Their people want to prove they're better than the old guard. Of course, usually, they're taking on a losing franchise, so there's plenty of room for improvement. Antonelli's guys can't complain about the product on the ice, so they have to focus on front-office issues—the biggest being the fact that the franchise isn't making enough money."

Walking over to the windows, they started eating.

"At least Marty seems prepared to listen to us before making any decisions," Callum said. "We've prepared as best we can. If he overrules our recommendations, we won't give up. We'll try to score on the rebound."

Scott nodded. "For sure."

As people from both factions joined them, they deliberately turned the conversation to more neutral topics—like which of the prospects at training camp would make the big team during the season. The debate grew lively with everyone making their predictions, yet it remained good-natured.

Although Sapphie took part in the discussion, Scott noticed that she avoided meeting his gaze. He tried not to take it personally, equating it to a pregame warm-up—when players avoided contact with longtime friends on the opposing team. Still, he didn't like it. She was skittish enough; he didn't need anything knocking them off balance now.

After tonight he and Sapphie would start a fresh phase—they'd effectively be dating—one he'd been optimistic about. He figured the no-commitment thing was only a temporary hurdle he planned to do his best to encourage her over. Starting with the coming weekend.

Anticipation had been growing as he'd thought of how they could spend the two days before Sapphie had to leave for Chicago. Casual, fun things—a walk along the High Line in the city, a ride on the Staten Island Ferry, maybe a trip to the shore. And yeah, things that might entice her to visit the East Coast more often.

Now he wondered whether he'd been foolishly overconfident. Was he kidding himself that he had a chance with her?

By the time Marty returned and everyone re-took their seats around the table, there were indications of a thaw between the two sides. Scott took it as a positive sign, though he was fully aware that it wouldn't last long once he began to speak.

Sapphie was the last to sit. Her body language was deceptively laid-back. Only someone looking closely would notice the glint in her blue eyes. Scott recognized a game face when he saw one.

Callum took the first shift, outlining the strengths and weaknesses of the organization as his management group saw them. Since many of them had already been highlighted by the other team, there wasn't much argument.

The air was definitely less tense by the time Scott strode to the head of the table and revealed the proposals he and Callum had developed. He spoke slowly, clearly, ensuring he made eye contact with those on both sides. He didn't attempt to engage Sapphie.

Within a couple of slides, the atmosphere had changed. It was clear that the two groups were coming at the key issues from different angles. Both had profitability at their core, but while Sapphie's team looked to streamline and cut, at least in the short term, Callum's looked to expand and develop.

All pretense of being laid-back now gone, Sapphie leaned forward, making copious notes. She said nothing, but it was only a matter of time. Part of him wished she'd challenge him. He'd always preferred a direct attack, relying on his wits and gut instinct to survive and win.

Wondering what would come made Scott edgy. He wrapped up with his final slide, then returned to his seat and awaited the onslaught of questions.

Before that could happen, Marty spoke. "Well now, that's very interesting."

He thanked both groups for their proposals. "Usually when I acquire a business, the issues and solutions are pretty clear. More often than not, the existing management is either unaware of the problems or unwilling to acknowledge them, let alone able to provide a comprehensive program of change designed to address them."

He tapped his forehead with two fingers. "I salute you and your team, Callum. It's not often I'm surprised or impressed, but you have done both. You clearly understand what's wrong and have strong opinions about how to fix the problems, without forgetting the all-important bottom line."

Looking round the room, it appeared Marty had taken the wind out of some of his own group's sails with his comments. Cocky Kid didn't look so arrogant now. But Scott knew success wouldn't be that easy.

Sure enough, Marty's next words threw down the gauntlet. "The floor is open for comments and discussion. I'll remind those of you new to my way of doing things that all criticism should be constructive."

There was a murmur of agreement around the table. Morgan volunteered to make notes about the decisions and actions on the whiteboards.

Callum started the discussion by supporting one of Sapphie's suggestions regarding travel expenditure. "There are definitely economies that could be made by negotiating for both your basketball team and the Ice Cats. Given deals achieved by Making Your Move over the past couple of years, I suggest we give them that project."

"Excellent choice." Sapphie smiled. "Because of their connection to this organization, I've researched them extensively." It was commonly known that the key partners, Tracy and Maggie, were married to Ice Cats players. "They give outstanding service to all their clients. Even our rivals have nothing but praise for them."

Sapphie then supported their recommendation regarding donation of goods and services rather than money for charities and projects in the local community.

"Excellent." Marty rubbed his hands together. "Note it on the board, Morgan."

After the polite opening gambits, both sides moved on to areas where, with minor tweaks, there could be agreement. Once the less contentious points were covered off, they began to tackle more complex issues. The debates grew more heated and compromises were harder fought, but eventually the majority of the operational proposals were approved in principle.

Things came to a head with the sales, marketing and sponsorship recommendations.

"There was no cohesion in the promotions run over the previous few seasons," Sapphie said. "They didn't follow a theme or purpose. Sponsorship of the promotions was ad hoc. Deals and giveaways should benefit not only the team but also the sponsor. It will encourage repeat support and hopefully increase revenue."

Scott responded, "That's why the marketing program we want to implement this season and going forward is multilayered and ties into promotions we run in the team shops, on the website, through social media and in the community." He outlined some examples.

Sapphie countered with the same marketing plan as apparently worked for Antonelli's basketball team, citing numbers to support its success.

Scott chose his words carefully. "What works in one sport doesn't necessarily translate to others. Big promotions that benefit a small number of people don't appeal as much to our fans as those that benefit a lot. Give a row a pizza or toss out a bunch of T-shirts every game and they'll be far happier than if they got the chance to win a holiday."

Sapphie's smile didn't reach her eyes. "Naturally, we want to promote goodwill within the arena, but we need to look beyond that to encourage the casual fan. And be more responsive to market dynamics."

From her position by the whiteboard, Morgan joined the debate, supporting Scott's position. Cocky Kid jumped in to back Sapphie. Tones grew more strained and the language less diplomatic as the two sides lined up against each other.

Scott defended his proposal. "One of the issues we had under the previous ownership was that decisions were dictated by nonbusiness factors, like the state of personal finances. Or what their wives thought was a good idea."

"I hardly think we're talking about such whimsical tactics," Sapphie retorted.

Scott noticed that everyone was watching their disagreement with the avid interest of spectators at a play-off game. Though he and Sapphie remained in their seats, it felt like they were fighting toe-to-toe. Neither gave an inch, until Marty stepped in.

"Let's table this discussion."

Sapphie's gaze clashed with Scott's. He couldn't miss her irritation and frustration. He didn't flinch. Too bad. He wouldn't roll over to make her happy. If they had to be on opposite sides to prevent plans that he felt were wrong from being implemented, so be it.

Regardless, he didn't like being at odds with her. He'd never liked conflict in his personal life. Perhaps that was why he'd gone to such great lengths to avoid it with Celine. Heading out for an extra session at the gym was easier than arguing with his wife.

He was glad this meeting would be over soon. Only a couple more issues to resolve. Then he had to get through the rest of the afternoon without saying something inflammatory and they'd be safe.

Easier said than freaking done.

Callum fought their corner effectively and aggressively. Sapphie also took more of a backseat, speaking only to clarify or emphasize a point. The sun set, the boardroom lights were switched on and still the two sides battled. One thing they agreed on—no one wanted the meeting to stretch into a second day.

Finally, only one point remained—supplier invoicing.

Scott was starting to breathe easier, figuring they were in the last minute of play, when Cocky Kid spoke up.

Callum and Scott exchanged a look—much as they wanted to let it ride, they couldn't.

Knowing he was about to blow his best intentions out of the water, Scott took a deep breath and said, "We can't agree to a strategy that will strip away the goodwill this organization has built over decades with the people who do work for us."

Sapphie arched an eyebrow. "How does making sure the business is fiscally tight do that? Suppliers get fair pay for good work and they get paid in a timely fashion. They are granted exclusive status that is renewed through a proper pitch system, not based on who's best buddies with the owner. The organization gets proper quotes and pays competitive rates to the best suppliers. In addition, all work costs are transparent, enabling sound budgeting and financial control. Surely, that's a win-win?"

"In principle, you're right," Scott acknowledged. "However, let me give you an example of where that can fall down. Imagine Joe Schmoe, a plumber and a big Ice Cats fan, has been doing work for us for years. For major jobs, he follows the route you laid out. However, for small repairs, he receives payment in kind—a pair of season tickets and an advert in every program."

Sapphie's lips tightened with disapproval, but she nodded for him to continue.

"Some years, he'll make out like a bandit. Other years, he'll lose out. Either way, he's happy and a loyal supporter of the Cats. Take away his tickets and advert, then make him invoice every job, and while he might technically be better off, you've ticked him off big-time. Is it worth fiscal tightness for that?"

"He has a point." Marty looked to Sapphie for her riposte. Naming a figure that was equal to the salary of a top forward like J.B. Larocque, her counter was as sharp as a well-placed one-timer. "That's how much money was lost because of payment in kind. Not to Joe Schmoe and his service-providing pals, nor to charities, foundations and good causes like supporting our troops or celebrating a local hero, but to businesses in the area for nothing more than 'goodwill.'" She emphasized her words with air quotes as she gave Darren a pointed look. "Imagine what the organization could have done with those funds."

Scott couldn't argue. "So one size doesn't fit all."

"No, but one starts with best practice and works from there."

Scott opened his mouth to reply, but Marty

tapped the barrel of his Montblanc pen against a water glass. "We've come a long way today and everyone needs a break."

The room was silent, waiting for him to announce the next step.

"There are points of value from both proposals. You have shown examples of where compromise, creativity and the spirit, rather than the letter, of a rule can provide enormous benefits. And where rigor, structure and proper process can, too." Marty's smile encompassed the two groups.

"I'm sure, with more time, a comprehensive plan that will benefit from the best of both worlds can be created. But the season starts in a little over a month and I don't want to go into it with unnecessary uncertainty. Therefore, a plan must be in place before the puck drops on opening night."

Suddenly, Scott knew where the owner was going. His stomach tightened as his gaze snapped up to meet Sapphie's. The dawning realization and a touch of dread showed in her eyes.

"I want both sides to work together and come to an agreement that incorporates the best of each proposal," Marty said. "Sapphie and Scott, you'll spearhead this project and come back in four weeks with a recommendation that you are happy to put your names to." He fixed them with his steely gaze. "Any problems?"

What could Scott say?

Nothing short of death would be an acceptable

excuse for saying no. For sure not the fear that Scott would lose the progress he and Sapphie had made personally. Marty wouldn't care that his demands were a game changer.

Less than a day to go before he was to have been more than a business associate to Sapphie and now Scott's plans were going up in smoke. What would the next month do to his chances with Sapphie?

He looked at her. Despite her carefully schooled expression, challenge glittered in her eyes. That told him all he needed to know. An already-bumpy road had turned into a potholed four-wheel-drive-only track.

None of that mattered as far as his owner and his boss were concerned.

"Cracked it," Callum murmured. "You can rock this."

Hoping his smile didn't look as grim as it felt, he said, "No problems from my side."

The ball was firmly in Sapphie's court.

YEARS OF PRACTICE with unpredictable clients—Marty was definitely top of the list—helped Sapphie keep her expression neutral. Okay, so she bit her tongue to stop a "Hell yes, I have a problem" from escaping.

This was *not* how these negotiations were meant to go.

She'd had it all planned. Her time with the Ice

Cats would end today. She'd been looking forward to putting business aside and seeing where the weekend took her and Scotty. True, she'd anticipated a late-night finish—this type of proposal presentation always ran over. She'd even assumed she'd have to return for a follow-up at some point because of the complexity of the situation. Not to mention the strong opposing proposals.

But four more weeks? Working with Scotty. That definitely hadn't been in the plan.

She wasn't happy about this. She didn't want the lines blurred between them and this threatened to do exactly that. She didn't want to wait a month.

"Sapphie?" Marty interrupted her thoughts, looking at her expectantly, though he knew there was no way she'd refuse.

One of the issues with being on retainer for Marty was that she had to stay on her toes, ready to duck and dive as needed. The rewards were worth it—Sapphie's future was secure thanks to him. Still, she knew better than to give in too easily. He occasionally needed reminding that she had other clients and that he shouldn't take her for granted.

Sapphie pulled up her calendar on her phone and studied it for a few moments before answering. "I'll have to rearrange some things in my schedule, as I was due to finish up here today. I definitely need to be in Chicago for the beginning of next week, but I should be able to return late Wednesday."

"Your deadline is set in stone, so how you organize your time is up to you." Marty smiled, acknowledging her game. "I know you'll deliver, so I'm not worried."

"Then we're good."

After that the meeting ended and the room emptied fairly quickly. Sapphie lingered to have a private word with Marty. Not to try to change his mind—that would never happen—but to get a better feel for what he wanted to see from the revised recommendation.

"Interesting meeting," she said.

Marty chuckled. "Scotty Matthews is the same in the boardroom as he was on the ice. Quietly goes about his business until someone steps out of line. Then, boom!" He smacked his fist into his palm. "I think he and Hardshaw make a good team."

Scotty had impressed her, too. He clearly suited a role behind the scenes better than one in front of a camera. Although she'd disagreed with his position and felt some of his suggestions were naive, he'd performed better than most of her rookie consultants. In other circumstances, she'd have offered him a job. High praise, given she recruited only the best.

"I agree," she said. "They'll certainly keep you hopping."

"You know I prefer a challenge. That's why I changed the GM of my basketball team. I couldn't stand having a guy who rolled over every time I spoke up."

"Worse, he flip-flopped anytime anyone disagreed with him. Remember his panicked expression when you and I argued about the arena sponsor. He didn't know which side to support." She sighed. "The weird thing is he'd been a leader in the locker room. But in the boardroom, he crumbled at the first sign of conflict."

"Goes to show that you can't tell how these guys will work out. It's a crapshoot. Like you and me, they have to have it in here—" he patted his stomach "—and in here—" he thumped his fist against his chest "—as well as plenty up here." He tapped his fingers against his forehead.

"You make it sound like a bad dose of the flu," she teased.

"So, can you get along with our former captain?" Marty's dark eyes had a knowing look.

The man always saw more than she'd wanted him to. He was one of the most perceptive men she'd ever worked with. And not only on the business side. But as avuncular as he appeared, Sapphie wasn't comfortable letting him see her vulnerability.

"Shouldn't be a problem. There will be some things he'll have to compromise on and others

I'll have to back down on. But it will all benefit the Ice Cats."

"Good, because I sensed an underlying tension." Though it was a statement, his tone made it sound like a question.

"We both feel strongly about our respective positions and care deeply for this team."

Marty gave her a searching look. For a moment, she thought he might probe further, but he let it go. "Glad to hear it. I like passionate, committed people working for me. Nothing gets in the way of your drive to succeed."

She knew he meant it as a compliment, but Sapphie couldn't help the sharp sting of pique. Strange, as she'd always prided herself on that determination. After what she'd gone through as a child, she never wanted to be dependent on anyone else for her well-being or her success.

Still, Marty's words bothered her. It sounded like there was nothing in her life but work. That nothing else mattered.

Isn't that the truth?

Sapphie ignored the voice inside. She saw friends, went out with men, had a good time. She was happy. This was probably disappointment that a project she'd thought was in the bag turned out not to be.

And that her chance to enjoy a personal relationship with Scotty had been delayed for at least a month. Drinks, dinner, dating…not going to happen.

Marty patted her on the shoulder. "I know my decision has thrown a wrench in your schedule, but I need this fixed ASAP."

"Of course. I'll make it work."

"I know you will. Now I'd better head out. Gloria is hosting a fund-raiser tomorrow and will doubtless have a honey-do list as long as your arm." His smile was indulgent. "Do you want my plane to make a stop in Chicago on our way?"

She had to deal with Scotty first. "Thanks, but I have some things to sort out before I leave. I'll ask my assistant to get me tickets for tomorrow morning."

As it happened, there was nothing available until noon the following day. Not ideal, but at least she didn't have to rush around like a lunatic. She could still make her evening plans with Scotty, but it was probably wiser to cancel them.

Sapphie was packing up her briefcase when she heard a knock on the door. Looking up, she saw Scotty leaning against the doorjamb. His expression was hard to read.

"Sorry, I can't make dinner tonight," she said brightly. "I decided to head to Chicago early. I need to catch up with my people first thing Monday morning. That way I'll be ready to return midweek and we can get cracking on—" She paused. "See, babbling again."

His smile was strained at the edges. "I'd hoped you could at least stay until Sunday so we could have dinner tonight and maybe do something tomorrow."

She stopped in midaction sliding her laptop into her case, ridiculously tempted to stay. Just a little longer.

No. "That wouldn't be smart. We'll be working together closely for the next month and anything... social...would only confuse things."

He straightened. "We've been through this. We both know where the line is and how to avoid crossing it."

"But that doesn't mean we won't *want* to cross it," she said softly. "Far better to wait. It's only four weeks, and then we'll be free to do whatever we want, without having to worry about muddying the professional water."

"So you don't want to have drinks together anymore?"

Drinks led to dinner, which led to walks in the moonlight and...

Again, *no.* "It's not that I don't *want* to. I don't think we *should.* Look, the sooner we get all those issues hammered out and a proposal ready for Marty, the sooner we can enjoy ourselves."

"Yeah, that's a great incentive." He made it sound like the complete opposite.

If she was truthful, she felt the same way. "I'm sorry, but I think it's for the best."

"I don't." He scrubbed his hand over his face.

The rasp caused by his five-o'clock shadow made Sapphie want to run her fingers over his jaw.

He continued, "And I don't see how anything's changed. We managed fine these past few weeks."

"But we hardly saw each other. Now we'll be constantly together. Negotiating terms and pulling together a workable plan. Then getting everyone to buy in."

"How does that affect us going out together? I'm perfectly capable of sitting in the same room as you all day and not giving in to my baser instincts. Nothing will happen that you don't want. Your body is safe from me."

She was just as capable of withstanding the attraction. Although she didn't find it quite as easy to deny that she wanted him. "We both know the game changed during that walk at Grey's. Lovely as that kiss was, it can't happen again. At least, not while we're working together," she amended.

"Why not? It was just a kiss. Not a marriage proposal."

She pushed aside her irritation at his easy dismissal of the heat that had flared between them. "Thank goodness, because the answer would definitely be no."

"Trust me, I'm not desperate to get hitched again so soon either," he retorted. Unfortunately, his defensive tone gave away more than his words.

"The point is that I will *never* want to be tied

down." She massaged her temples, where she could feel a headache brewing. "We've been over this. What if we date and I want out before the end of the month? That'll make things awkward for us finishing our work."

"I'm sure we can be adult about it." Scotty sighed. "We agreed on the rules of engagement the other night. If we both know where we stand, what's the harm?"

He made it sound so simple. Ordinarily, it would be. Hell, ordinarily, she'd be the one re-assuring the guy that she wouldn't be clingy if things went south.

With Scotty, it was different. He made her feel things no one else had ever made her feel. And when it came to rules, he made her think not about bending them but about breaking them.

That couldn't happen. She lifted her chin. "I don't want to hurt you. We may last longer than a month. We may not. For however long we're to-gether, I'm sure we'll have a wonderful time. But at some point, it *will* end."

"I get that. I don't need you to handle me with kid gloves."

Still, the insecurities of her childhood came flooding back. Ruthlessly, she forced them into the dark recesses of her mind while acknowl-edging that this man had the ability to make her vulnerable to all of that. This was why she had those rules. She couldn't…wouldn't…go through it again.

And yet she couldn't deny that he could also make her very happy. That weekend… Definitely not helpful for those memories to surface.

Scotty walked toward her. He came close enough to touch her but didn't. "Okay, what if we go forward as we have been for the next month, on the understanding that if you want to walk away, I won't try to stop you."

Why couldn't she be as single-minded about this, about them, as she was about business decisions? "You can opt out at any time, too."

"Of course." He tilted his head in acknowledgment.

Suddenly, she was tired of fighting him. Why deny herself what she wanted? "All right, you win."

"Let's seal that deal." He stuck out a hand.

She shook it, enjoying the warmth of his palm against hers. And that familiar, delicious tingle that danced up her arm.

Scotty's winning smile said he felt it, too. "So now that we've agreed on terms, will you have dinner with me?"

Sapphie wanted to, but she needed time to regroup. For once, she managed to restrain the urge to babble. "I'd love to, but I have things to do before my flight tomorrow morning."

Scotty didn't argue. "What time's your flight? I'll take you to the airport. I'll even throw in breakfast."

"That would be lovely. Thank you." She told him when she had to be at the terminal.

"Thank *you* for giving us this next month." Scotty brushed his fingers over her hair. He hesitated, as if debating whether or not to kiss her.

Sapphie held her breath—wanting him to and not wanting him to in equal measure. Well, not quite equal. Her lips parted in anticipation.

He kissed the tip of her nose, then stepped back. "I'll pick you up at eight."

After he'd gone, she remained where she was, staring into space. She'd made the right decision. She'd gotten everything she'd wanted out of the negotiation. So why was she nervous? And why did she have a feeling that the next month would define her future, in more ways than one? For better or worse. Her stomach twisted at the phrase. Her gaze dropped to the deliberately naked third finger of her left hand.

No matter how long they lasted, that was one outcome there was absolutely no chance she would allow. She'd walk away first. The problem was she knew at some point that's exactly what she'd have to do.

CHAPTER NINE

"MOM DRANK THE grocery money again."

Sapphie should have known when her younger sister's name appeared on the caller ID that the Saturday-morning phone call from North Carolina would be bad news. She phoned Emerald every Sunday evening, so anything that varied from the routine was definitely trouble.

She sank onto her suitcase and looked at the clear blue sky, trying to draw strength from the beautiful morning for the conversation ahead. Having been cooped up in the Cats' office building for too long this week, Sapphie had decided to wait for Scotty outside her condo. With impeccable timing, the never-ending drama that was her family reared its ugly head.

"Has Mom spent it all?" Sapphie asked wearily, knowing the answer already.

Emerald blew her nose. "I found a twenty-dollar bill stashed in her underwear drawer, but the rest is gone. I locked away the one unopened bottle of Jim Beam she had left. Thank the Lord I paid the bills day before yesterday, or we'd be in real trouble."

"Oh, Em. You know how devious she is. I thought we agreed you'd change where you keep the cash box every time you got your paycheck."

Sapphie had given up trying to convince Emerald that she should keep her money in the bank account Sapphie had set up. Even though the thought of her sister with a checkbook, or worse, a credit card, sent shivers through her—especially if their mother could lay her hands on them as easily as she did the cash box—Sapphie had hoped it might provide some protection for Emerald. But like most everyone in town, her sister didn't use the account; she paid cash for everything.

"I did. This week, I put it out in the shed, behind the tools. But I have a date with Jimmy Lee tonight and I wanted to buy a pretty dress in Simpson's and I don't get paid again until Monday. So yesterday I borrowed some of the grocery money and put the tin in my bedside cabinet to remind me to repay it from my wages. I forgot it was there, until I found Mom passed out on her bed, with the empties beside her. I'm sorry."

"That's okay. Don't worry. We'll fix this."

Sapphie rubbed her forehead. Though she was only four years older, she'd been taking care of her sister for as long as she could remember. The pull of drink had always been stronger for Ruby Houlihan than any maternal instinct. Their mother took advantage of Emerald's gentle nature whenever she could.

Sapphie loved Emerald dearly, but her sister was a naive, little bunny in the den of a conniving fox.

This kind of mess was why Sapphie had left her hometown as soon as she could. And why she never went to visit for longer than a couple days. She still regretted that she hadn't taken Em with her, even though her sister hadn't wanted to leave any more than Sapphie could have stayed. And she felt guilty that the money she sent Em every month wasn't the same as being there in person. But it was the best Sapphie could do. It was a solution that suited everyone involved.

She checked her watch. It wasn't too late to get money to Emerald today so there would be food in the house for the weekend. "As soon as I hang up, I'll wire you some money to tide you over. Like always, you should be able to collect it when you go to the store."

"Thanks, Sapphie. You're the best."

Financial crisis averted, the sisters chatted briefly about Emerald's new boyfriend—a guy from a couple towns away who was as sweet natured as she was. Sapphie hoped the two might get serious, getting her sister away from their mother's grasp.

"When are you coming home?" Em asked wistfully. "I miss you."

"I miss you, too. Remember you're coming to visit me for Thanksgiving." She and Issy had arranged for their sisters to visit Jersey, rather than the other way around, this year.

"I can't wait." Emerald sighed. "Mom's not happy. She's angling to come, too."

No way in hell.

Her sister continued, "She says Thanksgiving is a family holiday."

Yeah, right. Like their mother gave a damn about family. Ruby cared only about herself and who she could beg, borrow or steal her next drink from. Her attempts at a guilt trip hadn't worked on Sapphie for years.

"There isn't room for her to come, Em." Sapphie softened her refusal. "If she gives you a hard time, I'll speak to her."

Just then, Scotty's black SUV pulled into the parking space in front of her building. He waved as he climbed out.

Her heart gave a little thunk. He looked good in his khaki shorts and red polo shirt. The man had great legs. Must be all that skating.

"I have to go, Em. My ride is here. I'll speak to you when I get to Chicago."

While Sapphie finished her phone call and wired the money to her sister, Scotty put her suitcase in his car.

She finally put her phone away and smiled at him. "Sorry, family troubles."

"I hear you." He held open the car door for her,

then closed it and went around the other side to climb in. "Everything okay?"

"Not really, but it's not serious." She was embarrassed to share the details of her dysfunctional family with him. "My sister needed some money."

"Been there, done that, got that T-shirt."

"Really?" She looked up, surprised, from fastening her seat belt. "You have sister problems, too?"

"Hell yeah. My mom's great, but my sister is a pain in the ass." He drove out of the lot. "Mom runs a bar in a nowhere small town in northern Canada. My father isn't in the picture. He worked on the oil pipeline and hooked up with Mom one weekend in Edmonton, then disappeared into the Northwest Territories."

"Nice. Not."

He shrugged. "Happens a lot. At least he didn't marry her and abuse her."

"True." Sapphie thought of her own father, who had married Ruby when he'd gotten her pregnant. They'd both been mean drunks who liked nothing better than to scream at each other and anyone who got in their way.

"I have a half sister who either doesn't talk to me or harangues me with the Bible because—" he lowered his voice, as if talking about something shocking "—I play *hockey*—an evil, violent, godless game. She lives at home and works in Mom's bar. When I say *works*, I mean that loosely. Her father never married my mother either and isn't on the scene." He looked at her and grinned. "Enough problems for you?"

"I definitely don't feel abnormal anymore."

What she didn't get was why he was so determined to have a relationship when he clearly hadn't grown up in a happy family and his own marriage had fallen apart. She'd have thought it would be the last thing he'd want.

Scotty flicked the indicator, then joined the slip-road for I-95. Once he'd merged into traffic, he asked, "So, what's your story?"

"It's almost as pitiful as yours. Although my sister, Emerald, is a sweetie."

"Seriously? Your parents named you after gem-stones?"

Sapphie twisted her lips. "It's a Southern thing. My mother's name is Ruby. My granny was Pearl, and I have aunties called Opal, Garnet and Topaz."

"Go figure."

Despite what he'd shared, Sapphie was just as embarrassed as she always was when it came to explaining about her family.

"I grew up in the same kind of nowhere place but in North Carolina. A lot of poor folks, very few jobs and a lot of hand-to-mouth living. Issy's mom used to sum it up perfectly—'not enough money to live, not enough money to leave.' Her parents and mine were best friends who loved to party together."

She decided not to sugarcoat the grim reality of her background as much as she usually did. She needed Scotty to understand why she felt so strongly about relationships and commitment. "When my parents worked, they drank their paychecks, and when they were unemployed, they drank what anyone else got them. They didn't care about their kids, only about getting loaded. As soon as I was old enough, I took care of myself and my sister. I was the one who made sure there was food on the table and a roof over our heads. I also made sure my sister went to school and did her homework."

Scotty looked a little shell-shocked. "Your sister still lives at home?"

"As soon as I could afford it, I helped her buy her own place, hoping to get her away from our parents. It worked for a while, but when our father was killed in a drunk-driving accident, Mom told Em she couldn't handle living on her own and my softhearted sister bought it."

Scotty whistled through his teeth. "Man, that's tough. I never would have guessed where you came from and what you've been through."

She didn't need his pity, just for him to get why she was determined never to be shackled by family and responsibilities again. "I've worked hard to leave it behind."

"At least my mom always looked after us. And she was the one who got me into hockey, which gave me my ticket out. When I moved into billets, I got lucky with a nice family. I stayed with them until I got married and had my own family."

Sapphie realized that while on the surface their pasts seemed to have a lot in common, their stories had taken different turns, with different results. Scotty, like Issy, yearned for stability through marriage and family. For Sapphie, stability came through her financial independence. Freedom and control of her own life mattered more than anything.

Scotty must also have seen how their paths had diverged, because he asked, 'Is this why you don't want to date?"

"I won't be dependent on anyone else for my happiness or well-being. I also don't want the responsibility for other people's lives."

"You're still taking care of your sister."

"She has her own life. She works a couple jobs—at the local pharmacy during the week and at the hardware store on weekends. I mainly send her money to help out when she needs it." He didn't need to know about her guilt.

Scotty didn't look convinced by her airy tone. "What about your business? You look after your employees."

"Sure, but I don't have to worry about them beyond work. What happens in their personal lives isn't my business." That wasn't strictly true—she wasn't heartless—but telling him wouldn't help her case.

"It's funny how similar stories led to different outcomes. Despite my unconventional upbringing and my wife leaving me, I haven't given up on marriage or family."

Sapphie didn't want to pry, but curiosity overrode her good intentions. "I read that your split was amicable."

"It was, in the end—I just didn't expect it. I thought when I retired, we'd spend time together, doing all the things we never had a chance to when I was playing. But she wanted her own life, which I didn't fit into."

She wasn't sure what to say. "I'm sorry."

"It was tough at first, but I'm okay now. With the benefit of hindsight I can see that we'd grown apart. And I have two fabulous children who I adore and am very proud of. I've tried hard not to let the divorce come between us." He shot her a quick smile. "As for the future, the right woman is out there for me and this time it will work."

Although he didn't add that he wanted that woman to be her, it was in his eyes.

Sapphie looked away, pretending an interest in the passing scenery as they exited the freeway for the main street of a nearby town.

This conversation proved her concerns. He was looking for someone to settle down with. To have the retirement he'd wanted with his wife. That wasn't her. Would never be her.

"Don't worry," he said with a heavy sigh. "I won't break the rules."

Sapphie hoped not, because she really didn't want to hurt him.

She didn't have to come up with a response, because he turned into the parking lot of an old-fashioned diner.

"It may not look like much, but it has the best pancake breakfast anywhere." He turned off the ignition.

Sapphie had driven past the stainless-steel building many times but had never stopped, despite the number of cars outside. She regarded the place with new interest. "I love pancakes."

"It's family run, been owned by the same folks since the '50s. It was even featured in that TV show about the best diners."

"In that case, definitely bring it on."

Breakfast turned out to be every bit as delicious as Scotty had promised. Sapphie deliberately kept the conversation away from serious topics, asking him about his career before the NHL. In return, she shared stories from her college days. How she'd turned part-time office jobs into consultancy projects and then into a top-ranked business.

All too soon, though, it was time to head for the airport.

Scotty parked in the short-term lot, then helped

her with her case, even though she told him he didn't need to. He also insisted on wheeling her carry-on as he accompanied her through the terminal toward security.

Having someone there to see her off was a little weird, but she had to admit, it was also kind of nice. Walking together through the crowds of travelers felt good. Sapphie almost wished she didn't have to leave.

Almost.

Riding the escalator to the security level, there was a moment of envy. A couple entwined in a passionate embrace made her want some of that for herself.

That wasn't in the rules.

She turned her gaze away from the pair and said, "Thanks for breakfast. You were right—those pancakes were amazing. I'll definitely go there again. Of course, I'll have plenty of time over the next month…" She trailed off as he grinned. "That wasn't babbling—it was enthusing."

"Uh-huh." His grin widened. "Maybe we can check them out together next weekend. Brunch on Sunday?"

Brunch was in the rules. "I'd like that."

"Great. I'll look forward to it."

When they arrived at the security clearance area, she dug in her purse for her passport. As she started to say goodbye, she thought to hell with the rules. She twined her arms around his neck and pressed a hard kiss on his mouth.

Instantly, he let go of her carry-on and pulled her tightly to him, wrapping her in his arms. Parting her lips, he deepened the kiss, until she lost all sense of where they were. The sounds of the airport faded; the people around them disappeared. Her entire being was focused on him and the desire pumping through her veins.

Slowly, reluctantly, they parted. Sapphie resisted the urge to touch her lips, preserving the taste of him.

"There's another one of those waiting for you when you get back to Jersey." The husky rasp in Scotty's voice added a sexy layer of promise to his words, as did the fire burning in his eyes.

"Great. I'll look forward to it."

His smile at her deliberate repeat of his earlier reply was wicked. And tempting. She wanted to accept the invitation and kiss him again until he was the one battling temptation.

Instead, she cleared her throat. "See you next week. Probably Thursday or Friday."

Sapphie took her carry-on and walked over to security.

Scotty kept pace with her until she was ready to go through the machines. "Text me to let me know you got back safely."

His request should have bothered her, but it

didn't. "Okay, but if there's a problem, you'll know about it soon enough."

"Humor me."

"Yes, sir, Captain." She grinned and saluted him.

"Sadly, that's former captain."

"But you'll always be captain to me."

"Somehow I don't think that gives me any special privileges."

"You never know."

Despite her teasing tone, electricity arced between them, charging the air. Sapphie looked away first when the line ahead of her shuffled forward.

"You'll let me know your return flight details?" Scotty asked. "I'll meet you."

"All right. I'll send them to you once they're confirmed."

Once Sapphie had cleared the scanners, she gave him a final wave before setting off toward her gate. She was surprised by the sense of emptiness once he was no longer in sight. She'd never hated saying goodbye before. She'd also never missed a man before.

The feeling lingered as she boarded the plane and strapped in. Instead of pulling out files, she stared out the window at the ground crew bustling around the plane, prepping it for departure. She was still looking out as the plane took off, giving her a spectacular aerial view of Manhattan. One she didn't usually see because she had her head down working.

Maybe there was a message there. What else was she missing?

Once they were through the clouds, it was like a switch flipped in her brain. Thoughts of Scotty were pushed aside and her business came to the fore. She had a lot to do before Monday morning's meeting with her staff. Opening her case, she pulled out her laptop and files and got into what she did best.

MAN, IT WAS good to be on the ice.

As the Zamboni rumbled through the gate, Scott stepped out onto the surface that still glistened with water. Laying on a burst of acceleration, he headed around the rink like he was competing for the fastest skater in the All-Star Skills Competition. His laugh echoed around the empty facility. Like he'd ever been fast enough to compete in that.

Speed had never been his game. At his best, he could back-check the best in the league with devastating consequences. He could block shots, deliver a pretty mean hip check and, when necessary, drop the gloves and go the distance with all but the toughest goons. He'd stopped that once he'd gotten the C, but he reckoned he could still give most fighters a decent pounding.

Today wasn't about any of that. It was about

taking a necessary break after the past few weeks in the office. All the long hours with Callum, going over their plans and proposals before the review meeting, followed by yet more scrutiny as they revisited everything in light of the opposition view, all on top of the regular Cats business, meant that Scott hadn't had time to hit the gym or the rink for a proper workout. A couple of long runs on the weekends hadn't cut it. His body ached with the need for physical exercise.

After a couple dozen laps, Scott felt better than he had in days. Like he was where he belonged. It still frustrated him that he didn't—that his only role for the team now was behind the scenes. He couldn't imagine a day when he wouldn't miss playing. Still, even though he couldn't play any longer—not at the highest level and anything else was pointless—the ice would never stop being his home away from home.

He filled his lungs with the crisp, cold air tinged with the smell of popcorn and hot dogs and listened to the clacking of his skates as they moved in perfect rhythm. Yeah, this was what he'd needed. And there was nothing like a fresh sheet of ice. The feel of his blades scraping the smooth glass-like surface. The extra glide with each stroke, almost like he was flying. Heaven.

Scott had gotten to the practice facility early so he could get some time on the rink by himself before his friends arrived. This time was his.

Just him and the ice. As he slipped into his old warm-up routine, his body went on autopilot. He could always think better when he was skating. Perhaps because when he was growing up, it had been his only chance to separate himself from all the issues at home. Later on with the Cats, particularly when he'd been captain, it had given him the space to gain perspective on whatever was bothering him or his team. During his marriage breakup, it had been a respite and a sanctuary.

Today his mind was a jumble of thoughts, most of them tied up with the future of his beloved team. As if they didn't have enough on their plates bedding down with the new ownership, Callum was still trying to plug some gaps in the depth of their lineup before the season started. Scott had done a lot of legwork, alongside Scouting, to evaluate potential targets. Now they were clear about Marty's position on the team's finances, he and Callum could talk turkey with agents about some of the players still on the market.

Pushing himself into a complex routine of crossovers and stop-starts, Scott's mind turned to the situation with Sapphie. She was supposed to be back tomorrow and he couldn't wait to pick her up from the airport.

Interesting times ahead, definitely. They would literally be working side by side—Doreen had prepared the office next to his for Sapphie. What would it be like spending so much time with her—

in and out of the office? Part of him was nervous. They'd get to know each other pretty well over the next month, showing their best and worst sides. How would that affect things on the personal front?

He was already uncertain about how it would pan out because he and Sapphie hadn't spoken since she left, though they'd exchanged texts. He couldn't deny that he'd wanted—hoped for... expected—more communication while she was away. He appreciated that she had a lot going on, but something more than the occasional one-liner wasn't too much to ask, was it?

If it hadn't been for that kiss at the airport, he would have thought he'd pushed too far, too fast. Made her retreat into her safety zone. He understood why she was skittish. She'd had one hell of a childhood. But after that kiss, he'd thought that she'd begun to feel more comfortable with him. Now, after four days with nothing more intimate than a "Hey, how are you?" he wasn't so sure.

Despite telling himself to be patient, go slow, he was hungry for more.

Which brought him to that kiss. It shouldn't have been special. It was just a goodbye. But it was one *she'd* initiated. One *she'd* wanted to give him. Whether she admitted it or not, it was a definite step forward.

Scott lost an edge, landing flat on his ass at center ice, like a toddler who'd strapped on skates for the first time. Man, he hadn't done that for years.

Catcalls, slow claps and laughter echoed across the rink as his so-called friends leaned over the barrier and rated his performance like a figure skater.

"Five-point-eight," Ice Man called out. "I deducted marks for flailing arms."

Chance shook his head. "Five-point-six. You landed on the wrong part of your anatomy."

"I give you a perfect six for artistic interpretation." Monty grinned as he opened the gate and stepped onto the ice.

The three men skated over to join Scott as he jumped to his feet. They knocked gloves and exchanged backslaps before heading off round the rink in a group.

"You're all showing your age," Scott retorted. "They haven't used that scoring system in over a decade."

"Which one of us is retired?" Ice Man shot back.

Scott punched Kasanski's arm and told him where to shove his stick. His friend's retaliation had them scuffling and tussling until Rivera separated them.

"How's it going in the front office?" Monty asked. "Taking it easy while us poor schmucks have to work for a living."

"It's the off-season and you've been sunning your ass for the past few weeks. Besides, when have you ever worked, Net-Boy?"

"You wimps only manage a couple of minutes at a time before you have to take a rest. Only me and the zebras put in a full shift."

"Right. Because moving from side to side in the blue paint and the occasional swan dive can be compared to actual skating."

"Yeah, yeah," Monty said good-naturedly. "I've saved your bacon often enough. And I have the Jennings Trophies to prove it."

"Maybe once or twice," Scott conceded.

"You guys obviously need to get rid of some of that hot air," Chance said wryly. "Do I have to put you through a bag skate?"

Ice Man clutched his chest. "Oh no! Not the bag skate." He put on an angelic expression and drew a halo in the air above his head. "We'll be good. We promise."

"Speak for yourself." Scott laughed.

With the season about to start and his workload showing no signs of easing, he worried these sessions might be few and far between. He'd have to find a way to get to practices every now and again.

The guys got down to business. Training camp was a week away, and with physicals the day before it opened, the players were expected to be in decent condition. Even if they weren't game fit, everyone needed to be ready to pick up where they left off in June. Which was tough. The downside of a Cup run was that they didn't get the rest their bodies needed.

After a few sprints and drills, Monty set up a practice net at one end while Ice Man dragged out the bucket of biscuits. The arena soon resounded with the bang and clang of pucks on boards and pipes and the shouts of the men. After a short break, J.B., Taylor and Kenny joined them. The intensity ramped up as the younger guys challenged the older ones.

By the time the horn blew for the end of their session, they were all gasping and dripping with sweat. Scott's only consolation was that the young guns were puffing as much as he was. Which he and the other old men didn't hesitate to point out while they cleared away their stuff and hit the showers.

Damn, he missed this, Scott thought as he tossed his gear into his bag.

"Any of you up for a drink?" Kasanski ran a comb through his wet hair.

"I wish I could, but the babysitter needs a ride home and it's bath time for the twins." Chance grabbed his bag and headed for the door. "Give me a shout if you're doing this again before our session on Sunday."

J.B., Kenny and Monty followed Rivera out.

J.B. was going home, Kenny to his mom's, and Monty was apartment-hunting. Scott, Mad Dog and Kasanski had no plans, so they decided on burgers and beer at their favorite bar.

"I hear you're opening a sports bar," Ice Man said as they waited for their food.

Scott told them about the place he was in the process of buying. "It's a good investment and something to fall back on if this front-office gig doesn't work out. With Grey and Sapphie I have two partners who know more about the business than I ever will."

"Sapphie?" Mad Dog frowned. "She's based out of Chicago."

"Sure, but she works all over," Scott said. "You know we've been working together, right?"

"I knew she was consulting for Antonelli on the Ice Cats, but how does that turn into buying into a sports bar with you?"

"She came to check it out with me and asked to buy in. He'll oversee the food and staff, Sapphie will do marketing and I'll provide the memorabilia and my name."

"The investment isn't all she's interested in, from what I've heard." Ice Man winked.

"What's that supposed to mean?" Taylor's gaze swung between the two of them.

His aggressive tone reminded Scott that Mad Dog had once dated Sapphie.

Scott pushed aside the twinge of jealousy. That relationship had been over for a while, but did Taylor still have feelings for Sapphie? Man, that would be awkward.

Seemingly unaware of the undercurrents, Kasanski continued, "I hear that sparks flew at the board meeting with Antonelli. Plus they'll be like this for the next month." He held up two crossed fingers.

Mad Dog's face turned thunderous.

Before he could explode, Scott explained what had happened.

"That's all there is to this—business?" Taylor looked skeptical.

"It's complicated," Scott admitted, not wanting to reveal details. He didn't kiss and tell, and discussing Sapphie with one of her former boyfriends was just plain weird.

"What's so complicated? Are you dating her or not?" Mad Dog demanded.

Even if he'd wanted to, Scott wasn't sure how to explain what he had with Sapphie. "Sorta."

"What the hell kind of answer is that?"

Taylor's attitude was pissing Scott off. "Is there a problem here? I thought you two were just friends, bro."

"We are. Which is why I don't want to see her hurt."

"Why would dating me hurt her?"

"You're on the rebound from your marriage.

You haven't dated in, like, forever. She's pretty and hot with it—"

Scott shot his palm up in front of Mad Dog's face. "Don't even think of going down that route. This is not a freaking midlife crisis."

"I know about your weekend together," Taylor retorted.

"And...?"

"I thought it was a one-and-done. I didn't realize you were her new sex buddy."

Scott gave him a crude, anatomically impossible suggestion. "It's not like that. And don't be disrespectful to Sapphie."

Taylor jabbed him in the chest with his forefinger. "Oh, so because you've slept with her, you think you own the right to stand up for her?"

"That's the pot calling the kettle black."

Kasanski made a time-out sign. "Take it down a notch or five, will you?" He shot Mad Dog a stern look. "This is Scotty, man. He's not a horndog."

Taylor paused, looked at Scott, then said, "Yeah. You're right. Sorry."

When Scott didn't say anything in response, Ice Man nudged him under the table.

But Scott wasn't in a forgiving mood. "Where do you get off accusing me? Sapphie and I are unattached adults. We can do whatever we like and it's none of your damn business."

"The hell it isn't. Sapphie's my friend. I've known her longer than you—"

"A year," Scott said. "You met in Antigua last summer."

"It's a year longer than you've known her, so that gives me the right to make sure you're not going to mess with her."

"I don't plan to do anything she doesn't want me to."

"Nice." Taylor's lips twisted. "Already double-talking like a suit."

"Jeez." Kasanski threw up his hands in disgust. "Calm down, the pair of you. You're putting me off my beer."

Scott and Taylor glared at each other, jaws set.

Mad Dog backed down first. "Look," he said quietly, "Sapphie isn't as tough as she seems. Despite how she acts, she's not a hard case."

"I know." Because he knew his buddy's concern was genuine, Scott swallowed his sarcastic retort. "The last thing I want to do is hurt her. Fact is she's more likely to break my heart than the other way around."

Though he kept the words light, it was the truth. "We're just dating casually right now. If that changes, we'll take it a step at a time. Which still isn't any of your damn business."

"Fine. Just so you know, if you hurt her, I'll hurt you."

"You and which army?" Scott exhaled. "Whatever. Just don't take out your own problems on me."

"What problems?" Taylor asked.

"Come on, you screwed up with Lizzie at J.B.'s wedding and you're mad."

"That's got nothing to do with this."

"Right."

"Enough already." Kasanski groaned. "If you can't play nice, I'm cracking skulls."

"Another round?" Taylor signaled their server. "I'm buying."

"Just a soda for me." Scott accepted the olive branch. "I'm driving."

"I'll take another beer," Ice Man said.

Once their drinks and burgers arrived, the conversation turned to the Ice Cats.

"I heard there are a couple professional tryouts coming to training camp." Ice Man smothered his fries in ketchup. "Skilled guys, too. Man, I hope I never get to the point where I'm touting my skills at a PTO."

"You and me both." Mad Dog clinked his glass against Scott's, then Kasanski's bottle. "I'd rather retire."

"Easy to say." Scott put down his burger. "You're a long time retired, so you don't want to hang them up too soon. Teams want to go younger and cheaper, and good guys are left on the outside looking in."

"It's still a hell of a comedown to have to prove yourself against a bunch of green kids." Mad Dog grimaced.

"I couldn't do it, but kudos to those who do."

Kasanski turned to Scott. "Anyone interesting joining us?"

"I can't mention names," Scott hedged, "but Callum's talked to a few decent veterans."

They discussed available free agents and some of the young players who'd be up from the minor-league team for training camp.

As they were leaving, Scott took Taylor aside. "Are we good?"

"Yeah." His friend sighed. "I guess I can trust you to treat Sapphie right. Not many guys I'd say that about."

"Good." Scott clapped Taylor on the back. "I hope you fix things with Lizzie."

"Appreciate it, but not gonna happen." He raised a hand in farewell. "Later, man."

Scott mulled over their conversation as he drove home. He'd just pulled into his garage when his phone rang. It was Angela.

He turned off the ignition and got out of the car. "Hey, sweetheart. What's up?"

"I'm planning a quick visit home for the weekend. Are you going to be around?"

"Sure. And I haven't rented out your room, so you can stay."

She laughed. "Funny. I should be there sometime Saturday afternoon."

"Great. Are you around to hang out with your old dad on Saturday night or will you be out partying with friends?"

"I'll see a couple of people while I'm there, but I saved the evening for you. I thought you could take your favorite daughter out for a meal."

"I'd be happy to take my only daughter to dinner. Where would you like to go?"

They discussed possible restaurants, settling for Angela's favorite Italian place.

"Mom gets back from her trip on Saturday. She wants to take me out for brunch on Sunday. She said you could come, too."

Even though he and Celine were civil to each other for their kids' sake, the last thing he wanted to do was spend time with his ex-wife. But he didn't want to cause problems for his daughter or upset her by declining. Looked like he'd have to go along and grit his teeth for a few hours.

"I have time booked at the practice facility," he said carefully. "But I could grab a bite with you and your mother before you leave."

"Great. I'll see you Saturday."

He tossed his phone onto the couch and turned on the baseball. The Yankees weren't playing, so he checked out the Mets. Bottom of the seventh, and they were blowing out the Phillies. Not worth watching with the result in the bag. He flicked through the channels, but nothing caught his attention, so he turned the TV off. Dropping his head against the back of the sofa, he stared around the room. He really needed to do something about this place. Either redecorate or sell it.

What would Sapphie think of—

Crap. He sat bolt upright. He already had plans for brunch on Sunday. How could he have forgotten? His curse echoed around the silent room.

Talk about putting himself between a rock and a hard place. He knew which one he'd rather cancel, but that would also give him the most aggravation. Not to mention that, once again, he didn't want to have to make explanations. Not to his ex-wife and certainly not his daughter. Especially when he wasn't sure how long, or even if, he and Sapphie would last.

He'd have to rearrange with Sapphie. Canceling wasn't how he wanted to kick off this new phase in their relationship. He just hoped this wasn't a sign of things to come.

CHAPTER TEN

"I'M NOT DISAPPOINTED," Sapphie muttered to herself, for the tenth time, give or take, as she leaned against the plush leather seat of the town car that was ferrying her from the airport to her apartment.

She understood why Scotty couldn't pick her up. Work had to come first. Besides, she was all for him and Callum pouncing on an unexpected deal for a player who could shore up their blue line. It was the double whammy of also having had their brunch canceled…postponed…whatever. Especially since she'd spent extra-long hours the past few days clearing the decks with her staff so she'd have time to enjoy her date with Scotty on Sunday.

That was why she was later returning from Chicago than she'd originally planned. Knowing she had a little over three weeks to rework the proposal to be ready to re-present it to Marty had meant ensuring everything in her own business was in tip-top shape. Just because her plans had changed, didn't mean her clients should receive anything less than the first-class service she prided her company on providing.

But it had been necessary to take the extra days to organize it all, so she'd flown into Jersey on Friday afternoon.

Sapphie was supposed to be using the drive to her place to check her emails, but she didn't have the concentration to deal with them. So she gave up and let her mind wander to Scotty and their postponed brunch.

She couldn't compete with family, even if one part of that family was definitely ex. Nor did she want to. Wasn't that the point she'd been trying to make to Scotty all along? She didn't want to get involved because of exactly these kinds of issues.

Still, it hurt that she was pushed aside so easily.

Sapphie seemed to be experiencing a lot of unfamiliar feelings since she'd slept with Scotty. What was it about him that turned everything upside down and unsettled her?

She was saved from that troubling turn of thought when her cell rang.

"Welcome back," Issy said. "I'm always happier when you're in town. I like knowing you're close by."

Warmth filled Sapphie. This was one friendship she could count on not to change. "Me, too."

"Would you like to come over? J.B. will be at the practice arena this evening, so Sophia and I are on our own and would love your company."

Sapphie's spirits lifted. "An evening with you

and my practically perfect godchild is exactly what I need."

"Great, because Sophia wants to show off her new trick. She started to crawl this week."

"I told you the child is a prodigy. She only learned to roll over a few weeks ago."

Issy laughed. "You might be the teensiest bit biased, but she can scoot on her butt pretty fast."

"I'll drop off my stuff, get cleaned up and come over." Looking out the window, she gauged how far she had to go. "I'll be with you in an hour and I'll bring dessert."

After she'd hung up, Sapphie's good mood lasted for the rest of the journey. Energized, she whizzed through the emails she'd abandoned earlier.

But when she arrived at her apartment, the unsettled feeling returned. As she padded to her bedroom, she looked around. It was a conveniently located, fully serviced pied-à-terre that suited her needs. For the first time, though, she was aware that the apartment looked like what it was—a place where she spent a lot of time, but it certainly wasn't home.

Identical to her other apartments, it was sleek and efficient, with every convenience. High-end appliances and equipment, designer furniture and decor. It was also as impersonal as a hotel room.

Not one thing in the apartment belonged to her. Nothing of hers decorated the place—no knick-knacks, no photos. More to the point, she didn't *have* anything personal to put in the apartment. What did that say about her?

Sapphie stepped into the shower. Letting the water pound her body, she tried to get her head out of the strange place it seemed to be in.

This was what she wanted. No muss, no fuss, no responsibility.

So why, as she washed her hair, was she thinking wistfully of the heartwarming coziness of Issy's place? By contrast, this apartment seemed cold and bland and characterless.

Sapphie winced—she'd scrubbed her skin raw with the massage sponge. Good job she'd already shaved her legs or she'd be cut to ribbons. The sooner she got out of here, the better. Leaving her hair to dry naturally, she dressed in navy shorts and a red short-sleeved top. She slipped on red wedge sandals, then grabbed her purse and headed out the door.

En route to Issy's apartment, she picked up a few quarts of ice cream. Thankfully, the closer she got to her friend's place, the more that weird feeling dissipated.

When Issy opened the door, Sophia threw herself toward Sapphie with a squeal of excitement. Sapphie dropped the shopping bag to catch her, settling the infant on her hip.

"Someone's very pleased to see you." Issy laughed, retrieving the ice cream and leading the way upstairs.

Sapphie nuzzled her goddaughter's nose. "I'm really happy to see her, too."

"Bad week?"

"Just busy and a bit intense," Sapphie replied lightly, not sure she could explain the strange feeling. "But then, when isn't my life like that?"

"True. Well, you can chill out tonight." Issy poured drinks, then set the glasses on a tray already laden with their dinner plates. She indicated for Sapphie to precede her outside. "I thought we could eat out there."

"Sounds perfect."

Sapphie put Sophia in the playpen, where she showed off her crawling skills to her godmother's admiration. The friends ate overlooking the lake as the sun set.

Sapphie took a long drink of her wine. "Ah, I needed that."

"You and me both. I thought the first few months were tiring, but since Sophia started to move about, she's running me ragged." Issy rolled her eyes. "Once she sets her mind on something, nothing will make her veer off her path."

"Hmm, I wonder where she gets that from," Sapphie said, smiling.

"Her father, for sure."

"Uh-huh. Because you're so easygoing."

"Of course."

Issy caught Sapphie up on what the other Ice Cats and their families were doing. Most of them had returned to Jersey and were prepping for the new season.

"That was lovely." Sapphie sighed and pushed her chair back from the table. "I'm stuffed. If I eat another bite, there won't be room for ice cream. As it is, I need a breather."

"Me, too." Issy lifted Sophia onto her hip. "We can save dessert for when I've given little madam her bath and put her to bed."

"Oh, fun. I'll help."

"No need. You can relax out here."

"I want to."

Issy arched an eyebrow. "Only because she's angelic for you. She saves her hissy fits for her poor mom."

Sophia's halo was shining as Sapphie bathed her. Sophia loved the bubbles and water and soon had her godmother covered in both. Sapphie didn't care—she enjoyed playing with Sophia. Maybe because it was something out of the ordinary. Taking care of a precious child who wasn't her responsibility was different from having to look after her sister when she was growing up. It also wasn't a requirement. Sapphie chose to do it.

Once Sophia was clean and in her crib, she fell asleep almost immediately. The friends then returned to the balcony and dug into the ice cream.

"How's the house hunting going?" Sapphie asked.

"Slowly. There still isn't much on the market

that we like. But there's no rush. Something will come up."

"You don't sound too worried about it."

Her friend was normally one for detailed plans and didn't like them disrupted. Also a function of their childhood, when they could rely only on each other.

"I'm not." Issy shrugged. "I don't know why."

"Perhaps because you're settled here, so you don't want to start over somewhere else."

"You could be right. Plus I'm not sure I want to move with the season about to start. Much as I love J.B., I know what he's like once he's playing. He'll be so focused on his game that little else matters," Issy said fondly, though at one point in their relationship, that single-mindedness about hockey had almost split them up permanently. "It doesn't matter to him where we live as long as it's an easy drive to the arena and the practice rink. I'll keep looking, but I won't mind if we don't move before spring."

"I don't blame you. I can't imagine the up-heaval." Sapphie gave an exaggerated shudder. "All that packing and unpacking. It's much easier to travel light." She ignored the twinge in her chest that reminded her of how she'd felt earlier.

Issy gave her a penetrating look that saw too much. "Maybe, but it makes me happy that my home is full of things that are special to me."

"And it's lovely." Sapphie cut off the wistful

tone, saying briskly, "That wouldn't work for me. Plus I need more than one place."

"You could still create a home out of your apartment in Chicago, although I wish your home base was here."

"Funny you should say that. I was thinking along similar lines myself. Maybe I should put an offer in for your apartment when you're ready to sell."

Issy stopped, loaded spoon halfway to her mouth, and stared at Sapphie. "Excuse me. Did you just mention *buying* somewhere?"

"I was thinking that maybe it's time I have a place that feels more like me." She cast her mind to her earlier inventory of her apartment. "Maybe have my own furniture. I don't even have a fork to my name."

"What's brought this on? You've never cared about owning stuff before."

Sapphie shrugged. "Maybe it's time I did. Now I'm on the downward slope to forty—"

"You're thirty-one." Issy waved off that excuse.

"Well, I can't keep up this pace forever. Once I start to slow down, it would probably be nice to have somewhere to live that is mine, with my things in it."

The thought had never crossed her mind before— in fact, she'd always rebelled against the idea—but now that it had, she wondered if she should start building a base for the future.

Issy's spoon clattered into her bowl. "Okay, who are you and what have you done with my best friend?"

"Ha-ha. Very funny."

"I'm serious. Are you all right? Is something going on you haven't told me about?"

"I'm fine. Possibly just a little tired of feeling like I'm always on the move."

"You're sure you're not sick?"

"I'm perfectly healthy." Sapphie hoped that Issy wouldn't dig deeper to things she didn't want to discuss. "Anyway, I thought about having my home base in Jersey rather than Chicago. Maybe because I've been spending more time here lately. Obviously, you're here, too, and my gorgeous god-daughter. In fact, all my friends are here."

Issy frowned. "I guess that makes sense. But what would you do with your own place? How would you find the time to decorate and furnish it? And you'd still need services to look after it. Plus you'd be responsible for everything that went wrong with it."

Issy was only trying to help by playing devil's advocate. Still, Sapphie started to feel unsettled again. The warm glow of having her own place began to be replaced by the sensation of ropes winding around her, tying her down.

Was she taking things a step too far because she was having a weird day?

She took a deep breath. "I don't have to do it all

myself. Tracy or Maggie at Making Your Move could find me someone to help set up the apartment and then get someone to manage it."

Something in her voice must have given away her uncertainty, because Issy backed off.

"Well, you can have first dibs on this place if we sell. And if we don't move, I'd love to have you as a neighbor. These apartments come up for sale all the time. There's one several doors down that's going on the market soon. I'll give you their number and you could get ahead of the game."

Those ropes tightened a little further. "Great. I can at least look into it."

"This sudden desire to settle in New Jersey wouldn't have anything to do with a certain retired captain?"

Trust her friend to nail it. "Perhaps. I don't know," she replied honestly.

"How are things going?"

"I thought it was okay. That we'd come to an understanding. Now I'm not so sure."

She explained what had happened prior to leaving for Chicago, including that kiss. Then how he'd changed plans, not once but twice. She didn't admit how much that had stung.

Issy grimaced. "Ouch. That can't be fun for him. Having to appease your daughter by being nice to a woman you don't like anymore. Why do kids always assume their parents should be friends once they've split up? There's a reason they got divorced."

Sapphie shrugged. "Anyway, I didn't want to cause trouble for him, especially when there's nothing serious between us."

"Still, not the best start."

"No. Maybe it's a sign that we shouldn't be seeing each other."

"Give it, and him, a chance. There's obviously something between you that's worth exploring. You'll regret it if you don't."

"Maybe." Or maybe she'd regret it more if they did.

Before Issy could say anything more to convince her, J.B. arrived home.

Sapphie left a short while later. Like a reverse of her earlier journey, she grew more and more unsettled the closer she got to her apartment. Walking inside, she felt suffocated. Sapphie strode to the sliding doors and opened them, breathing deeply. The breeze off the river soon permeated the apartment.

It was still too early to go to bed, so she poured herself a drink and grabbed the thriller she'd started reading on the plane. After a few minutes, she realized she wasn't in the right frame of mind to read about a serial killer targeting single career women and set it aside. Instead, she walked onto the balcony, drink in hand, and looked out over the Hudson at the lights of Manhattan.

Maybe she'd been premature in her thoughts about changing her life. Not that it was a bad idea, but perhaps right now wasn't the best time. There was too much else going on. Too many variables to consider. She should take it slowly and really think about what she wanted for the future.

Meanwhile, she'd be perfectly satisfied to keep the status quo.

Her phone rang. Surprised to see Scotty's number, she almost dropped the phone. "I thought you were meeting with your agent."

"I am. We're at Grey's and waiting for Andy to show. He's caught in a traffic holdup in the Lincoln Tunnel. I wanted to make sure you got in okay."

She was touched he'd called, but her edginess remained. "Of course. I'm an old hand at traveling." Then, worried that sounded a little abrupt, she added, "Thanks for checking."

"I'm really sorry I canceled. You know I wouldn't have changed our plans if it hadn't been important."

His sincerity eased some of her tension. "It's fine. I've been over at Issy's enjoying a pretty sunset and cuddles with my goddaughter. Not to mention a huge bowl of ice cream."

Scotty's deep chuckle sent tingles dancing over her skin. "I can't top that, so maybe it was for the best."

"It will be if you get the deal signed, sealed and delivered."

"The signs are encouraging. Speaking of which, Grey confirmed that our offer for the Brew House has been accepted."

"That's good news."

They talked about what that meant in terms of timing for the project. Then Scotty had to hang up because his agent had arrived. "See you on Monday."

"I'll be there, bright and early."

As she disconnected, it occurred to her that even without buying a place to live here, she'd just tied herself to New Jersey. And to Scotty. She hoped she hadn't made a terrible mistake.

PAINFULLY POLITE.

Two words Scott would never have thought he'd use to describe working alongside Sapphie. Yet that was exactly what the past four days had been.

From the moment she'd arrived at the Cats' offices on Monday morning, they'd taken part in a cagey dance. Unlike in the locker room, where guys told him straight up something was a load of crap, he and Sapphie disagreed using cocktail-party-style niceties. Every comment, every response, was measured.

If keeping on his verbal toes all day long wasn't tough enough, working so closely with her was a different kind of torture. The underlying attraction in the air. The constant battle against the urge to touch her—even simple gestures like smoothing a stray strand of hair from her cheek. The way her scent lingered long after she'd gone home. Not to mention his daily fight to hide the fact that he spent from nine to five in a near-permanent state of arousal.

Their days followed the same pattern. She'd be in her office working when he arrived. He'd bring her coffee and they'd head to the meeting room to tackle the list of projects from the review. Over lunch Sapphie went to her office to have a sandwich at her desk, while Scott stretched his legs and got some air. He'd ask her to join him, but she always declined.

He'd wondered if her cooler attitude was because he'd screwed up last Sunday. But when he'd asked yesterday if anything was bothering her, she'd denied it.

Scott swiveled his chair to stare out the window at the people arriving for work. He and Sapphie couldn't continue like this. He had to change things up. Fix what had gone wrong between them.

But how? Work would only get more contentious. They'd started by tackling simpler issues that could be solved easily. Unfortunately, they'd exhausted those yesterday. The outstanding issues were the most complicated and the ones where they were most at odds.

Still, he had to try. It would make the next few weeks more comfortable, at least. He decided to test the water by cashing in the rain check for last Sunday's brunch.

With a strategy in place, he strode to the meeting room and set his things on the table. He paid no attention to the wall opposite, where a line of flip-chart pages—detailing their agreed position on each of the resolved issues—hung, walking instead to the wall where the charts contained the problems still to be discussed. He'd barely glanced at the first one before Sapphie walked in.

His heart kicked. He should be used to that—it happened every time he saw her—but he wasn't. Today's summery yellow dress hugged her curves and skimmed her knees, emphasizing her shapely calves. Matching peep-toe pumps showed an enticing glimpse of red nail polish. She looked smart, professional and delicious.

"Good morning. We have a lot to get through today, if we want to keep to schedule. Especially as you'll be observing some of the training-camp sessions next week."

At her brisk tone, he snapped his gaze up from her legs. "Before we get started, I still owe you brunch. How about Sunday?"

Her blue eyes widened. "You don't need to do that."

"I'd like to. This time, I promise I won't change plans at the last minute."

When she didn't respond right away, deliberately arranging her papers, laptop and phone on the table, he added, "I enjoyed our breakfast together. I thought you did, too."

She looked up and nodded slowly.

"Don't allow unfortunate circumstances to spoil us having a good time. What happened was a one-off. I won't let you down again."

"Okay." Her lips curved in a half smile. "Brunch on Sunday would be nice."

Relieved and more buoyant than he'd felt all week, he said, "Then let's tackle these problems."

"Hit me with your best shot." She fisted her hands, held them up to her face in a boxer's protective stance and blew on her knuckles, right, then left.

He laughed, mocking a jab. "Remember to keep your fists up, Rocky."

The light camaraderie lasted an hour before they began to slip into their firmly entrenched corners. Tension seeped in. Their comments grew sharper.

"I see your point." Sapphie rested her hip against the edge of the table, hitching the hem of her dress. "But, with respect, I don't think it will work."

He ignored the glimpse of smooth thigh as he crossed his arms and squared his stance. "Depends on your perspective. You're looking at short-term return, whereas I'm thinking longer term. An investment for the future."

Her back straightened. Finally, some sign of emotion. "Of course we need to consider both, but without the short-term financial return, there won't be a future."

"I understand that, but we can't sacrifice the future either."

"What sacrifice? It's simple math." She strode to the wall of charts and pointed a finger at the ones in her handwriting. "These proposals will bring in greater revenue. If implemented correctly, they could pay for themselves in a few years, enabling you to do some of the things that your team wants."

"But they don't generate loyalty. They don't encourage the fans of the future." He joined her, waving his hand at his charts. "We're putting forward ways to bring hockey into the lives of ordinary folk who could become loyal season-ticket holders for generations. Not fat cats in luxury boxes and big companies who buy expensive seats they never use."

"Last year worked because the team won the Cup." Sapphie stepped closer, her scent teasing his nostrils.

Scott silently cursed the instant tightness in his pants. "For sure. But if you can entice someone to a game, chances are they'll be hooked. Maybe even convert them to season tickets next year. The return far outweighs the cost."

"But there's a limited amount of money and we need to get the best bang for our buck. Which is why the focus initially has to go to building up those who pay the big money—your fat cats and big companies." She leaned past him, her arm brushing against his chest, and circled some numbers in red on both sets of charts.

That brief touch seared him and sent fire straight to his groin. He stalked to the table and leaned against it, crossing his legs at the ankles.

"It burns my butt to give more to people who least need it, at the expense of those who cheered for us through every minute of every game, every season."

"Tight finances mean tough choices."

At some points, he thought they were getting closer to a resolution, and at others, he realized they were as far apart as ever. They worked through lunch—Doreen brought in sandwiches—and into the afternoon.

All the while, Scott carefully kept his distance from Sapphie, creating a virtual no-go zone around her. He felt like an agitator hovering on the edge of a goaltender's crease.

At around three, his patience snapped. "I don't know why we don't make our lives a hell of a lot simpler and make the fat cats and businesses pay for the real fans."

Sapphie blinked, as if a bright light had come on, and tilted her head to one side. "Of course. That's where we've been going wrong. We've been letting ourselves be restricted by what's written on the charts."

He frowned.

She jumped up, ripped the flip chart they'd been using to record their progress off the wall, then tossed it onto the floor. "A cascade is the perfect solution."

Enthusiasm tinted her cheeks pink. The memory of a similar blush after they'd made love the first time momentarily distracted him. "A what?"

"We cascade money down the chain—so one thing pays for another, turning our smaller pot into a much bigger one and killing several birds with the same stone." She picked up a marker and sketched out a diagram to illustrate.

"I get it. We get corporate sponsors to fund discounted food and drink packages and cheap ticket deals—like students' night—as well as merchandise giveaways?"

"Exactly. We invest here." She drew an arrow at the top of the diagram. "They invest here and here." She added two more arrows. "We get butts on seats and the benefit of both short-term financial gain and longer-term regular income." The firm click of her replacing the cap on the marker punctuated her point.

Scott went to stand next to her. "To make this

work, we need to ensure what we're doing in marketing, sales and corporate sponsorship dovetails." He grabbed a blue pen and drew a circle around her diagram. "Why don't we make them one department?"

Sapphie opened her mouth but snapped it shut again.

"You're right." She tore off the flip-chart page and put it on the table before sketching an organogram on the fresh sheet. "We can set up a new VP role to oversee the three departments."

After that, the ideas flowed thick and fast. Pages of issues were ripped down and replaced with pages of solutions.

Sapphie stuck the last chart to the wall, then stood back to survey what they'd achieved. "I think we've cracked it."

Scott scrubbed his hand over his jaw. "Either that or we'll blow everyone's minds."

"That, too." She laughed. "I like this a lot. Marty will love it. I know he will."

He slung his arm across her shoulders and gave her a brief one-armed hug. She didn't stiffen or shrug him off. Oh yeah, a good day's work all round.

She looked up at the clock and did a double take. "Wow. Check out the time."

He glanced up. "Nine thirty? Seriously?"

The silence and stillness of the building sank in. All the offices were dark.

Sapphie took a sip from her glass and grimaced. "We did fantastic work today. We should celebrate with something better than warm water or cold coffee."

"I'm starving and you must be, too. How about we walk to the Pubbe? I think they serve food until midnight on Friday."

"Sounds perfect. Before we go, we should get these charts down and ready for next week."

They carefully stacked the pages in ordered piles, which they divided between them. After stowing them in their respective offices, they returned to the meeting room to clean up.

They were pushing the chairs under the table when the lights clicked off, plunging the room into darkness. Fluorescent emergency lamps out in the hallway flickered to life almost immediately, casting a faint bluish light into the room through the glass walls.

"Time to get out of here," Scott said, heading toward the door.

"Definitely." Sapphie pulled out her phone and switched on the flashlight app. "I'll grab my purse and briefcase."

They met at the elevator. Inside the car, the dim light created a cozy cocoon. They stood, slightly apart, staring forward. As the elevator descended, the desire Scott had struggled to keep under control all day began to pulse through his veins.

He turned his gaze slowly and saw her watching him. Her dark, wide pupils seemed to show the same hunger that was pounding through him.

She moistened her lower lip with her tongue.

He longed to follow the same path with his. Instead, he shifted his body so he was facing her. Almost touching, but not quite.

Without dropping his gaze, she turned toward him, taking the extra half step that brought them flush against each other. Thigh to thigh. Chest to chest.

Her head tilted upward. His lowered until their mouths were barely separated.

Her lips parted in invitation. One he couldn't refuse.

There was nothing polite about their kiss. Nor about the way their bodies fused together. His arms banded around her, pressing her closer. Hers wound around his neck, her hand holding his head firmly in place. Like he'd want to pull away.

The judder and bump of the elevator reaching the ground floor gave scant warning that the doors were about to open, exposing their kiss to the foyer. For a moment, his grip tightened. Hers, too. Then they drew apart, returning to their original positions as the doors slid noiselessly apart.

The security guards barely raised their heads from the small TV showing a baseball game to say good-night.

Striding ahead purposefully, Scott focused on getting to the rotating door. Beside him, Sapphie's heels clicked steadily, marking the distance to freedom.

Once outside, they maintained the semblance of normality until they were round the corner and heading toward the pub. At the central fountain, they stopped and burst out laughing.

Their eyes met and the laughter faded.

Suddenly, the pub seemed too far away. Dinner, an unnecessary waste of time.

Scott's stomach rumbled. He hadn't eaten since that quick sandwich at lunch. But by the time they had some food, the moment would be gone.

"We could get takeout," Sapphie said quickly.

Once again her mind was in sync with his. Thank God.

"There's a pizza place around the corner from my house. We can order now and pick it up on the way."

She smiled. "Thin crust, anything but anchovies and pineapple on mine."

He pulled out his cell and called in their order. "They'll be ready in twenty minutes."

"Then we should get going."

He held out his hand and she took it. Fingers entwined, they hurried toward the parking garage.

They barely stopped on the way home—the lights were in their favor and the pizzas were ready when they arrived.

There was a moment of hesitation as he approached his house.

Somehow, she must have sensed his hesitation, because as he pulled into the driveway, Sapphie laid her hand on his thigh. "Are you okay about this? We can go to my apartment."

He wanted to grab the out she'd offered him but shook his head as he reached for the garage-door opener. "Uh...the pizza will go cold."

"It can be reheated. I have the necessary appliances and know how to use them." Her smile was understanding. "Besides, it'll go cold regardless."

Scott stopped the car. His finger hovered over the button of the opener. Delicate moment. It had taken too long to get to this point. He didn't want to blow it.

Sapphie gently pushed his hand toward the wheel. "You know the way. Step on it."

He didn't argue and headed for her apartment.

The elevator ride to her floor was different from the one earlier. This car was brightly lit and they weren't alone. Although Scott and Sapphie stood against the rear wall, she was tucked into his side while his arm circled her shoulders. She carried the pizza boxes, he both their briefcases. They smiled politely at the seemingly endless stream of people who got on and off, delaying their arrival.

Finally, it was their turn. They exited the elevator sedately and walked down the corridor to her apartment as if there were no hurry. At her door, Scott took the boxes, while she dug in her purse for her key.

No sooner was the door closed and bolted than everything hit the floor—bags, briefcases, boxes—as Scott and Sapphie came together in a kiss that threatened to heat up those pizzas all by itself. Shoes were toed off. Jackets joined them.

"Bedroom?" he murmured against her lips as he finally worked the zipper of the sunny yellow dress that had driven him crazy all day.

She tilted her head backward, indicating the end of the hallway, as her fingers unbuttoned his shirt.

The only awkwardness was managing the removal of clothes while not letting go of each other or breaking off the kiss. By the time they reached her bedroom, they were naked. They tumbled to the bed, still entwined.

The crisp white sheets were cool against Scott's heated body. Compared to the smoothness of Sapphie's skin, they felt scratchy and rough.

He tried to hold back, but Sapphie encouraged him, demanding what she wanted. He didn't resist.

Her slick, wet heat welcomed him as he plunged inside her. She encased him, drawing him deeper until it wasn't a matter of *if* he could hold on but *when* he would give up trying.

She came with a cry, pulsing around him. Barely a breath later, what little control he had left slipped away and he succumbed, too.

CHAPTER ELEVEN

THE SUNRISE OVER Manhattan was a glorious sight.

Wrapped in Scotty's arms, Sapphie watched the colorful lights of the City that Never Sleeps wink out, turning the buildings into that famous silhouette against the pink-and-orange Sunday-morning sky. Curled up on one of the lounge chairs on her balcony with a sheet covering them against the cool air, she felt as though New York put on a show just for them.

"I wish I was a photographer and could capture the beauty," she said softly.

"Yeah, me, too." The tender note in his gravelly voice told her he wasn't talking solely about the view.

Sapphie leaned against his shoulder and kissed his jaw. He turned his head slightly and captured her lips. A soft, gentle kiss that made her heart catch with its simplicity and leap with its power and emotion.

They'd barely left each other's sides since her apartment door had closed behind them on Friday night, sealing them away from the rest of the world. After a midnight feast of reheated pizza, they'd spent most of yesterday in bed, emerging only to accept a lunch delivery of subs from the local deli. Which they enjoyed in bed. In the evening, they'd showered together, then moved to the sofa, had another delivery—Chinese—and watched classic movies on TV.

They'd carefully avoided defining the present or looking to the future, content to enjoy being with each other. Aware, though nothing was said aloud, that their time together was short.

Biting back a yawn, she said, "We really should get some shut-eye. A couple hours in the past thirty-six are not enough to sustain me anymore."

Scotty's chuckle reverberated against her back. "There was me thinking it was only my aging body that couldn't cope. You've worn me out."

"I think your aging body has coped very well." Her smile was sultry. "Any better and we'd both need medical assistance." She trailed a finger over his thigh, delighting at the stirring in his groin. "Retired or not, your stamina is impressive."

"I never thought I'd be grateful for all those hours training. But don't tell my coaches that I might have found a better use for that stamina."

"Might have?" She arched an eyebrow and withdrew her hand.

"Definitely have." He guided her fingers to where they'd been, then rested his hand over hers. "Much as I'd love to prove that to you, I definitely need some z's before I attempt anything more. The problem is I don't have the energy to move."

"Me neither." This time, the yawn escaped. She snuggled against him and closed her eyes. "We can rest right here for a couple of hours."

"Good idea." His voice was drowsy, as if he was already half-asleep.

Her last thought before she drifted away was that she'd never before felt comfortable enough with a man to simply sleep with him.

THE SUN WAS high in the sky when they awoke.

The angry cawing of two seagulls fighting over a prawn cracker on the railing of her balcony wasn't the gentlest alarm, but it was entertaining viewing. Especially when the birds' tug-of-war ended with them losing the cracker over the edge. As they dived after the falling treasure, Sapphie shook her head.

"See, if they'd worked together, they'd each have half a cracker. I might use that example in my next talk on teamwork."

"I'm with the gulls." Scotty tucked a strand of hair behind her ear. "Who wants half a cracker when you could have it all? You play to win."

She laughed. "Somehow I figured you'd side with the birds."

"I'm hungry enough to go down and fight them for the food."

"Me, too." She twisted her lips. "It's Sunday

and you promised me brunch and I won't be denied. I've been looking forward to my pancake breakfast for two weeks."

"Like I'd dare to keep you from those pancakes. We'll go as soon as you're ready."

"Let me grab a quick shower."

"I'll do the same, if that's okay? I'd like to stop by my house to change my clothes."

"Of course." She started to move when he stopped her.

"Have you got to work this afternoon or can you play hooky?"

She should decline whatever he wanted to do—she'd already lost one day of the weekend. Instead, she wanted to say to hell with the tasks waiting in her briefcase and on her laptop. Would it hurt to take another day off? She could make up for it later. Especially as they'd soon be going their separate ways.

Her stomach dropped. She didn't want to think about the end.

Her silence must have given him a clue to her thoughts, because he said ruefully, "We haven't actually had a date. Partly my fault, I know, having to cancel last week's brunch. And partly because of the long hours we've been putting in. Anyway, this could be our first official date."

Sapphie didn't know why his words made her nervous. He wasn't pushing, trying to charm her into giving in by being endearing—that part came naturally. Still, no one had ever made her consider putting work aside before.

Overthinking it much?

"What did you have in mind?"

"Taking the ferry into the city and heading to Central Park for the afternoon. I'll even treat you to an ice cream."

"You're not going to suggest one of those horse-and-carriage rides everyone thinks is so romantic, are you?" She wrinkled her nose. "In this weather, the stink of the horse manure will be unbearable."

He laughed. "I was thinking more of a stroll, maybe catch a softball game or see if there's a theater-in-the-park performance on."

Despite the butterflies in her stomach, she couldn't resist. It was just one afternoon.

"Okay, let's do it. Brunch—because you're not getting out of that—followed by an afternoon in the park."

"Great." His grin did naughty things to her insides.

"Make yourself at home while I take that shower. I won't be long."

"You don't want me to help scrub your back?"

"You know I'd love that, but we'd get—" she kissed the tip of his nose "—distracted—" then the curve of his chin "—a lot." She pressed her lips to his, quick and hard. "By the time we surfaced again, I'd have missed my brunch." She jumped up and quickly moved out of reach of his grasping hand, taking the sheet with her.

Which left Scotty naked.

She feasted her eyes on his magnificent body—from his broad chest to his flat stomach and deliciously, impressively lower—for a few moments. Okay, more than a few.

He grinned unselfconsciously and laced his fingers behind his head, to give her an unfettered view of his finely honed muscles and his proud erection. "Go ahead. I'll wait here for you."

"Not fair," she admonished, even as moisture pooled deep within her. "Those pancakes are calling my name."

"Something else is, too. Loud and clear."

She released a put-upon sigh and let the sheet drop to her feet. "I can't leave you in that state. But we'll have to be quick."

"I'm primed for *quick*. I'll make it up to you with *slow* later."

"In that case..." She deliberately swayed her hips as she sashayed to him, climbed onto the lounger and straddled him.

She closed her eyes at the waves of pleasure that rippled through her as she lowered herself slowly onto his hot, hard length until he filled her completely.

For a few seconds she couldn't move—the sensation was exquisite.

All thought of food was pushed from her brain

as it focused on a completely different hunger raging through her body. One that couldn't be satisfied with maple-syrup-drenched pancakes. That could be slaked only by the man she was riding.

Brunch could wait.

SIMPLE PLEASURES.

The sun on her back, an ice cream in her hand and a gorgeous man by her side. Sapphie and Scotty sat on a bench, watching a hard-fought coed softball game between the blues and the reds. The grassy area around them was filled with families and couples on blankets. The path behind them had a steady stream of passersby—sunburned tourists, sweaty runners and in-line skaters, parents with kids in strollers and dog walkers—all taking advantage of the Indian summer.

It was the perfect afternoon. And she hadn't once felt guilty about the work she should have been doing.

They'd made it to the diner for brunch—by the skin of their teeth.

While he'd showered, Sapphie had put on a floaty dress and flat sandals. She'd also found a broad-brimmed straw hat that would protect her face and shoulders. Then they'd headed to Scott's house.

Sapphie had waited in the car while he'd gone inside to get changed. She'd sensed his discomfort

Friday night and had understood how difficult it might be for him to take a woman into what had been his family home. She hadn't seen the need to force the issue. It wasn't like she would be the new Mrs. Matthews.

Admittedly, she had been curious to see inside his home. It hadn't been what she'd expected at all. She'd imagined something solid and traditional. Historic, even. Brick and aged wood, with gingerbread trim on the gables, colorful shutters and a wraparound porch.

Instead, the house was a sleek, white-stone-and-smoked-glass ultramodern McMansion. Sure, it would have suited any number of the millionaire young bucks lighting up the NHL. But it seemed totally wrong for Scotty. Even the manicured lawn and artistically shaped shrubs seemed out of place. Where were the old trees—perfect for tire swings or a tree house?

She'd hoped, for his sake, there was somewhere inside that was more suited to him. If ever anyone had needed a man cave, it was Scotty.

But perhaps she had him wrong. How well did she know him, after all? A couple weekends tearing up the sheets didn't make her an expert on the man. Strangely, she found herself wanting to know him better, even though she knew that would be unwise. Maybe there could be a middle ground between knowing only his preferences in bed and knowing everything about him.

A roar from the winning blues interrupted her thoughts. Sapphie looked to see both teams converging on the mound to exchange good-natured backslaps. She noticed one guy in red getting a lot of cuffs to the back of his head from his teammates.

"That'll teach him," Scotty said with a chuckle. "No matter how cute the blonde, you've got to keep your eye on the ball. That dropped catch cost them the game."

"Some blondes are too attractive to ignore." She fluttered her lashes at him. "We're much prettier than some silly old ball. Or puck."

Squeezing her shoulder, he pulled her toward him and dropped a kiss on her lips. "I'm glad you didn't have seats on the glass when I was still playing."

"There was me thinking you'd be spurred on to break your own scoring records."

He laughed. "That wouldn't be hard. I was never much of a scorer. With you to inspire me, I'd probably have tallied double digits in goals— assuming I didn't trip over my laces trying to impress the gorgeous girl in the expensive seats."

"I could have held up a homemade sign for you. I Heart Scotty."

"As long as you didn't promise some poor kid a puppy if I scored."

"And break his heart? I think not."

"Ouch. Thanks for the support."

"Aw, you know I've always been your number-one fan."

He frowned. "You won't break my ankle with a mallet because I retired, will you?"

"As if. That would be totally counterproductive under the circumstances."

"Phew." He mocked wiping the sweat from his forehead, then eyed her curiously. "You didn't have the hots for Bad Boy or the Russian Rocket?"

"Nope. I'm a tried-and-true captain's girl."

His grin was smug. "I like getting one over the pretty boys."

"I'm sure you've had your share of devoted fans over the years."

"Maybe back in the day, but it was so long ago I don't really remember. They seem to prefer the guys with the quick hands to the ones who can block a puck."

"Personally, I think your slow hands are perfect."

"Correct answer." He planted another kiss on her lips. This one was slow, to match his hands. "I guess we should head back."

Sapphie was pleased to hear the reluctance in his voice that matched her own. "I suppose so. We both have stuff to do to get ready for tomorrow."

"Yeah." He got to his feet and held out a hand to help her. "There's no rest for the wicked. But, man, was this weekend worth it."

Twining her fingers with his, she smiled. "Definitely."

Following the dispersing crowd, they wandered through the park, heading toward the southern edge. When they reached the line of famous horse-drawn carriages, the eau de manure was as pungent as she'd predicted. She and Scotty looked at each other and laughed as they watched a family of Japanese tourists wearing cotton masks clamber aboard.

"Don't think that'll keep the smell out."

Scotty and she sat on the top deck of the ferry to Jersey. His arm was around her shoulders. Her hand was on his thigh. They didn't say much, as if concerned that words would break up the magical cloud they'd been wrapped in.

The short ride to her apartment seemed to take no time at all. She wanted to invite him in but sensed that would be a mistake. She was also a little scared—partly that he'd refuse, but also that he'd accept.

Scotty walked her into her building and waited for the elevator with her.

"So, I'll see you in the office, bright and early," she said, trying to sound like she wouldn't miss him. Which was crazy. It was one weekend.

"I'll be there, ready to tackle those flip charts. I swear I'll see them in my dreams. Marching along like some weird animation sequence."

"Thanks for that. Now I'll have 'The Sorcerer's

Apprentice' stuck in my head all night." She sang a few bars, then rolled her eyes. "That was the singing equivalent of babbling." She puffed out a breath. "I've had a lovely time."

"Me, too. I'd like to go out again, before next weekend."

Her heart thumped. "Okay."

"The Cats' first preseason game is on Thursday evening. Would you like to come with me? I'll be in the team's suite, so we'll be surrounded by people from work, but we could grab something to eat afterward."

"Some girls prefer diamonds and shoes—I'm definitely partial to a nice pair of Louboutins or Zanottis—but the way to my heart is paved with hockey."

"Then it's a date." The word had a deliberate emphasis.

"Absolutely."

Scotty leaned forward to kiss her, just as the elevator arrived with a loud ding.

"Damn bell." He slammed his hand against the open door to keep it there, then continued with what he'd started—a leisurely kiss that set her body alight and her pulse racing.

He stepped back. "Sleep well. Sweet dreams."

"You, too." She smiled. "Scratch that. I want your dreams to be anything but sweet."

"Yeah. That won't be a problem."

She blew him a kiss as the doors slid closed.

Sapphie was still smiling, and her body was still on fire, when she arrived at her floor.

Her apartment seemed even more empty and cold than when she'd arrived from Chicago. Sapphie poured herself a drink and wandered onto the balcony. She leaned on the railing and watched the ferries sailing across the Hudson. Despite the view and the sunset—which was as pretty as the sunrise—she felt restless. She should head inside and tackle the work waiting for her, but she couldn't be bothered.

What was Scotty doing? Was he home yet? Was he thinking about her? Missing her?

For crying out loud. Sapphie straightened. Next she'd be sitting wistfully by the phone, wondering if he'd call. This was a bad sign. It couldn't continue. She wouldn't let it.

When her phone did ring, it was Marty.

"How's it going?" he boomed. "No word of a body disappearing to rest with Jimmy Hoffa's in the Meadowlands, so I take it you haven't killed each other yet."

"No. The bloodshed has been minimal. Actually, it's going pretty well." She gave him a heads-up on the direction they were taking. "We've still got a way to go, but we'll have this nailed by the time you get here."

"I never doubted it. Sounds like you've found a good solution."

"I believe we have. Plenty of opportunity to

make the franchise financially sound in the short term, with the potential for strong growth in the medium-to-long term."

"And you've tried to make it results-proof. We both know that a couple of poor seasons, especially if the team misses the play-offs, can turn an organization upside down."

"Exactly. We smooth out the peaks and troughs, which also protects the team's ability to get and keep the players it needs."

"Great. I look forward to the final presentation. Now that all you have left is to pull it together, you'll already be thinking about your next job."

She didn't want to admit she hadn't really given it much thought. "Of course. I'll head to Chicago for a week, and then I have to be in Minneapolis to oversee a project."

Somehow she'd find her way to New Jersey, even if only for a weekend. She did it for the occasional hockey game, so why not for her favorite retired player?

"Is your passport up-to-date?"

"Of course. Why?" Her curiosity was aroused. Another deal must be in the works.

"Because you might be needing it soon. I'm looking into some stuff in Europe. If it works out, I'll need you to evaluate the business."

"Europe sounds nice. London, Paris, Rome, Munich…" She trailed off, hoping for a clue.

He was too smart for that. "All I'll say is that it involves a round ball."

Marty was looking at a soccer franchise? She knew there were several available for purchase in each of the countries and that he enjoyed the sport.

"Interested?" Marty's tone said he knew her answer was a foregone conclusion.

"Definitely." Her mind raced ahead. Which team? Which country? She should watch some games from each of the main professional leagues.

"Get your ducks in a row, because if it works out, you could be heading across the Atlantic in less than a month."

"That shouldn't be a problem."

By the time she hung up, Sapphie was totally in work mode. She fired up her laptop and opened her emails. The clock was chiming midnight when she finished.

As she crawled into bed, she spotted the pillow that still had the indentation of Scotty's head. That was when she realized she hadn't thought about him in hours.

See, not a problem after all. What happened earlier was a blip. She could handle this dating thing. She just had to keep it in perspective and not get caught up in the romance.

Still, as she drifted to sleep, she thought about the weekend. About their time together. About his touch. And how the bed felt lonely without him.

"I'LL HAND OVER to Sapphie for the next part of the presentation."

Scott took his seat, relieved that his section was over, and drained his glass of water. Beside him, Sapphie smiled supportively before rising to take his place in front of the screen. As she began to speak, Scott surveyed the boardroom, which looked and felt different from the meeting three weeks ago.

Marty hadn't brought his full team with him, so there were gaps around the table. From the Cats' side, Callum and the heads of the departments were all present.

The atmosphere was less combative. Partly because Scott and Sapphie had chosen to show a united front by sitting next to each other. Also, they'd made sure to get buy-in from Callum ahead of today's meeting. The GM had been very supportive and pleased that they'd pulled together a plan he could back 100 percent.

Of course, they weren't out of the woods yet. Marty still had to approve. Sapphie believed he'd back their play, but Scott had learned never to assume the win was in the bag until the final horn sounded. Too many last-second goals had taught him well. There were the key department heads who would be affected by the organizational changes. At least one would be very unhappy.

Still, the nervous twisting in his gut was caused by something else entirely. The project was all over save the implementation—which would be left to Callum and his team. There was no reason for Sapphie to stick around.

Scott had known this day was coming and thought he'd gotten his head around it. But now it was here, he wasn't so sure.

It had been a great couple weeks. They'd spent every moment they possibly could together, both at work and outside. Lunches, dinners and even a couple breakfasts after nights of the most amazing lovemaking he'd ever experienced. Last weekend had been a mirror of the previous one, except they'd headed to Battery Park and, like a couple of tourists, had taken the boat tour to the Statue of Liberty and Ellis Island.

But as much fun as they'd had together, they'd carefully avoided talking about how they'd handle what came next.

In the short term, Sapphie was heading to Chicago and then to Minneapolis. There was an underlying assumption they'd continue to see each other when their schedules allowed. She wanted to be here for opening night and Scott would accompany the team on their early-season road trip, which included a game against the Wild, at the same time as she'd be in Minnesota.

She'd been a little cagey about her plans after that. He suspected she might be waiting until they discovered how things worked between them once she was no longer in Jersey.

Scott was happy enough to play it by ear. For now.

"With that in mind, this is the new structure we propose for those departments." Sapphie's words interrupted his thoughts.

The organogram that appeared on the screen was a sign that she was winding up the presentation. The moment of truth was here.

A quick glance around the room was encouraging. Aside from Darren, who was scowling, the mood seemed to be upbeat. Success was definitely in the air.

Marty's face was impassive. That wasn't unexpected—it was how he rolled. But Sapphie had worked with him long enough to be able to gauge his support depending on what he did after the presentation was over. If Marty asked Callum for his thoughts, that would be a clear marker that they were good. If he replaced the cap on his fountain pen and aligned it on his notepad before he spoke, then he had a major issue.

"Better to hear it and deal with it," she'd said. "Frustrating as they can be, Marty's objections always add value."

Now, as she returned to her seat, everyone turned to the boss.

Marty leaned back in his chair, picked up his pen and rolled it between his fingers. "Thank you, Sapphie and Scotty."

Scott felt the room collectively hold its breath.

His pulse sped up like it did the moment before the puck dropped.

Marty tapped his pad with the pen and said, "Before I give my views, Callum, what are your thoughts?"

Sapphie exchanged triumphant grins with Scott. So far, so good.

After Callum said his piece, Marty nodded approvingly. "Nice work all round. This is a solid plan that should deliver exactly what the franchise needs. I have some points where I'd like clarification and also some thoughts to add."

Marty asked a few questions, then made several suggestions for improvements. There were a couple areas he didn't like and they debated them with him. On one, they changed his mind and he instructed that their idea be rolled out to his other franchises. On the other, he was immovable, and he insisted they fall in line with those other businesses.

"Let's get this done." Marty pushed away from the table. "Callum and Scotty, I'm confident I'm leaving the business in good hands. I'm only a phone call away, so I hope you'll feel free to use the brain cells I have before they're gone."

Everyone laughed, more as a release of tension than anything else.

"And now I suggest we celebrate. This has been a tough job, but you've all handled it really well. Congratulations are in order for Morgan on her new position as the VP in charge of marketing, sales and sponsorship." Marty waved his hand and Doreen walked in carrying a tray with bottles of champagne. "Dinner has been arranged at my club so we can continue the party."

With the meeting officially over, the volume in the room rose as various conversations started and overlapped. A group gathered around Morgan, congratulating her. Most people seemed to be satisfied with the outcome of the project. All except Darren, who stalked out of the room, his expression thunderous. Scott wasn't surprised—he and Sapphie had expected the restructure would put Darren's nose out of joint.

When the champagne came round, Scott grabbed a couple flutes and gave one to Sapphie. "Before the main toast, I want to make one to you. It was a pleasure working with you." He lowered his voice. "But I'm glad it's over and we can move forward with a more...personal project."

Her blue eyes twinkled as she clinked her glass to his, reminding him of the private celebration they had planned for later. "Here's to future collaborations. May they all be as successful as this one."

"I'll drink to that." Callum joined them and raised his glass before taking a sip. "Great job, both of you. I have a good feeling about the upcoming season now that everything's settled and we have a strong strategy in place."

"Not to mention the defending Stanley Cup champions on the ice." Sapphie laughed.

"Never hurts," Callum agreed. He slapped Scott on the back. "And this guy backing me up in the front office is turning out to be an even bigger bonus than I expected."

Pleased about the praise, Scott said, "Well, this job is already a hell of a lot better than yapping in the booth."

"Don't think you've had an easy escape yet," Callum warned, smiling. "Wait until I send you out to deal with the media hordes during a Cats bad run and they want Coach Macarty's head, and mine, on a platter."

"I'll be ready. I've already started watching film of you handling the vultures and made notes. There are several quotes I can borrow. Like 'Every season has its ups and downs' and 'No team wins eighty-two games.' And my personal favorite, 'The Cup isn't won in November' or whatever month we're in."

"I told you he was a quick learner." Callum turned to Sapphie. "So, what will you be tackling next?"

The slight hesitation before she answered and the quick glance she shot at Marty triggered a hint of unease in Scott's gut. Was there another project for Antonelli? She hadn't mentioned anything. Obviously, it was good news for her company, but most of Marty's holdings were on the West Coast.

How often would she be able to make it to Jersey under those circumstances? How would that impact their relationship?

"I'll be catching up with everything that was pushed aside for my extended stay here," Sapphie said lightly. "No peace for the wicked."

"But you will be here for opening night?" Callum asked. "We'll be raising the championship banner."

"I wouldn't miss it." Sapphie's gaze met Scott's.

The promise in her eyes eased the tightness in his gut. She didn't play games, he reminded himself. He shouldn't borrow trouble by trying to second-guess her words and actions. Or their future.

Jeez. He'd never wondered so much about a woman's behavior. Probably because he'd never had to. He'd missed out on all that crap when he was a teenager. Now he seemed to be paying for that.

A short while later, the meeting broke up. People went to their offices to clear the decks before heading to Marty's club. Their owner had arranged transport so no one had to worry about drinking and driving.

"We knocked it out of the park today." Scott walked with Sapphie to her office.

"Great teamwork." She began gathering up her things. "It doesn't always work out so well. Even when I'm on the same page as the client. Egos can get in the way over the smallest points."

"That's not something we had to worry about." He leaned against her doorjamb. "I barely noticed that you had two more slides in the presentation than I did."

Sapphie laughed as she unplugged her laptop and slipped it into her case. "Three, if you count the summary chart."

"Hmm. You may need to soothe my bruised ego later."

"I'll do my best to make it up to you." The husky edge to her voice was as effective as if she'd caressed him.

He shifted to cover the tightening in his pants. "How long will dinner be?"

"Too long. But the sooner we get there, the sooner we'll be able to leave."

"Good plan. I'll get my stuff sorted and meet you here."

He barely made it to his office door when he heard someone snarl, "I want to talk to you, bitch."

What the hell? He swiveled in time to see Darren grab Sapphie's arm.

Scott started to move forward to tell the ass to get his freaking hands off her, but Sapphie caught his gaze through the glass and shook her head. He held off, prepared to let her handle things. For now. He edged closer to her door, just in case.

"That VP's job should have been mine. Not Morgan's."

"Get your hands off me." Sapphie wrenched her arm out of Darren's grasp and stepped away from him. "You've done nothing to deserve the promotion. Your numbers are pitiful and your contribution to this project has been zero. Now get out of my office and consider yourself lucky I don't have you fired."

The icy note in her voice should have been a warning, but Darren was too riled to notice.

"You can't do that. Don't you know who I am?"

"In case you hadn't noticed, your uncles don't own the team anymore."

As Darren lunged forward to grab her again, Scott stepped into the office.

"You're making a scene." His voice was low and even. "Walk away. Now."

Like a playground bully, Darren didn't like the interference of someone he perceived as stronger than him. His chin had a belligerent tilt as he slammed out.

Once he'd gone, Sapphie turned to Scott. "I was perfectly capable of dealing with that ass, but thank you for backing my play."

"Anytime."

"Hopefully, there won't be another time. Darren's just done you and Callum a favor and written his own marching orders."

"The sooner he's gone, the better."

"Exactly." She shooed him out of her office. "Now, let me get packed up so we can get out of here."

As he returned to his own office, Scott realized that the incident had brought back the uneasiness he'd felt earlier. Specifically because Sapphie's reaction had reminded him how fiercely independent she was.

Why did that bother him? He'd never had a problem with strong women who could take care of themselves. He'd always respected them—from his mom to his billet mom, even his ex-wife.

Sapphie's independence, her need to have everything on her own terms, came from a darker place, he knew. He respected that, too. Still, he couldn't ignore the niggle of concern.

How long would it be before he became a casualty of that fierce independence?

For now, with things ticking along between them as they were, all was fine. Their relationship went from day to day, with their plans fluid. It suited them both for different reasons—the requirements of his new job, the demands of her business.

But he wanted more. More of her time. More of a sense that he mattered to her as much as she mattered to him.

The problem was that the moment he shared that with her, she'd be off like a shot.

If he were smarter, he'd probably end things

now. Before she got scared that they were getting too close. Before he got in too deep.

But he also wanted more of what they'd shared. It was special, he knew, even if she didn't—or couldn't—recognize it. Special enough that, despite the risk, despite the odds, he had to give them a chance.

And because deep inside was the kind of hope that had sustained him throughout his life, when his dreams—of playing professional hockey, of making it to the NHL, of winning the Cup—had also seemed against the odds. This time, the hope was that he could be the one to change her mind and that they'd have a future together.

CHAPTER TWELVE

OPENING NIGHT HAD always been special. More than his birthday or Christmas. Although, Scott reflected, that was possibly because during a normal year, he was either playing or traveling on those other days.

The season began for real on opening night. Everything up to that point was simply a rehearsal and didn't count. What had happened the previous season didn't count either. Whether you'd won the Cup in June or hit the golf course in April, there was a clean slate for every player and every team from the minute the puck dropped on that first face-off.

It was a time fresh with possibilities, hope and belief. Favorites hoped they'd start strong to deliver the ultimate prize. Underdogs believed they could beat the odds of every sporting pundit. As for the ones in the middle of the pack, it was a long eighty-two games and the only thing you could guarantee was that there would be plenty of surprises.

From here on in, every game, every point, mattered.

Standing behind the team bench as the Cats went through their morning skate, Scott felt the buzz in the air and the energy of the players preparing for tonight's game stir his blood. Man, he wanted to be out there instead of watching. The only reason he was here was to check on the arena operations team as they got ready for the pregame ceremony and the raising of the championship banner.

But even as his heart yearned to feel the ice beneath his blades and the puck on his stick, Scott's joints ached in protest. He needed to be ten years younger and have had less than ten years' worth of injuries to have a chance of keeping up with the kids. The last few seasons he'd played had proved that. It had taken longer to recover from each game and prepare for the next one. It had been harder to get himself into peak condition. Harder still to maintain it. Being a veteran gave him no quarter, especially not from the youngsters. Today's rookies were fitter, stronger and faster than when he'd broken into the league. Not to mention some of them were the same age as Angela and Wayne.

A spray of ice cut into his morose thoughts.

He cursed and wiped the melting flakes from his jacket. "Watch the suit, Kasanski. I need to look sharp when I'm wining and dining the important guests and watching you ice-dance."

Ice Man's lip curled as he climbed over the boards. "Drinking champagne is for wusses."

"It's a tough job, but someone's got to do it so you don't play to empty seats. Don't worry. You'll be in my shoes soon enough."

"Ah, but I've got lucky genes that mean I can keep skating and playing like a kid."

"Is that why you spend more time on your ass than your skates?"

Before Ice Man could reply, the whistle blew and the team headed to the bench for a breather and some water. The players greeted him with the usual mix of good-natured jabs and insults.

"Suit and tie." Chance, who'd skated up beside Kasanski, shook his head sadly. "How the mighty have fallen. I bet you'd give your left nut to be skating drills with us."

Scott would slice off said nut before admitting that. "Are you kidding? I like waking up in the morning and not hurting."

"Man, that sounds good," current captain Jake "Bad Boy" Badoletti groaned. "I can't remember the last time I didn't hurt."

"Me neither." Ike Jelinek flipped up his mask and drank deeply from a bottle before squirting water over his face. "Some mornings it takes me ten minutes to ease out of bed."

"I think that has more to do with your hot wife," Monty said.

Ike's face softened at his backup's words. "She does make those aches go away."

Ike's younger brother Kenny made a gagging sound and held up two fingers like a cross warding off evil. "TMI, bro. Way too much information."

"You're just jealous."

J.B. laughed. "That's for sure."

"I don't need a wife." Kenny shuddered.

It was good to be jawing with the guys. There was nothing like the give-and-take with them. At least that never went away.

Scott noticed that Mad Dog didn't join in, but hung off to one side, giving him weird looks. Not the stink-eye, but odd nonetheless.

A short blast of the whistle and the trainer holding up two fingers warned that work would start again in a couple minutes. Most of the players made a final comment to their former captain, then skated to center ice, ready to scrimmage.

Scott laid a hand on Taylor's arm, holding him back momentarily. "I thought we were good about Sapphie."

"We are."

"So what's with the attitude?"

"Nothing. Just a little surprised that you're still with her. I thought it would have fizzled out now that she's finished working with the Cats. She's normally quick to move on."

Even though Scott had wondered the same thing over the past week—especially when they'd barely had a chance to talk for more than a few minutes each night—he was pissed at Mad Dog's comment. Like somehow he wasn't good enough to hang on to Sapphie.

"Don't get me wrong," Taylor continued. "I think it's great. She seems happy. And it's way past time she had more than a fun-and-done with someone."

The unspoken *but* hung in the air. As did the knowledge that the relationship would end sometime.

Mad Dog clapped him on the shoulder. "Patience. Even though you'll want to hold on tight, you have to give her enough slack that she feels comfortable. It's the only way to win her trust."

It was Scott's turn to be surprised. "I'm trying."

"You've already gotten further than any other man, so stick with it." Taylor tapped his glove to his forehead in a salute. "She's coming in later, right?"

When Scott nodded, Taylor added, "Bring her to the team dinner. Trust me, that'll be a big score in her eyes."

Before Scott could splutter an excuse, Taylor skated off and practice started again. Sticks clashed and bodies thudded into each other. Shouts echoed around the rink.

Over the years, as more and more guys had gotten married, women had become part of the postgame dinner. Generally, once kids came along, the wives tended not to show up as much. Girlfriends who were included were usually fairly steady. And, of course, the queen of the puck bunnies and her entourage always made an appearance for the single guys.

Would inviting Sapphie be too much, too soon?

Scott mulled that over as he headed to the office. He hadn't quite made his mind up when his phone rang.

It was Cam Lockhead returning his call. Scott had been trying to get hold of Cam for several days and was getting worried.

"Hey, Bullet. How's it going?"

"It's going." His friend's flat tone set off alarm bells.

"What's up, bro?"

"I've quit the Seattle job. I couldn't stick it out anymore."

There was more to the story, Scott sensed. "I guess that was inevitable. Sounded like you were about done last time we spoke."

"Yeah. I feel bad for letting the team down, but they were okay about it." Bullet sounded like even talking was too much of an effort for him.

"Well, hopefully their loss is our gain. I spoke with Callum and there's an Ice Cats ambassador's role open for you anytime you're ready." Scott filled Cam in on what he'd agreed on with his GM.

"Thanks, man. I appreciate you going to bat for

me." The lack of emotion belied the words. If he couldn't even get himself up over a new job, one he'd asked for, there was something really wrong.

"You want to tell me what's going on, Bullet?"

There was a pause. Long enough that Scott thought his friend might be prepared to share whatever was bothering him.

"I'm just a little tired. I haven't been sleeping well."

"Right. This is me you're talking to. Give me the truth."

Bullet sighed. "It's been a rough week. My head's bothering me worse than usual."

One of the problems with concussion, especially in the long term, was the accompanying depression. Scott was no expert, but his friend didn't sound good. "What does the doctor say?"

"Everyone has times like this. I'll get through it."

The mechanical parroting of the medic's opinion didn't ease Scott's concern. "Can't he give you something for when your head's bad?" He was careful not to specify antidepressants, knowing Cam would consider them a sign of weakness.

"Yeah. I have some other pills. But they make me feel like crap."

Scott felt helpless. "Have you spoken with Grey yet? He said he'd been trying to get hold of you, too."

"Nah. I've been kinda tied up with the whole

Seattle thing. I'll reach out to him now things are settling down."

"You'll feel better once you're in Jersey, where you belong, instead of out there with the weird Left Coasters."

"For sure. Laurel will be glad to move back."

"There's no rush to start. Take some time to rest, then let me know when you're ready to get motoring."

"I'll talk to the boss lady and we'll figure out a plan. Sooner would be better for me, but I don't have to organize the logistics." His dry laugh was an improvement but still lacked the buoyancy Cam usually had.

"Any help she needs, we can give. We use a firm, Making Your Move, who can look after all that for her."

"I'll tell her to call you."

By the time he hung up, Cam had started to sound more normal. But that didn't ease Scott's concern, so he dialed Grey's number. When his friend answered, Scott updated him on the conversation and his worries. "There's something in Bullet's voice I don't like. I'm worried he's worse than he's letting on."

"Damn, I should have called him." Grey sighed. "I've been busy and haven't had a chance to track him down. I'll try again tomorrow. Maybe if we exchange war stories, I can get him to open up. I'll let you know how I make out."

"Thanks, man. At least we'll get him back in the fold soon and we can keep a closer eye on him."

After the call was over, Scott made a note to follow up with Bullet within a few days.

As Scott got into the elevator, the sound of heels clicking on the marble floor of the foyer caught his attention. Although he knew Sapphie wasn't coming in until later, he tried not to be disappointed when Morgan joined him.

"Going my way, Scotty?" she joked. She now had the office next to him.

It had felt strange the first few days after Sapphie had gone. He'd missed her enough without the empty office as a constant reminder that her stint with the Ice Cats was done. The number of times he'd looked up, even started to rise from his chair to share something with her, only to remember she was gone, was ridiculous. Especially since she'd been there only a short while. He'd missed talking to her, sharing stuff with her, even arguing with her.

One night after everyone had gone, he'd sat in her office, in her chair, thinking about how to solve a particularly thorny problem. The air, still faintly scented with her perfume, had seemed to clear his head, enabling him to see a solution. The next day when Doreen had moved Morgan into that office, he'd felt a crazy sense of betrayal.

Then he'd gotten over himself. It was just an office, not a freaking shrine.

Still, it took some getting used to, seeing Morgan at that desk, in that chair.

He paused in front of his office to confirm a detail for tonight's program with Morgan, then turned and stopped in the doorway.

"Sapphie?" It took a moment for him to realize she really was seated behind his desk. "I wasn't expecting you until later."

"That's a warm greeting," she teased, looking up from her laptop. "I finished up quicker than expected and caught an earlier flight."

"What a nice surprise." He walked around the desk to lean down to kiss her. "Hi."

The second kiss was longer, deeper. "Welcome back."

The third kiss practically blew his socks off and made him forget he was in an office with glass walls. He wanted to take her right there on his desk.

From her uneven breathing and the fluttering pulse at the base of her throat, it seemed she had similar needs.

Scott wanted to take her home and lose himself in her. It had been a long, lonely week. The too-brief calls each evening hadn't been nearly enough.

Unfortunately, there was too much to do before tonight to play hooky.

He lifted his head. He should probably have eased her out of his arms, but a minute more couldn't hurt. "I'm afraid I need a couple more hours here. But then I'm all yours. For the whole weekend."

"I can't wait." Her smile said she planned to take advantage of that promise. "In the meantime, I'm going to see Issy and Sophia. We'll all come to the game together. So should I meet you here or at the arena?"

"The arena is probably best. Call me when you get there and I'll find you."

She stood, bringing her body flush against his. She tilted her head, pressed a quick, hard kiss to his lips, then stepped back. "Don't take too long."

He laughed, his heart lighter than it had been all week. "That's the pot calling the kettle black. I don't suppose you were playing computer games on your laptop."

Sapphie shut her machine down and slipped it into her case. "Not just now, but I might have indulged on the flight."

"Yeah, right. You worked the whole way." There was no rancor in his voice. It was what she did. Who she was. Even if he'd wanted to—and he didn't—he couldn't change her. As long as there was time for him, too, what did it matter?

"Busted." She grinned unrepentantly. "But only so I'd be free for the weekend." She slung her purse over her shoulder. "I assume you have grand plans for us."

"I do. Starting with the game tonight, obviously." He walked her to the elevator. "If you're up for it, I thought we could have dinner with the guys later."

Her eyes widened. "Go to one of the famous postgame dinners? Won't I be intruding?"

"They all know you and you're part of the bigger circle of family and friends." He added honestly, "Taylor suggested it, if that makes you feel more comfortable."

"All right." She fist-pumped. "I'd love to come. I promise not to be too much of a fan girl."

He leaned forward and kissed her. "As long as you don't forget who your favorite player is."

She sighed theatrically, hand to her heart. "Dinner with Bad Boy. A dream come true."

"Hmm, forget the invitation." He tweaked her cute nose.

"I'm kidding. You know you're my number-one guy." She waggled her fingers, then blew him a kiss as the elevator doors slid closed.

Scott sauntered to his desk, hands in his pockets, fighting a broad, cocky smile. Well, that was one for the books.

Sapphie had missed him.

"I CAN COOK well enough. I just choose not to most of the time."

Sapphie hefted the paper bag of groceries onto

her hip and followed Scotty, who carried his own bags, into his house. "I'm happy to contribute salads to our meal."

He laughed, leading the way into the impressive kitchen filled with state-of-the-art appliances. "Hey, opening bags and taking lids off pots is cooking in my eyes."

"I recall your offer of dinner included something about relaxing on your deck with a nice glass of wine. And being your personal cheering section as you grill the steaks to unsurpassed perfection."

"Mock all you want, but you'll be weeping tears of thanks from the first delicious mouthful." He put his bags on the butcher-block table and removed two bottles of wine, which he put in a separate beverage refrigerator. "Of course, other forms of gratitude will also be accepted." He held his arms out for her to walk into, which she did.

"Consider this a down payment."

The banter helped dispel the awkwardness of walking into his house. She knew his ex-wife hadn't called it home for over a year, but his children stayed here during college vacations. So it was still the family home, and invited or not, she felt like an interloper.

She hated the feeling of not belonging. It was often accompanied by the sense of not being good enough. Though she'd left the poverty of her childhood behind long ago, times like this made her feel like the kid in the mended thrift-store clothes. The long-past—but not forgotten—feeling of being trapped by her circumstances and responsibilities bubbled up from the back of her mind, where she'd ruthlessly shoved it.

You've come a long way, baby. As Sapphie emptied the groceries onto the counter, she wiggled her toes in her cute suede Charlotte Olympia flats. No more hand-me-downs. *Look who's riding high on the wave now.*

The mini pep talk gave her a boost of confidence. She could hold her own with the best in the business, as well as the best dressed. She could afford her own mansion, if she wanted one, complete with fancy kitchen. As for not belonging, Scotty had invited her and she'd agreed to come. She had nothing to feel uneasy about.

And she was damned if she'd allow her normally well-hidden insecurities to spoil what had been another near-perfect weekend.

Then she noticed a red stain on her blouse—something in the grocery bag had leaked. Sighing, she dampened a paper towel and patted at the mark. "I look like I've been stabbed in the stomach."

"You can wash it here." Scott led the way to the laundry room.

He plucked a clean Ice Cats T-shirt from the pile in the basket and handed it to her. "In case you want to preserve your modesty, though don't feel you have to on my account."

"That's most generous of you." Sapphie laughed as she stripped off the blouse and tossed it in the machine, then put on the soft, faded T-shirt.

It felt strangely intimate to be wearing something that belonged to him, surrounded by the clean, fresh scent she associated with him. She shoved back the unsettling thought.

In the kitchen, she accepted a glass of wine and perched on a stool at the granite breakfast bar to watch him perform his magic.

"The secret's in the marinade." Scotty put the steaks in a red-wine concoction, then covered them with foil. "While we let them do their thing, we can sit outside."

He led her out to the deck. The evening was surprisingly warm for mid-October, though the sun was already setting. A light breeze brought the scent of autumn leaves and cut grass. For a few moments, they stood at the rail, sipping their wine. Sapphie leaned her head against his shoulder and he rested his temple against the top of her head as they let the peace of the evening wash over them.

Any remaining stress seeped away, leaving Sapphie feeling relaxed. This was nice. Comfortable. A lovely ending to a lovely weekend.

It had kicked off with the Ice Cats' resounding win against Philly, followed by an enormously fun dinner with the team. She'd enjoyed being treated as one of the gang and she'd managed to avoid squealing like a fan girl as she was surrounded by her favorite players.

She hadn't been so reserved with their love-making that night. The hunger that had engulfed them both the minute her door had closed behind them hadn't abated until this morning. Plans to spend the day exploring the city had been abandoned as they'd explored each other in her bed... and other parts of the apartment. She didn't know about absence making the heart grow fonder, but it was clear Scotty had missed her as much as she had him.

Sapphie hated to admit that she wasn't looking forward to heading to Chicago, then Minneapolis, and another week's separation. She'd never felt this way about a man she'd been seeing before and it made her uncomfortable and wary. She kept telling herself it was probably because they'd been in each other's company so intensely for the past month. As she returned to her normal life and got used to not seeing and speaking to him all the time, she was sure it would wear off.

Nonetheless, earlier she'd delayed her Sunday-evening flight to early tomorrow morning so they could have this night together. Scotty's pleasure at the unexpected change had matched her own and they'd celebrated in style.

"Your seat, my lady." Scotty indicated the teak lounger. "I need to get the grill fired up."

Sapphie made herself comfortable while Scotty prepared the charcoal. "I thought you'd have a gas super-grill to match your restaurant-quality kitchen."

"You can't beat the flavor from charcoal." He lit the briquettes and tended the flames. "Besides, I like stuff to be simple. The kitchen was for Celine. She had to put up with crappy appliances until I started earning big money. So when we moved here, she remodeled and put in top-of-the-line everything. Hell, I'm not even sure what some of those appliances are for."

"I'm glad you said that, because I'm not sure I recognized all of them either."

Scotty sighed. "This whole house was for Celine. Pretty much everything about it is by her design. I often feel like I'm the one thing in it that doesn't come up to spec."

Relieved she wasn't the only one who felt like that, she was also curious. "So how come you're the one living here?"

"After we split up, she wanted to travel, so she preferred a low-maintenance place that she could lock up and leave. I didn't care where I lived and I didn't want the kids to lose their home, so I kept it for them." He shrugged. "The things we do to make sure our children don't suffer in a divorce."

"I guess." Since her parents hadn't cared how their actions impacted their children, Sapphie found it a little hard to comprehend. "I'm sure if you moved to somewhere you actually liked and felt comfortable in, they'd get over it."

"I'm thinking about it. My son doesn't mind where I live, so once my daughter graduates next summer, I'll probably sell."

"What kind of house would you like?" She was curious to see if she'd pegged him right.

"Something smaller—I don't need eight bedrooms and six baths—and also less…modern. Definitely older, more traditional. With a wraparound porch and a yard meant for enjoying with big trees and lots of color."

Pleased to have nailed it, she couldn't help feeling a little sad that she wouldn't get to see him in that house. Their relationship would be long over by next summer. Although, if they remained friends… No. Somehow she didn't see that happening.

And yet an image of the two of them sitting on that wraparound porch, watching the sunset over the old oak trees and mature garden, insisted on floating through her brain.

"Sounds lovely." She tried to ignore the hint of wistfulness in her voice. Not appropriate. Not right.

Scotty looked at her thoughtfully. "Based on your apartment, I'd have thought this—" he waved a hand to indicate the house "—would have been your taste."

"Nope. I've always preferred traditional and

vintage. But my place is conveniently located, has a great view, is fully serviced and reasonably priced. It's a rental, so I don't have to like the style as long as it delivers what I need it to."

"I guess. If you were to buy a place, what would you go for?"

"An apartment like Issy's. It's cute and homey, with nice features—wood floors and painted cabinets. Also a balcony or a patio. I love being able to sit out in the evening and enjoy the view. It doesn't have to be of the city—Issy's apartment overlooks a pretty lake."

He nodded. "Somewhere that feels like a home, not just a place to live."

Interesting that he'd zeroed in on the thing that bothered her about both their current abodes. They were both living somewhere they weren't happy with.

Despite the panicky feeling of being tied down, the idea of buying Issy's apartment hadn't gone away. Over the past few weeks, Sapphie had thought about it several times. But she wasn't prepared to admit that to Issy, let alone Scotty.

She gave him the same line she'd been giving everyone for years, even though this time it sounded a little hollow. "I don't have the time to look for a place, let alone buy one, decorate it, furnish it and then take care of it. I know there are people who can sort all that out for me, and maybe someday I'll get around to talking with them. But right now, I'm happy as I am."

"It doesn't bother you that you don't own your home?"

She shook her head, though the answer didn't seem so clear anymore. "That would be too much of a commitment. I like not being tied down."

Scotty frowned. Her answer obviously didn't sit right with him.

Then it occurred to her that his ex had wanted somewhere with less commitment, too.

She changed the topic. "How's the grill coming along? I'm starving."

He grinned. "It's about ready. All it needs are the steaks, which should be tender by now. I'll get them."

"I'll start dishing out the salads and sides." She gathered their empty glasses. "And top these off."

"Good idea."

Sapphie almost ran into him when he stopped abruptly in the doorway. He swore under his breath.

Startled, she took a step back. "Is something wr—"

A young blonde woman threw her arms around Scotty.

"I could smell the grill firing up halfway down the block, Dad. I hope you have two more steaks for me and Sean."

"Hey, sweetheart." His voice was strained. "I wasn't expecting you until next weekend."

His daughter? Sapphie's stomach twisted sharply, her earlier misgivings flaring.

Scotty stood stiffly, seemingly unable to move. Meanwhile, the bubbly blonde, wearing cutoff shorts, a college T-shirt and cute sandals, turned and headed toward the refrigerator. Clearly, she hadn't seen that Scotty had a visitor.

"I wasn't planning to stay. But Sean was playing a gig at a club nearby last night, so I thought we'd stop by and you could check him out. He's checking his precious drums in the van and will be in shortly." Angela laughed. "I think he's nervous about meeting you."

Scotty still hadn't moved. "I'm not sure there will be enough food for everyone."

Angela got the bag of prepared salad leaves from the crisper, then reached for a bowl. "Can't you get some more steaks out of the freezer?"

Sapphie waited for Scotty to mention her presence, but he didn't. Although his brain had probably frozen the minute he'd seen his daughter, his omission made Sapphie feel out of place again. Which stung, when she was the one who was meant to be there.

Since Scotty seemed unable to make the necessary introductions, it was up to her.

"We're not ready for the salad yet," she said calmly, pushing past Scotty and into the kitchen, where she put down the glasses, then took the bowl from Angela and put it aside. "I'm Sapphire, by the way."

Angela's jaw drop was almost comical. She recovered quickly; her blue gaze narrowed and did a head-to-toe examination of Sapphie, lingering briefly on the too-large T-shirt.

"Dad? You have a guest?" Her question had an accusing edge.

"I do." Scotty kept his tone even, though he squared his stance. "Sapphie, this is my eldest, Angela."

"Nice to meet you." Sapphie smiled. "I've heard a lot about you from your dad."

Angela didn't smile back. "Does Mom know about *this*?" She waved her hand between him and Sapphie.

"Sweetie, your mother and I are divorced," he reminded her gently. "Which *she* wanted."

The tension level ratcheted up a notch. "How long has this been going on? Sapphire's wearing your T-shirt." Her lip curled as she said Sapphie's name. "Very cozy."

"She spilled something on her blouse and had to change. Though I don't have to explain that to you," Scotty said carefully. "I'm—"

"And I don't have to stick around and watch you entertain some puck bunny."

"Enough. Sapphie isn't—"

The doorbell rang.

"That's Sean." Angela turned on her heel

and stalked off, tossing over her shoulder, "I've changed my mind about you meeting him."

The front door slamming echoed through the house.

Scotty closed his eyes briefly, then heaved a sigh. "Sorry about that."

"It's fine." Sapphie busied herself with the sides they'd purchased so he wouldn't see how much Angela's visit and her antagonistic attitude—not to mention that puck-bunny dig—bothered her. "Shouldn't you go after her?"

She was startled when his arms wrapped around her. He pulled her into him and rested his chin against her head. "Better to let her cool off. Anything I say now will only rile her further. I'll call her in a day or two and set her straight."

His tone said that was a discussion he wasn't looking forward to having. She couldn't blame him, yet something about the way he said it unsettled her.

Although the situation had taken the edge off her appetite, Sapphie turned in his arms, kissed him, then said brightly, "Where are those to-die-for steaks?"

Gratitude shone in his eyes. "Coming right up."

The rest of the evening went more smoothly. The steaks were indeed the best she'd ever tasted. The lovemaking that followed was intense and passionate. They finally slept, curled in each other's arms, legs entwined. As if neither wanted to let go, even for a moment.

Early the following morning, Scotty held her hand as he drove her to the airport. He stood with her as she checked in, then lifted her case onto the scales. Their goodbye was quiet—little said, a lot unsaid. Her throat tightened as she walked away.

Sapphie looked back only once as she cleared security. Scotty's serious expression broke into a grin and he blew her a kiss, making her laugh.

She was still smiling when she slipped into her seat on the aircraft. As the cabin crew went through their last-minute tasks before takeoff, Sapphie's mind was further afield. With a certain retired hockey captain. Wondering whether it would be so bad to get serious about him. Whether they could actually make a relationship work.

And why the thought of all that, which should have terrified her, instead made her happy.

CHAPTER THIRTEEN

"YOU'RE STILL SEEING that woman, aren't you?"

Every phone call with Scott's daughter after her unexpected visit six weeks ago had followed the same route. At least, it had once Angela had started speaking to him again, which had taken a couple weeks.

"Give me a break, sweetheart," he said calmly, biting back a sigh. "We've been over and over this. I'm sorry that my dating Sapphie upsets you, but I'm a divorced man who is free to date whomever I please."

He leaned against the headboard of the hotel room bed. This was going to take a while. So much for his plan to chill out before he had to join the team for dinner. He'd worked nonstop in the office, then on the plane to Columbus and in the hotel once he'd arrived. He'd just gotten out of the shower when his cell had rung.

The conversation had actually been going better than usual, until Angela had started talking about Christmas. Since he'd been away over Thanksgiving—on a western road trip with the Ice Cats—and there was no hockey from Decem-

ber 24 to December 26, plus the team had a home
stand after, Angela wanted both him and Celine
at Christmas lunch.

"You'd rather spend Christmas Day with *her*
than your children."

"I've already explained that I'm going to J.B.
Larocque's place with some of the guys." He deliberately didn't mention that Sapphie would be
there, too. "You and Wayne will be with your
mother."

"Why can't you join us? You did last year."

His words were measured. "That was a one-off
to make things easier for you and your brother.
Next year, you'll both spend the day with me."

Angela huffed. "Is it serious—this thing with
her?"

He wasn't about to explain the situation with
Sapphie to his daughter. "We're dating. We have
fun together."

"Well, I don't want her in our house when
I'm home for the holidays." His daughter's tone
changed, growing angry. "I'll stay at Mom's. And
I won't come over to visit."

He shook his head. This was starting to degenerate into a familiar argument that he had neither
the energy nor the will to deal with. Especially
not on the phone from a hotel room.

"Cool your jets."

When she tried to interrupt, he cut her off. "I'm
a single adult who's entitled to live his life the way

he wants. To be happy. If that means you don't want to live in my house anymore or even see me again, I'm sorry. I won't like it, but that's your choice and so be it." He puffed out a silent breath. "I will not be held to ransom by you."

"Fine. Bye." The click of the line disconnecting was as effective as a door slam.

Scott tossed his phone onto the bed, then laced his fingers behind his head and stared at the ceiling. "That went well," he said. "Not."

He was not backing down. Even if things didn't last with Sapphie, it was the principle. He wouldn't go through this every time he started seeing someone.

Needing to get rid of the sour taste in his mouth, he called Sapphie.

"This is a nice surprise." The pleasure in her voice instantly brightened his mood. "I wasn't expecting to hear from you until after the team dinner."

"I had a couple minutes before I have to join the guys, so I thought I'd try to catch you and say hi."

"Hi."

How could she put so much sensual intent into one small word?

His erection sprang to life, as if she'd reached through the phone and stroked him. Then again, his body probably assumed this was foreplay.

Scott couldn't believe he'd gotten this far in his life without having experienced phone sex. It had simply never occurred to him before, but with Sapphie, it was an adventure. Fun, steamy and ultimately frustrating, despite the completion they both achieved. Solo satisfaction was nowhere near as good as being buried deep inside her, feeling her pulse around him as she came, then giving in to his own climax.

Still, intimate calls had been one of the ways they'd coped with their jam-packed schedules over the past month and a half. Though he'd managed to catch up with her in Minneapolis for one glorious night, the next Cats road trip to Detroit and Nashville had coincided with her being elsewhere. She'd made it to Jersey a couple times and he'd flown to Chicago once.

"Hi." His voice deepened with a husky edge. "Miss me?"

"Hell yes." She laughed. "If my office door wasn't open, I'd tell you in explicit detail how much."

His imagination fired. Scott shifted to ease an almost painful hardness. "Hold that thought for later."

"Definitely. Though I was planning to show you tomorrow when you arrive in Chicago. Unless you'll be too tired. I know you don't get in until late."

The Cats were flying to Chicago after the game against Columbus. Since they weren't playing until Sunday and Coach Macarty had organized a team-building activity for Saturday, Scott was free. He planned to spend every moment with Sapphie.

"I've been used to that kind of schedule my whole adult life. No matter how late it is, I'll be ready for you."

"Excellent. Be sure to eat your Wheaties tomorrow. It's been a long ten days since we were together and I plan to make it up to you."

Their plans had fallen apart the previous week, when Sapphie had canceled because of an issue with one of Marty's projects. Instead of flying to New Jersey to meet up with Scott, she'd gone to LA. He'd tried not to let on how much it had irritated him that he'd come second place to her business again, but that wouldn't stop him from accepting what she was offering as compensation.

He groaned. "I'm supposed to meet the guys in fifteen minutes. I can't show up with a raging hard-on."

"I could help you with that."

"I'm tempted, believe me. But I'm saving myself for the real thing."

"Me, too… Hold on a second." He heard someone talking in the background. Then she said, "Sorry, but I have to go. I have a videoconference with the Antonelli group."

"No problem. I'll speak to you later."

"I look forward to it." She lowered her voice. "I promise there won't be any interruptions."

"Great," he said, trying to sound upbeat while aching.

Once he'd hung up, he went into the bathroom and ran the cold water, splashing it over his face.

Although he didn't want to get ahead of himself—it was still early days—his relationship with Sapphie was going pretty well. And not just on the physical side. The long-distance thing was tough and it was difficult not to keep pressing for more from her. He'd dropped several hints about her making Jersey her home so they could spend more time together. He'd hoped it might also make their relationship more settled. But he had to tread carefully. If he pushed too hard, he'd scare her away. So he was schooling himself to be patient.

He shut off the tap and headed for the door, only to be stopped when his cell rang. In case it was his daughter calling to give him more grief, he checked the caller ID.

It was Cam Lockhead. Scott debated answering but let it go to voice mail. Their conversations over the past few weeks had become difficult.

Bullet had suffered a setback in his recovery from concussion syndrome. That had affected his move to Jersey. Even though Making Your Move was handling all the logistics for him and Laurel, Cam had found it hard to make decisions about the simplest things. So they'd slowed the process to make it easier for him to cope. At this stage, the move wasn't likely to occur until well into next year.

That had bothered Bullet, making him feel like he was letting everyone down. No matter how many times Scott had reassured him, Bullet had become depressed and withdrawn. Both Scott and Grey had teamed with Laurel to get Cam into counseling, but the man was stubborn as hell.

The phone fell silent. Scott heaved a sigh and opened the door. He felt bad for ignoring the call, but he wasn't up for dealing with Bullet right now. He'd call later, after dinner. His cell rang again when he was in the elevator going down to join the guys in the bar. Scott frowned, seeing it was Bullet again. Once again he let the call go to voice mail. This time because he was hardly in the right place to talk. He'd return the call downstairs, where he could step outside and get some privacy.

Scott bumped into Chance and Ice Man getting out of the adjacent elevator and they all headed for the bar together. From there, they went on to the team dinner and Scott didn't get a chance to check his phone until much later, when he was returning to his room.

His stomach dropped when he saw he'd missed nearly a dozen calls from Bullet.

Crap. Something must be seriously wrong.

His friend had stopped calling over an hour ago. Cursing, Scott fumbled with the key card, taking a couple attempts to open the door. Rushing inside, he was about to call Bullet when his cell rang.

Seeing his friend's name, he puffed out a relieved breath and answered. "Hey, man. I'm sorry I missed you earlier. You know what it's like on the road with team dinners."

There was a pause, then a female voice asked, "Is that Scott?"

"Uh, yeah." Who was using Bullet's phone? "Laurel?"

"I'm Candace, her sister."

"Is she okay?"

She hesitated. "Laurel asked me to contact Cam's friends. I hate to give you bad news over the phone, but I'm trying to stay one step ahead of the media."

His gut twisted hard. "Why? What's happened?"

"I'm sorry to tell you that Cam passed away this afternoon."

"What?" His legs suddenly felt weak. He grabbed the wall. How the hell did a guy die from a freaking concussion? "I thought he was getting better."

"We—" Candace cleared her throat. "We all did."

"So what happened?"

The silence went on for so long that he wondered if the connection had gone. Finally, she said quietly, "He hanged himself."

"You want me to go with you to London?"

Sapphie couldn't believe it. She almost pinched

herself to be sure she wasn't imagining what Marty had said.

It was a dream come true. She'd always longed to travel abroad, especially to England, but the opportunity had never arisen.

When Marty had told her he was thinking of buying one of the English Premier League soccer teams, she'd hoped that he'd send her to evaluate the business.

"Of course." He chuckled. "Who else would I trust to do the job? Besides, you know more about football, as they call it over there, than most of my staff. Almost as much as my soccer-mad wife."

Sapphie jumped to her feet and did a silent happy dance around her office, fist-pumping with the hand that held the phone. Then she sat again and took a steadying breath. "When do you need me to go?"

"Ideally, Monday. Tuesday at the latest. I know it's short notice, but the owner has finally agreed to sell and said I can have first refusal, so I want to get the ball rolling as soon as possible…in case he changes his mind again."

Sapphie would have moved heaven and earth to clear her schedule for this trip. As it happened, her next project, which required her to be in-house for at least the initial meetings, wouldn't start until January, so she was free. Also, with the holidays coming and December being notorious for disruptions, she'd focused her team on finishing their current projects, not starting new ones. She had intended to do some internal strategic planning, staff appraisals and general housekeeping to ensure a fresh start in the New Year. Other than the reviews, most of that work could be managed remotely.

"I'll check my diary, see if I can move a few things about and get back to you."

"Good, good. I'll get my assistant to email you the bare-bones schedule we have so far and you can adapt that as you see fit. I'll be there for the first week minimum. The club plays at home on the Saturday afternoon and I'd like to attend. I assume you will, too."

Even though the soccer team wasn't her favorite, she wasn't giving up the chance to watch a live game in the best league in the world. The only thing that would have been better was if they'd been playing her beloved Red Devils. Then again, she'd have found it hard to maintain a professional detachment and cheer for the appropriate side. "Definitely. I'll practice my chants."

"Make sure they're the clean ones. Some of those songs can be a little choice."

Sapphie grinned. "As if I'd do anything else."

They discussed what Marty wanted to get out of the trip. She chipped in with observations and suggestions of her own. It was a much more complicated acquisition than the Ice Cats had been, not least because of the regulations of both countries and the dictates of soccer's national and international governing bodies. There was a lot of due diligence to be done before Marty could make a final commitment.

"I figure that you and the rest of the team will need to be in England for the whole of December. Maybe longer if you run into any hitches or uncover any major issues."

She winced. "I need to be finished by Christmas. I have commitments to other clients in January that I can't shift."

"I understand. Plus Christmas is a family time. Although Gloria would understand, she really wouldn't be happy if I wasn't around for the holidays. I'm sure you'll work with the team to meet the timings." Marty added, "I realize this is a major commitment for you. It's a long time to be away from your business. I expect you to reflect that in your fees for this project."

"That's generous but unnecessary."

"Nonsense. It's smart business. You'll make it worth my while, I know."

Given how much money she'd made for him on previous projects, she knew that to be true. "I appreciate it nonetheless."

"While we're on the subject, when you return from London, I think it's time we discussed bringing your business into the fold."

Her mind was still on what she'd need to do before going to England, and it took a moment for Marty's words to sink in. "Excuse me?"

"I'd like to purchase your company. Make it part of the Antonelli group. Obviously, as with my other acquisitions, it would continue to run as a discrete business with you remaining in charge. However, you'd get the benefit of my financial backing and security for the long term. It's an opportunity for you to take your company to new heights."

Sapphie was flabbergasted. Marty acquiring her business was the last thing she'd expected. It wasn't something she'd ever thought about. Sure, she wanted to be successful and well respected in her industry and to make enough money so that she never had to worry again about where her next meal was coming from or how to keep a roof over her head. But she'd always assumed she'd make it on her own. Never as part of a conglomerate.

Honestly, she wasn't sure how she felt about it. Everything Marty had said was true, but on the flip side, her company would no longer be hers. She'd lose her independence and autonomy.

Was that a price worth paying for total financial security?

Realizing she hadn't spoken for several moments, she responded truthfully, "I don't know what to say."

Marty seemed unfazed by her lack of enthusiasm. "Obviously, it's a lot to take in and we need to discuss it in far more detail. I'm sure you'll hold my feet to the fire before you let me add you to my holdings. But there will be plenty of time to talk through everything once this deal for the soccer team is done."

There was no harm in hearing what he had to say, so Sapphie agreed to that much before ending the call. With so much to organize before leaving for London, she resolved to put thinking about his offer and her company's future aside until she had time to consider it properly.

Sapphie called in her assistant and they discussed travel arrangements.

"Pack an umbrella," her assistant teased. "I hear December is wet."

"But not as cold or windy as it is here." Sapphie looked out of the window at the blustery Chicago weather and saw that the sky was dark and the rush-hour gridlock had already begun to ease.

Scotty would be here soon. Smiling, she looked at her watch. His plane was due to land shortly.

He hadn't called last night. Sapphie had been a little surprised not to hear from him but had assumed dinner had gone on longer than expected and he hadn't wanted to disturb her so late. That he hadn't left a message or even sent a text was odd, but there could be any number of reasons for that. Dead battery, no cell coverage, phone dropped down the toilet...at which point she'd felt ridiculous for making excuses for him. He'd call when he could.

Sapphie's mind finally connected the dots that she probably should have joined up before. Going to England meant she wouldn't see Scotty until Christmas.

Damn it. That was a wrinkle she hadn't considered. Seeing each other once a week—usually on the weekends—had been working well. She'd already begun to miss him when they couldn't be together. And with each visit, the time in between had seemed to drag more and more. Phone calls and Skype were a poor substitute for being with him.

The next month would seem like forever.

Sapphie felt guilty that she'd been so caught up in the excitement of the trip she hadn't thought of Scotty before now.

Her guilt annoyed her. That was her problem with dating—expectations, responsibilities, commitments. Accepting the demands of their respective jobs was fine when all was going smoothly, but this could turn everything around.

Then she felt guilty that she'd been annoyed. Scotty hadn't put any demands on her, even though he'd made it clear that he wanted them to be a couple. She put those demands on herself.

What a mess.

She paced her office. There had to be a way to make it work. England was only a plane ride away.

Technically, it wasn't a lot different from flying from the West Coast to the East. The problem was that it wouldn't do the project any favors for her to fly home every weekend. Equally, Scotty wouldn't be able to travel to England. This was a busy time in the Ice Cats' schedule.

Still, where there was a will, there was a way. They'd managed to make things work so far. A solution would mean compromise, but it was only for a month. And it would be a good test for the future, seeing how they could work their relationship around these obstacles. This might be the first hiccup, but it wouldn't be the last.

Satisfied that there would be a way around the problem even if she wasn't sure what it was right now, Sapphie tidied her things and prepared to go home.

Her phone rang as she was putting on her coat. Scotty, at last.

"I'm sorry I didn't call." His voice sounded strange. Wooden. Tight.

Concerned, she asked, "Is everything all right?"

"No."

The single word came out with such force it took her aback. "What's wrong?"

"I'm at O'Hare."

"Great. I was about to head to my apartment. Are you going there or do you want me to meet you at your hotel?"

"Neither."

This was the strangest conversation. Not that he was ever a motormouth, but she'd never had to drag every word out of him before. "Okay. What's the plan?"

"I'm waiting for a connection."

She shook her head, confused. Had she missed something? "Connection to where?"

"Ottawa."

"Excuse me?" When no further explanation was forthcoming, she prodded, "Why are you going to Ottawa?"

Assuming it was something to do with the Ice Cats—seeing a player they might want to do a deal for, maybe—she wasn't prepared for his answer.

"My friend committed suicide." His words came out in a rush, as if saying them faster might somehow make them less horrifying.

Her mind raced as she tried to make sense of what he'd said. "What? Who? When?"

"Cam Lockhead."

An image of a broad-faced man with a menacing, gap-toothed grin came to mind. "The former Cats enforcer? The one Callum announced was going to be an ambassador for the team?" The one both Scotty and Grey had played with.

"Yes."

"I'm so sorry." Her words seemed so inadequate. "What a terrible tragedy. I don't know what to say."

"It's okay. No one does." His voice cracked on the final word. He cleared his throat.

Her heart ached for him. To lose a friend and teammate so young was bad enough. Knowing that he'd taken his own life must be devastating.

"So, why Ottawa? Isn't he with Seattle?"

"No. He'd finished with them in the summer. He's been at home. I'm going to see Laurel, his wife. Grey's flying up, too, and will meet me there."

At least he wouldn't be alone dealing with such an unimaginably awful situation. "Will you stay until the funeral?"

"No. Just until tomorrow night. Then I'll rejoin the team in Chicago and Grey will go home." His shuddering sigh tugged at her heartstrings. "I'm not sure what we can do, how much help we can be, but we have to go. For Bullet."

"Of course. I know there isn't anything I can do, but I'll be thinking of you. Will you call me when you get a chance?"

"I'll try."

"Send a text. Anything to let me know how you're doing."

"Sure."

"Even if it's only for a few minutes, I'd like to see you when you get back."

"Okay. Sure. I'd like that." A muffled voice spoke. "Gotta go. Flight's being called."

"Take care of yourself." Once again she felt inadequate.

"Yeah."

When she hung up, she sat for a long time trying to process the awful news. She hadn't known Bullet personally, as he'd left the Ice Cats long before she'd become friends with Taylor and the other players. But Cam had been a longtime fan favorite and his craggy face was well-known. There were still a large number of jerseys with his name and number in the stands at any game.

Whenever she'd seen him interviewed, he'd always seemed full of life. He was the classic goon—a fighting machine on the ice, but a placid, humble, generous and intelligent guy off it. A big family man. She recalled he'd had concussion problems, but she'd thought he was over them. He'd seemed pleased to be coming home to the team where he'd played the best years of his career. She found it hard to imagine that he'd felt desperate enough to end his life. Yet he'd clearly had some terrible demons.

Since her evening had now opened up, Sapphie considered staying at the office and working. But her heart wasn't in it. So she stuffed files and her laptop into her briefcase and headed to her apartment.

By the time she got there, the story had started

to hit the media. It was heartbreaking to see the photographs of Bullet with his teammates. Especially a much younger Scotty, Grey and Ike Jelinek. There was video of a classic fight between Bullet and Jake Badoletti, back when Bad Boy had played for Chicago. And pictures of Cam towering over his petite, beautiful wife, smiling at her as if she were the most precious thing in the world. His expression seemed to say "How the hell did I get so lucky?"

It was sobering to see his picture added to the growing list of players—far too many, far too young—who'd also suffered once their careers were over and who'd chosen the same ending Cam Lockhead had.

The irony that Bullet's life had ended in misery and despair just as hers had taken a huge upswing was not lost on Sapphie. It reminded her of all the times growing up when the opposite had been true. When other people's lives had seemed so bright and brilliant, so full of joy and opportunity, while hers had sunk to another new depth.

How many times had she been at rock bottom? Overwhelmed by always having to be the responsible one, the one who sacrificed daily to make life bearable for her family? Had she thought that she couldn't take one more day? In her darkest moments, only the thought of escape and freedom had driven her to keep putting one foot in front of the other. Knowing that one day the only person she'd have to worry about was herself was enough to make her carry on and keep striving.

Still, there but for the grace of God, the Fates or whatever greater power people believed in. That could so easily have been her.

Sapphie poured another glass of wine and raised it to Bullet and all the players who'd passed far too soon.

Cam Lockhead's death reminded her that life was too short. There wasn't time to waste on anything that didn't make you happy. She looked around the apartment and thought again about moving her home to Jersey, being closer to Issy and her family.

Being closer to Scotty. He made her happy, for sure. Maybe he could be the man who was able to be a true partner, instead of someone who made demands. Who could support her as much as she supported him. Who could share the responsibilities and commitments, not expect her to carry the load.

She had no idea what the future held for them, but she had to give them a chance. Instead of putting up obstacles, finding reasons that they couldn't work, she should focus on finding ways to help their relationship to succeed.

She was going to do it. A new adventure. Sapphie laughed giddily. Instead of cutting ties, she would create them—a home and a man. It was scary, but it had worked for other people. Why not her and Scotty?

She leaned against the couch and thought about a very different life from the one she'd always imagined. The one she'd always thought she'd wanted. Happy in her relationship, happy in her work.

Work.

She sat bolt upright on the couch, her stomach tightening. She hadn't told Scotty about her new job for Marty.

THE LAST THING Scott expected when he walked out of O'Hare's secure area into the arrivals hall was that Sapphie would be waiting for him. Yet there she was, looking fresh and beautiful and so damn alive his heart ached with joy.

He saw her a second or two before she noticed him, which gave him a chance to watch her blue eyes light up when she spotted him and then see that happiness spread to her face. Ah, how the sight of her soothed some of the raw pain that had been scraping his insides since that horrible phone call.

Guilt stabbed him. How could he be happy when Bullet was dead? What right did he have to be looking forward to a night with his woman when Laurel would never again see her husband?

The moment he cleared the cordons, Sapphie threw her arms around him. Scott wrapped her tightly in his embrace and bowed his head to rest it against hers. Breathing in her scent eased some of the tightness in his chest and reminded him of what—or rather *who*—made him happy. If only he could stay like this forever.

Somebody's case banged against his legs, reminding him where they were. He lifted his head and smiled ruefully. "I guess we're blocking the way."

"That's okay." Sapphie pulled gently out of his embrace. "Come on. We can get a cab. I thought we could go to my apartment and you'd have a chance to decompress before you rejoin the team."

Not wanting to lose the connection with her, he slid his hand along her arm and entwined his fingers in hers. As they walked toward the exit doors, he cleared his throat, trying to ease the lump that made it hard to speak.

"Thanks. I didn't think I'd see you until tomorrow at the game."

"I wasn't sure if you'd want to be alone. Or if you'd rather join the guys at the hotel. Or meet up with Callum and get right back into it. Some people prefer that. Anyway, I spoke with Callum and he said to do whatever you needed and he'd make things work at his end." She wrinkled her nose. "For sure, you don't need me babbling at you."

His laugh sounded as rusty as it felt. "Actually, that's exactly what I need. *You're* exactly what I need."

She squeezed his hand. "Then you're in luck."

As if understanding that he couldn't talk about his trip right now, she chattered away while they waited for a taxi and then rode to her apartment. He didn't know exactly what she talked about, because his mind kept disappearing into the protective fog that had surrounded him for the past twenty-four hours, blurring the edges of the waking nightmare. Luckily, she didn't require any contribution from him.

Once inside her apartment, she ushered him to the large sectional couch while she got him a drink and something to eat. From where he sat, he could look out of the floor-to-ceiling windows at two completely different vistas—tall city buildings on one side and the lake on the other. In his frame of mind, he couldn't appreciate the great views. Instead, he leaned back and stared at the ceiling. When Sapphie set the loaded tray on the coffee table, he knew he should move, but he didn't have the energy.

This trip had been bad enough. He couldn't even face the thought of how awful the funeral would be.

When Sapphie sat beside him, he pulled her to him.

Her thoughtfulness, the way she'd stepped up to take care of him, touched him. "Right now I'm not up to questions and sympathy. It's well-meant, but it's hard. You know?"

She nodded, stroking her hand down his arm. "I can't imagine what you're going through. You can talk about it if you want, but equally, you don't have to say a word. Whatever makes you feel better."

"I'm not sure myself." He puffed out a breath. "Man, how does Laurel do it? This must be a million times worse for her."

"How is she holding up?"

"On the one hand, she's completely destroyed. The man she's loved since she was eighteen and who worshipped the ground she walked on took his own life. With no warning." He shook his head. "The worst must have been explaining it to their two sons. They are…were…such a close family. But her incredible strength amazes me. She's the one organizing everything and everyone. She's the one comforting people who loved Bullet, like me and Grey."

"She sounds like a special lady."

"Laurel is a far better person than I am. She's the one speaking of forgiveness and understanding, and of what Bullet had been through. That he wasn't different from those people who have painful and debilitating diseases and who cannot take the suffering anymore. I can't get my head around it. How bad it must have been for him to…end it."

What he couldn't say aloud was that he kept wondering what he could have done to help his friend. A question that would haunt him for the rest of his life.

They sat quietly for a while, both lost in thought. Then they talked a little about Bullet. Scott shared memories and told her about the last conversations he'd had with his friend.

As the evening wore on, Scott was grateful for how easy Sapphie was to be with. And how she was able to give him what he needed. She let him talk when he had to and was silent when he couldn't speak. She didn't rush to fill the gaps with platitudes or keep pressing him to share his feelings. She made him eat, and then when exhaustion overtook him, Sapphie helped him to bed and held him until he fell asleep.

She held him throughout the night, every time he woke and the shock and horror came crashing down on him again. When the tears—hot, angry and bitter—fell. When he railed at everyone and everything, not the least his friend. When he kept asking why.

Then, when he'd needed the reassurance of life, she'd made sweet love to him.

The following morning, Scott was drained. Empty. His head pounded and his mouth was parched. His guts felt like he'd swallowed acid. It was as if he were hungover, but there was no freaking hair of the dog for this situation.

A shower and breakfast, which Sapphie cooked for him, had him feeling halfway human.

"Don't get used to it. This is a one-off, because of the circumstances," she'd warned.

"I would say it's almost worth it, but…" He couldn't finish the thought.

"I know and I appreciate the sentiment."

Scott pulled her onto his lap. "Enough miserable talk. Tell me about you. What's your week been like?"

For the first time since he'd arrived, she seemed a little hesitant to speak. "Oh, you know. Busy, busy, busy."

"I thought everything was winding down with the holidays coming up."

"There's always another contract and another project. Some you just can't say no to."

"Such as?"

She waved a hand and said airily, "I don't want to bore you with tales of my work. I bet tonight is one of those times when you really wish you could strap on your skates and play a hard sixty minutes with the team."

"Definitely." He accepted the abrupt change in subject, but it made him more curious as to why she didn't want to discuss work. "Ironically, given the circumstances, I'd be happy to drop the gloves, too. Going a round or two with an enforcer would probably do me a world of good right now. And save me busting my knuckles by hitting a wall."

"I understand the principle, but fighting, you're more likely to get a busted jaw."

"Only because I'm not in the peak shape I was in when I was playing."

She waggled her eyebrows at him. "I think your shape will do."

"As long as it satisfies you."

"Any more satisfied and I wouldn't be able to walk straight."

"Then you'd be the one busting your nose against a wall." He kissed the tip of her nose. "That would be a shame."

"Oh, I think you could make even a bruised nose worth it." She brushed her lips against his, then settled into him as she took the kiss deeper.

When they broke apart, breathing heavily, she said, "Mmm, definitely worth it."

Much as he was enjoying her efforts to distract him, he wanted to know what she was keeping from him. The way she kept deflecting the question made him nervous. She obviously thought he wouldn't like whatever it was.

"You want to tell me what's going on? I'm sure it can't be as bad as you're making me imagine it might be."

She sighed. "It's not bad at all. At least, not for me. And I'm not trying to hide anything. I just didn't think this was the time to talk about my work. Marty has given me another acquisition project to evaluate."

"That's great. Congratulations." She didn't

sound as excited as he would have expected. "I'd have thought you'd be jumping for joy."

Sapphie climbed off his lap and leaned against the kitchen counter, wrapping her arms around her waist. "It's a really nice piece of work, and financially, it will mean we start next year strong and sound."

"Okay, so what's the problem?"

Did this job mean they wouldn't be able to see each other as much? At this point in their relationship, when everything was still finely balanced, an extended separation was the last thing they needed. "Is Marty expecting you to be in LA for the duration?"

"No, but there is a complication." She explained that the project was evaluating a soccer team in England and what that meant for her schedule over the next month or so. "I'll have to be there pretty much until Christmas."

There it was. Her work was coming between them again. "When do you leave?"

"I'm flying to Newark tonight and taking the day flight to London on Monday morning. It'll get me there Monday night, so I'll get some sleep before— I'm sure you don't want to know the details."

"I see. So you won't be at the game." That shouldn't have bothered him. But it did.

"I wanted to go, but I couldn't get a later flight. I did think about hitching a ride with you guys, on the team plane, but figured that might be taking advantage of our relationship." She smiled tentatively.

He didn't feel like smiling back. "I guess this means you won't make Bullet's funeral next Saturday either."

"Uh, no." She looked startled. "I never thought about attending."

"Even though I need you there."

"I'm sorry, but it never occurred to me that you'd want me to accompany you."

He felt let down. "Why not? Isn't that what couples do—support each other?"

"I suppose so, but I'm new to this whole relationship thing. I assumed you'd be with your teammates and friends."

"Yeah, but it would have been nice to have you there, too."

"I don't know what to say, but I'm sorry. Again."

"Surely Marty will give you some leeway under those circumstances."

"He might if it was my family or a close friend, but I didn't even know Cam."

"I did. And we're together. That should count for something."

Sapphie straightened, her eyes stormy. "I know this is a difficult time for you, and I feel for all you're going through, but don't you think you're being a little unreasonable? There's a good reason I can't be there. I have a work commitment out of the country."

Truth was there would always be a work commitment that came before him in her priorities. Just when he'd begun to think that they were moving in the right direction. That they could make a go of their relationship.

"Is it unreasonable to expect the woman in my life to think it's more important to accompany me to my friend's funeral than to accompany her boss to a soccer game?" Crap. He didn't mean to strike out so viciously.

She arched an eyebrow at him. "It's not about me having a fun day out. It's about providing a service for an important client. I'd have thought, as an assistant GM, you'd understand that. You attend games for reasons other than to watch the Ice Cats play."

"That's different."

"It's not different at all. There are two rules here—one for you and one for me. How much flexibility would there be if the situation was reversed? You couldn't be home for Thanksgiving because you were on the road with the Cats. What if I'd made the same fuss because I wanted you to meet my sister?"

"It's hardly the same. I can meet your sister another time. Cam's funeral is a one-off."

"Look, I know it's not ideal timing, but it can't be helped. I knew it would upset you and that's the last thing you need right now. Which is why I was reluctant to bring it up."

"When did you plan to talk about it? When you started packing for your trip? When the car arrived to take you to the airport?"

"You make me sound callous. Honestly, I hadn't thought that far ahead. I just knew this morning that you needed a little time before facing another problem."

He could see that she was bewildered about why he was making such a big deal out of something she didn't see as that important. Sure, he wasn't handling it well—he blamed the emotional upheaval of the past forty-eight hours—but couldn't she understand that this was a defining moment of their relationship? At what point did she start taking what they had together seriously? When did she stop treating him like he was just a fling?

He ran his hand over his jaw. Maybe it was time he found out.

"What does this mean for us?"

CHAPTER FOURTEEN

HOW SAPPHIE DREADED any question about *us*.

Like the proverbial harbinger of doom, it inevitably signaled a conversation that wouldn't end well. Someone always got hurt and upset. No matter how well things had gone to that point, how happy both people had been, that one discussion always messed it up.

Why did relationships need to be defined and analyzed? Why couldn't they just be?

In the past, whenever the question of *us* had been raised, Sapphie had considered it the beginning of the end. Despite her constant reminders that she didn't do serious, the guy she was dating would want to take things to the next level. Some had wanted to go as far as living together. As if that weren't one small step away from marriage.

The mere thought turned her stomach.

She should have known her trip to England would trigger the dreaded discussion. Perhaps she had known, which was why she'd put off telling Scotty about it. As it was, she'd hoped a little reassurance on her part would prevent a blowup. That maybe she and Scotty, despite having been together only a relatively short time, had progressed to the point where they could deal with this hurdle sensibly.

Unfortunately, at the moment, he was being a jerk. Sapphie was prepared to cut him a little slack because of what he was dealing with, but he was dangerously close to the precipice of their relationship. If he didn't ease up, take a step back, there would be no future for them.

Sapphie really didn't want to end it with Scotty. If they could come to some kind of reasonable compromise, they might be able to avoid a decision that neither of them wanted.

"I know being on opposite sides of the Atlantic will make things difficult in the short term." She forced her voice to remain calm, measured. "But I'm sure we can find ways to deal with it."

Scotty rose and paced the kitchen. "Can we?"

His cynical tone made her wonder if he even wanted to try.

"Of course. It'll take some fancy footwork, but it's only temporary." When he didn't look convinced, she added, "We knew a long-distance relationship wouldn't be easy. The distance is just a little longer and the opportunity to be together is a tad more complicated than we anticipated for the next month."

"That's an understatement." He stopped pacing and jammed his hands in his pockets. "We won't be together until at least Christmas—if you can

make it then. Come January, you'll be off to…
Where is it again?"

"Houston."

"Right, then wherever else you need to go after that."

Sapphie gritted her teeth, trying hard to keep a rein on her temper. "I can't come back next weekend, but I'm not saying I can't make a trip to Jersey at all. Maybe you could fly to meet me for a couple of days at some point, too. I know it's different from what we'd planned, but we can make it work."

"I can't just take off. You know how busy this time of year is. The games come thick and fast."

"But you don't have to be there for every game," she said levelly, even though she wanted to smack some sense into him. "Surely you could miss one. If it's easier for you to fly over midweek, I can work my schedule around that."

"Like that'll happen. All it'll take is an important meeting and our time together would be a bust."

She wanted to reassure him but knew she couldn't promise. It would be tempting fate. "You're deliberately putting up obstacles instead of finding a solution."

"The obstacles are already there. The question is whether they'll ever go away. Whether you'll be committed enough to our relationship that it occasionally takes precedence over your work."

With each verbal dig, Sapphie's anger grew. Now she was the one pacing the kitchen. "I'm tired of being your whipping boy. So my project has thrown a wrench in our plans. Up to now, I've tried hard to make things work for us. But I'm beginning to wonder why I bother when you're stamping your foot like a child whose toy was taken away."

"Excuse me for expecting more from you than you're prepared to give. For feeling like the only one who gives a freaking damn about *us*." He waved his hand back and forth between them.

"That's not fair. The fact that we're actually in a relationship tells you how important I think *us* is." Why did she have to keep defending herself? "You knew what you were getting into with me. I made it clear that I'll never be the kind of woman who sits around waiting for her partner to have time to pay attention. I won't put my life, my career or my business on hold for any man."

Sapphie winced inwardly as he stiffened. That was a low blow. She knew one of the reasons his marriage had broken up was that his wife had wanted to put her life and interests first once he'd retired.

She changed tack slightly. "I have a successful business. I have to make tough choices to keep it that way. You were the one who insisted we could make our relationship work in spite of that. Have you changed your mind now that it's not quite so straightforward and we *both* have to make sacrifices?"

"Of course not." He crossed his arms over his chest.

"Feels that way to me. I can't turn my life and my business upside down to revolve around your needs. I won't. Just as I don't expect you to revolve your life around mine."

"Really? Seems to me that's exactly what you expect. Every time Marty or some other client snaps his fingers, you pick up and go. To hell with what we have planned."

"It's unfortunate, but that's the way it goes. You don't seem to have the same problem if the shoe's on the other foot. You expect me to roll with it and I do." She stopped short of mentioning that he'd canceled with her to go to Ottawa. She wouldn't use that tragedy to make her point.

"Because I can't do anything about it."

"Neither can I." This argument was going nowhere and that precipice was ever closer. "Let's take a step back and think about this rationally. We're talking about a month, not a lifetime. If you'd stop being so stubborn, I'm sure we can find a practical solution."

He stalked to the windows and stared out for a few minutes before turning to her. "That's where we're at odds." His voice had a note of resignation that set alarm bells ringing. "Because in reality, it isn't just about these next few weeks, or even months, is it? This will happen again and again. Marty is an important client and he's only going to get more so. And he'll keep on expecting you to drop everything for him."

Especially if she was to sell her business and become part of Antonelli Holdings.

Something in her face must have alerted Scotty, because he looked at her strangely. "There's more, isn't there?"

She wanted to deny it—telling him would only make things worse—but given the way the conversation was going, she might as well lay it out for him and let the chips fall however they may. "It's only preliminary, and I haven't decided whether or not to entertain the idea, but Marty wants to buy my business." She explained what Marty had said to her.

"Congratulations." He made it sound like the opposite.

"I don't think it will make a difference to how things work, or to *us*, but I'm sure you feel differently."

"Come on. Even if you don't move to LA, you'll be even more at his beck and call. And you won't be able to say no when he owns you."

"He won't own *me*. And where I'm based doesn't affect where my projects are," she said wearily.

She could have told him that she planned to move to New Jersey and that, if she agreed to sell, she'd make that clear to Marty, but what was the point? Scotty had already made up his mind that their relationship couldn't work unless she did things his way.

Scotty leaned against the breakfast bar. "Easy to say now, but our relationship will suffer. Seeing each other will go from every week to every couple weeks to once a month. I'm sorry, but I want more than the occasional flyby visit. I want someone who's prepared to commit to being with me. Who wants to be involved in my life and who considers me as important in her life as she is in mine."

"You think I don't do that." She threw her arms up in frustration. "Even though, in reality, the only person turning herself inside out to make her partner happy is me. I don't notice you making the same effort to adjust your life and your work to make me happy."

"It's not that simple. I don't have control over my schedule. Just because I'm in the Cats' front office, not playing, doesn't mean I'm not bound by the NHL's timetable. I can't blow off games or meetings because they're inconvenient."

"Neither can I."

"You run your own business and dictate the projects. You could find some flexibility if it was that important to you."

"I'm just as bound by my clients' needs as you are by the league." She was suddenly tired of going over the same ground repeatedly. She dropped onto a chair at the table. "You know what? You're right. Without both of us prepared to compromise and work at our relationship, this isn't worth continuing."

Sapphie saw the resignation in his eyes. The inevitable conclusion she'd wanted to avoid so desperately was here.

"I'm sorry," he said quietly. "I really thought we had a chance. I care for you a lot."

"I care for you, too." She gave it one last shot. She rose and went to stand in front of him. She wanted to touch him but was afraid that if she did, she'd lose her resolve, so she kept her hand at her side. "This is a difficult time. Is it really a good idea to rush this decision? Maybe if we waited and thought about it some more…"

He shook his head sadly. "It's because this is such a difficult time that it's important to do what's necessary. No matter how much it hurts. Life is too damn short. We can't waste a single precious moment on something that isn't right."

Sapphie couldn't argue with that, much as she wanted to. There was no point trying to fix something that only one of them wanted to work. "If only there was another way."

"Yeah." He ran his thumb across her cheekbone. "But we both know there isn't."

She turned away. She bit down hard on her lip

to keep from saying something she would regret. From promising something she couldn't deliver.

"I should go."

Determined to be strong until he'd gone, she said brightly, "Of course. You must have a lot to do."

"I don't regret any of our time together. Only that it can't work."

Because he wouldn't bend and she couldn't be what he wanted. "Take care of yourself."

"I'm sure we'll see each other around."

In a fit of childishness, she wanted to say "Not if I see you first," but merely nodded. She walked to the front hall and waited for him to collect his stuff and join her.

He reached past her to open the door, then stopped. He leaned down and pressed a brief, hard kiss to her lips, then walked away quickly.

The hollow thud of the door closing echoed the thud in her heart. She leaned against it for several moments, unable to move. Her eyes burned with unshed tears. Her throat ached.

Then, slowly, she slid down to the floor, staring ahead unseeing.

She couldn't believe it. The one time she'd broken her own rule and this was how it ended. She should have known—she *had* known—but she'd done it anyway. She'd actually begun to trust Scotty. He'd made her believe in them and the possibility of a relationship, a future, together. Then, like everyone else, he'd let her down.

Somehow, the disappointment and sense of betrayal were worse than they'd been for all the others. Sapphie was tired of always being the one who coped. The one who soldiered on.

She couldn't be strong anymore. Sapphie lowered her head onto her knees and, for the first time in her adult life, she cried.

WHOEVER HAD SAID that it was better to have loved and lost than never to have loved had been talking out of his ass. Scott would have been better off not knowing how good love could be. Because, yeah, he'd finally figured out that he'd fallen in love with Sapphie—when it was too freaking late. What he felt for her far surpassed the emotion he'd previously called *love*.

Yet that night in Chicago, every time he opened his mouth, he'd made mistake after dumb-assed mistake. His mind had been so screwed up he couldn't think straight, let alone fix the disaster he was making of a conversation that had quickly spiraled out of control. Grief and guilt over Bullet's death had twisted his insides every which way. He'd tried not to lash out but couldn't stop himself.

All he could see was that once again he'd come up second-best for a woman.

It hadn't helped that he could hear Bullet's voice

in his head reminding him that it was all downhill now that his playing career was done. Then there had been Laurel's voice warning him not to settle for less than what he wanted. Celine, Angela—they'd all had their say, too.

Now, sitting in his den in a dark, silent house, he understood how people went insane. The cacophony of voices had messed with his head so badly that he'd struck out blindly.

Fear of losing Sapphie had only made things worse.

He'd thought that if he didn't change her mind, they'd drift apart and he'd end up alone, miserable and back where he'd started.

So he'd held on tight. Too tight.

He'd ignored his years of experience as a captain and the countless times he'd mediated battles in the locker room. He'd tossed aside the logic and reasoning he'd been famous for. Tossed aside the knowledge that sometimes it was better to retreat and rethink the tactics than to keep plugging away with a plan that wasn't working.

Instead, he'd been a complete and utter jackass. So damn fixated on what he'd thought was the only answer that he'd lost sight of the heart of the issue. He and Sapphie should have been fighting side by side, not against each other. Together they should have been stronger than they each were alone.

Then he'd made the biggest, dumbest mistake

of all—he'd walked out on the best thing that had ever happened to him. And man, was he paying for it.

In the days since he'd returned home from Chicago, he'd been lonelier than he'd ever been before. It was worse than when Celine had left him. There was no sense of relief or peace. Just an awful emptiness that made every inch of his body ache.

The pain of loss cut deep. Every time he thought about Sapphie, it was like pouring acid on the wound. There wasn't a place he could go that he didn't think of her. Home, work, the arena, the city. Even the grocery store and the local pizza place brought back memories. His brain was filled with snapshots of their time together. Smiling, laughing, kissing, making love. Reminding him that not only had it not been bad, it had actually been pretty damn good.

Scott had thought about calling her so many times but had made stupid excuses for why he shouldn't. The time difference with England— she'd be in meetings or sleeping. She wouldn't want to hear from him. She'd hang up. She'd be with some amazing English guy who didn't have Scott's hang-ups and who was happy to take advantage of what he'd thrown away.

He ground his teeth as he imagined a man who looked like that famous actor everyone was crazy about, smiling at her, holding her hand, making love...

The doorbell rang, providing a much-needed interruption from the mental torture.

He frowned as he pushed to his feet and lumbered through the house. Who the hell was bothering him tonight?

A pair of familiar shadows was visible through the glass in his front door. Just what he needed. Not. Still, he opened the door.

Kasanski and Rivera pushed past him and into the house.

"Come in. Make yourselves at home," he said sarcastically as his friends headed straight for the kitchen and the drinks refrigerator.

They didn't blink when he slammed the front door and stomped after them.

"Grey's right." Chance pulled out three beers and handed them around. "It's worse than we thought."

Ice Man shook his head. "Never thought I'd see the day. You're a sorry mess, bro."

Scott twisted the cap off his bottle and took a swig. "Is there a reason you came over, other than to drink my beer and insult me?"

"We came to give you the benefit of our wisdom." Kasanski clapped him on the shoulder. "Not a minute too soon, by the looks of it."

Scott snorted. "This'll be the best laugh I've had all week. Grab a seat and have at it."

Chance walked to the living room. "Either you have to remodel or you need a new place. This one looks as comfortable as a bed of nails."

He wasn't going to admit he agreed with his friend. "So you're not only Dr. Phil but an interior decorator, too?"

"Just telling it like it is, man. Seriously, do people actually sit on that or is it just for show?" Chance dismissed the sofa, which was as hard as it looked, with a wave of his hand. "I'm going to your den."

While his friends plopped down on the leather couch, Scott leaned on the back of the matching armchair. "I'm listening."

Ice Man pointed his bottle at Scott. "Uh-uh. You need to talk first. Starting with what happened with Sapphie."

Scott inhaled sharply at the acid-on-the-wound sting. "I thought you knew everything."

"Only that you've been dragging around like a dog who lost his bone for the past couple days. Bad enough that Doreen called and told us to straighten you out."

That explained a lot. He hadn't seen any of his former teammates since the flight from Chicago. He'd kept to himself on the plane—put on his headphones and pretended he was dozing so no one would talk to him. Or see what a mess he was in.

He'd stayed away from practice and gone to

the game last night only to schmooze a potential big new sponsor. The Cats had been after the guy for years, but he'd become interested only after they'd presented the new program. The new program Scott had worked on with Sapphie.

Damn it. Just like that his chest squeezed so tight he could hardly breathe.

"Spill already," Kasanski said.

"There's nothing to tell. We…uh…broke up." It was the first time he'd said the words aloud. "It's over."

"Why? In Columbus you said you thought things were going well."

"More fool, me. Turns out we wanted different things."

Chance gave him a disbelieving look. "Cut the crap. Seemed to me you wanted the same thing. What went wrong?"

"Okay, you're right," Scott admitted. "We didn't know how to get what we wanted. We had different ideas for making it work. Ne'er the twain, et cetera, et cetera."

"How come? You're both smart and grounded. You should've been able to figure it out."

Knowing he wouldn't get away without telling his friends the whole story, Scott explained what had happened. He told them what he'd said, how he'd been feeling and what thoughts had been crowding his head. He didn't pull any punches. Not about what an idiot he'd been or about how he wished he could put it right but didn't know where to even start.

"Let me get this straight—you blew up your relationship because she's going to England for a month?" Ice Man looked shocked.

It sounded even dumber put that way. "It wasn't only about the next month, it was about the future. I get pushed aside every time. Her job, her career, her clients always come first."

Chance shrugged. "Hasn't hockey come first since the moment you laced up your first pair of skates? I know it has for me."

"But what about your twins? You were left to take care of them alone and they've been your priority ever since." Chance would walk barefoot through fire for his girls.

"They're important, for sure. But as much as I love them, I still have to put myself first on some things. If I didn't, I couldn't continue to play hockey. I'd be home all the time, looking after them. And that wouldn't be good for them or me."

Scott was confused. "But you always do what's best for them."

"Do I?"

"For sure."

"I do the best I can. For all of us."

"You're splitting hairs."

"Am I?"

"Explain."

"Leaving aside the financial issues, if I gave

up my career, I'd begin to resent them because I'd want to be doing the job I love. And I'm not Superman. I can't do it all. Hell, I can't cook more than the basics and I'm not the greatest at keeping the house clean. But I pay someone to do those things for me so I can do what I need to. It's a win-win. Do I make sure I'm there as much as I can be? Of course. Am I involved in everything I can be? You bet. Is it perfect? Not always. But it's the best compromise."

"I understand that. But my situation is different. Sapphie isn't twin toddlers. I can't hire a housekeeper or a nanny and make our problems go away."

"The principle is the same, numbnuts." Kasanski rolled his eyes. "Even I can figure it out. You want to be with Sapphie, don't you?"

"Damn straight."

"And, crazy as it sounds, she wants to be with you, too?"

Fighting through the pain, he thought over the nightmare conversation and realized that for the first time in their relationship she'd been the one pushing him. The one trying to find a compromise. She was right—she had been doing most of the giving and he'd been happily taking. She'd switched her schedule, arranged meetings in different locations and taken late-night and early-morning flights to spend time with him. He'd done his part, but it hadn't been as much. Truth was it hadn't been nearly enough.

Not only had he been a childish jerk, he'd been unfair to her. "She did. Whether or not she still does…"

Ice Man waved his hand dismissively. "Sure she does. So all we have to do is find a way to make it work that suits you both. How hard can that be?"

"Talk about stating the freaking obvious, Ice Man. The problem is her company is based out of Chicago, but she has contracts all over. She won't even commit to an apartment, let alone settle down or get married. How am I supposed to find a solution with all that working against me?"

Chance set his bottle on the table and leaned forward, elbows on his thighs. "Let's get the easy stuff out of the way. Do you care about getting married again?"

"Not right now. But at some point I probably will."

"So, deal with that at some point."

"What if she never changes her mind?"

"Come on, man. What's more important— marriage or being together? The alternative is never being with her again. Does a ring on her finger really matter so much?"

"Right." Ice Man got to his feet and walked to the cabinet displaying Scott's awards. "There's not one of us here that has had even a quarter of the success in our marriages as we've had in our careers. I, for one, would be happy never to say 'I do' again."

"I wouldn't say never." Chance shrugged. "You don't know what's around the corner. Plus there are my girls to think about. But if it came down to making the choice you have to, I'd ditch the ring for the woman every time. Wouldn't you?"

Put that way, the answer was simple. "Yeah. I would. But what about the separation? A long-distance relationship can only work for a while. I'm based in Jersey and pretty much all my work is here, except when I have to travel for the team. My home is here. So is my life. And my kids."

"Seriously? Your life. What life?" Kasanski laughed. "As for your kids, they're in college. They'll be gone, without a backward glance, before you know it. And I won't bother to give you my thoughts on your home. You could sell this place in a heartbeat and move to Chicago or wherever."

Scott hated to admit it, but Ice Man had a point. "But what about my job? I enjoy it and I'm pretty good at it. Sure, I could get another job somewhere else, but I don't have the experience to get something similar with another organization. I want to stick with this and try to make a career out of it."

"Patience, grasshopper." Chance drained his beer. "Now we know what you do and don't care about. None of it is impossible and the one thing you'd like to keep is your job. That gives you the perfect basis for a negotiation."

Kasanski nodded. "You offer to do the things you can and show her you're prepared to compromise. Then she'll tell you what she's prepared to compromise on, too, and you go from there. Maybe she'll want to set up an office in New Jersey. Maybe she'll sell to Antonelli and use some of the money to buy a place here or a private jet to ferry her back and forth to you. Who knows? But at least you have a starting point."

Scott tried to imagine Sapphie's response. All he could think of was more obstacles. "What if none of it is enough? What if we can't make it work?"

"What if you do?" Ice Man asked. "Jeez. Since when do you focus on the negative in everything? What happened to our never-say-die captain? Some of us would give our eyeteeth to have half the chance you've got." He stalked to the door. "I'm getting some more beer. See if you can talk some sense into him, Chance."

When Kasanski had gone, Chance said quietly, "Rick just found out that his ex is getting remarried. To that young guy she left him for. He's a little touchy because he found out via social media."

Scott swore. "Will he be okay?"

"I hope so. The drinking is getting worse, but now that he knows there's no way back, he might start coming out the other side."

"Keep me posted and let me know if he needs help."

"You got it." Chance cleared his throat and said in a normal voice, "Find out what you can give Sapphie that she really needs. Preferably that no one else can give her."

Scott thought for a few moments about Sapphie's past. About what she'd achieved and what was important to her. "She had a rough childhood. I guess she's looking for security."

"So what can you give her that represents security?"

"Nothing she can't get for herself."

"Sure, you can. Give her *you*. Your support. The knowledge and confidence that you'll be by her side when she needs you. That she'll never have to cope alone again. But make sure you also let her know that you'll respect her wishes, her boundaries and her independence."

Scott mulled over Chance's advice for a while after he and Ice Man had left. He'd nailed it. That was exactly how Scott could prove to Sapphie that he was the man for her and that they could have a great future together. He grabbed a flip chart, stuck it up on the wall and, just like when he and Sapphie had worked together, started figuring out the moves he wanted to make for himself. Then, in a different color, he added the moves he could make for Sapphie. Finally, in a third color, he added the ones Sapphie might want to make.

When he finished a few hours later, Scott slumped on the couch and looked at the picture the charts illuminated. He was chagrined to realize that there were plenty more overlaps than he'd expected. How had he missed that?

The emotionally draining exercise had also helped clarify a lot about himself. In looking to the future, he'd had to analyze the past and he'd come to some interesting conclusions. He'd also recognized some important truths.

Scott had been pretty self-contained all his life. He'd had to be. As much as he loved his mom and she loved him, she wasn't maternal in the traditional sense. Determined that he'd be able to survive in a hostile world, she'd encouraged his independence. Drilled self-reliance into him.

That had been invaluable during his time in billets and throughout his hockey career. It had probably helped his marriage survive for as long as it had. For sure it had allowed him to ignore the problems.

But the downside was that it had made him cautious of what he had with Sapphie. That she was so special to him, that she'd made him feel things he'd never experienced before, had been terrifying. Finding himself in unfamiliar territory, he'd retreated into the defensive habits he'd honed so well.

Scott could see that Sapphie had done the same thing. They'd both been protecting themselves from the hurt of being let down again. And nearly lost it all.

Well, that was about to change.

Scott leaped to his feet and stuck a fresh flip chart on the wall. He was surprised that his hand trembled as he wrote the number one at the top of the page. This was the most important action plan of his life. His future and his heart, his happiness, depended on it.

THE WEATHER IN London matched Sapphie's mood perfectly. Gray, drizzly, miserable.

Not that she'd seen much of the city since she'd arrived two days ago. Other than the limo ride in from the airport, she'd seen little more than the inside of her hotel room and the serviced office that Marty had rented for the duration of the acquisition project. The cab rides to and from dinner each night had given her brief glimpses of a few famous landmarks and she'd managed to see one of the well-known red telephone boxes.

Still, she had a long month ahead of her, so she could get out to play tourist at some point. There was no reason to go back to the United States now.

Sapphie pushed her chair away from the hotel room desk and turned to look out the window. The bright, pulsing lights of the winter fairground in Hyde Park in the distance reminded her that this was supposed to be the festive season. Normally, she liked Christmas, but this year she was with Scrooge and would be glad when January finally rolled around.

Maybe she'd have gotten over Scotty by then.

Her short, humorless laugh echoed around the room. Given how much she missed him, how much he'd dominated her thoughts and sleepless nights, that didn't seem likely anytime soon.

Sapphie couldn't believe how deeply she'd been affected by their breakup. Even though they'd been together such a short time, it felt like a piece of her heart had been cut out. Her body ached, as if she had the flu. She couldn't concentrate for long, as her mind would invariably return to that final conversation. Reliving and reworking it. Trying to find a way to change the outcome. Of course, she never succeeded. She never stopped Scotty from walking out of her apartment and her life.

Logically, she knew it was pointless. What was done was done. She should move on.

Yet she couldn't. More important, she didn't want to.

If only she could put things right without giving up the independence she'd fought so hard to achieve.

The alarm on her phone pinged, reminding her she was supposed to meet Marty in the hotel bar. He'd asked to get together early, before they met the others for dinner. Sapphie hoped he hadn't noticed that she wasn't at her best. She'd tried not to let her personal issues affect her work but knew she hadn't been as on the ball as she should have been.

Maybe it wasn't about that, she tried to reassure herself as she freshened her makeup. Maybe he wanted to talk about buying her business. She'd barely thought about his offer, and when she had, she'd found it hard to decide either way. Crazy, since not long ago, the answer would have been a no-brainer.

Downstairs in the dimly lit bar, Marty was seated in the far corner in one of a pair of leather armchairs with a glass of bourbon on the table beside him.

The nervous twisting of her stomach eased a little when he grinned broadly as he stood to greet her.

"Thank you for joining me, Bella Sapphire. What can I get you?"

"Sauvignon blanc, please."

They chatted briefly about the day's meetings, which had gone well. The owner, having played hardball until he decided to sell, was now bending over backward to make things easier. There was still a lot of work to do evaluating the soccer club, especially all the associated holdings, but she was quietly confident that the sale would go through in the New Year.

Maybe by the time the deal was done, she'd be back to her normal self.

Sapphie was caught off guard when Marty

fixed her with a searching look and asked, "Is something wrong? You've been quieter than usual these past few days."

Embarrassed that she hadn't done as good a job of hiding her feelings as she'd hoped, Sapphie tried to laugh it off. "I've never been good with travel across time zones, especially this direction. My body clock takes a while to adjust, so I haven't been sleeping well."

"Somehow, I don't think this is jet lag." He rested his elbows on the arms of the chair and steepled his fingers. "We've known each other a long time. If you need to talk to someone, you know that you can speak to me in confidence."

"I've always appreciated your friendship, advice and discretion."

Marty knew pretty much everything about her, especially her past, and had never said a word. Nor had he used it against her in their dealings. But this wasn't something she wanted to discuss with anyone. Not even Issy.

"I'll be fine. Just got some issues to sort through."

"Okay. As long as you know that you're not alone. In our game it's crucial to have someone whose ear we can bend when necessary. I'd never have lasted as long as I have without Gloria."

"You're lucky. Your wife is a special woman." She wished she knew their secret. Maybe it would have helped her with Scotty.

She couldn't resist asking, "How do you manage to balance work and home, without both suffering? You and Gloria make it look so easy."

"Don't be fooled," Marty said. "It takes work. I recognize what she gives up to support me, and try to make sure I do as much as I can to support her. I try never to take her for granted."

The joy in his eyes when he spoke about his wife was lovely, but it also poked at Sapphie's pain. She'd thought that was the kind of relationship she and Scotty were building. How had it gone wrong so quickly?

"Gloria's my sounding board and my conscience. She keeps me grounded. She tells me I give her pragmatism. I help her cut through the emotions and worries, to help her see a clear path." He smiled fondly. "Wherever I am, whatever I'm doing, I speak to Gloria at least once a day and always have. No matter how late it is when we're finished, we always share our days. The highs and the lows. I can't go to sleep without saying good-night to her."

"There must be more to it than that." She didn't mean to say that aloud.

"It's that simple and that difficult." Marty's gaze was too knowing. "What you have to remember is that work comes and goes. So does money. But love, real love, is constant. Nothing is more important than the one you love. Because once you lose them, all the work and money in the world won't make up for the loss."

His message hit uncomfortably close to home. "What if you've already lost them?" she asked quietly.

"You try your damnedest to win them back."

"And if it's too late?" Her throat tightened, so her words were barely more than a whisper.

"As long as you're both still breathing, it's not too late." He patted her hand. "I'll tell you a story. Years ago, when I was starting out, I fell in love with a girl. She wasn't anything like what I thought I needed for my wife. She was a thunderbolt and lightning strike rolled into one. Boy, did she shake up my world. But I wasn't brave enough to follow my heart. Instead, I went for the woman I thought would best suit a man with my aspirations."

He sighed. "Big mistake. I wasn't unhappy, but I knew inside that I wasn't as happy as I could have been if I'd been strong enough to make a different choice."

He was silent for a few minutes.

Sapphie couldn't help thinking about what had happened between her and Scotty. Had she made the most appropriate choice instead of the right one? For sure she'd chosen the easier path. The one she'd assumed would be the least likely to cause her pain.

How's that working out for you?

Marty grinned, startling her. "Of course, I was

smart enough to realize my mistake before things had gone too far."

"What did you do?" She leaned forward, desperate to hear something she could use.

"I risked it all for the woman I loved. Knowing that I might end up alone—I'd have preferred that to being with the wrong person—I broke up with my fiancée and went after Gloria." His smile turned rueful. "She didn't give in easily, which was only fair after I'd let her down so badly. But I kept after her, proving over and over that I wouldn't go away, until she forgave me. I've made sure she hasn't regretted it since. There isn't a day goes by, even after forty years, I'm not grateful that I had the balls to fix my mistake."

Do you? The question, unspoken, hung in the air.

"You have to decide, Bella Sapphire, what's the most important thing for you and what you're prepared to do to get it. Trust me, whatever it is you're scared of won't seem so bad if it means you and Scotty are back together."

Her jaw dropped. How did he know?

Marty winked and tapped the side of his nose.

Unfortunately, they couldn't discuss it further, because the rest of the team arrived for their predinner drinks.

Suddenly, Sapphie needed to be alone. She had to think. To figure out what she really wanted from her future. To understand what she was afraid of. To see, once and for all, if there was a way to make things work with Scotty.

Knowing Marty wouldn't mind, she pleaded a headache and excused herself.

In her room, she paced the floor. Her mind jumped all over the place. Finally, she resorted to what she did when faced with business problems—she got out her flip chart and started brainstorming. She jotted down her thoughts, filling page after page, until there was nothing else in her head. Then she took a step back and looked at what she'd written.

Just that easily, several things became clear.

She didn't want commitment because she was scared of losing what she had.

Her whole childhood had been spent a step away from being homeless and starving. When her parents had been flush, they'd spent lavishly and filled the house. As the money had dwindled and the call of the booze had grown louder, her parents had emptied the house and hit the pawnshops.

Sapphie had learned the hard way not to get attached to anything, because she wouldn't have it for long. She'd schooled herself to pull back from her home and her parents. Sapphie had been seven years old the first time she'd squirreled away what she might need, packed a bag with essentials and hidden it away from the house, just in case. Seemed like she'd never stopped waiting for the worst to happen.

It was a small step from that to not getting attached to a man.

The thing was she no longer needed to be scared about any of it. She'd been self-reliant since she was eighteen. Even if she never got another contract, she had enough money put aside and invested to live comfortably for a reasonably long life.

What's more, if the worst happened and she lost everything, she would survive. She was strong. She was resilient. Okay, and damn stubborn, too.

The time had come to stop being scared of what she might lose and embrace what she might gain. To start taking the same risks and make the same commitments in her personal life as she was prepared to for her business.

On a fresh sheet of paper, she started to make a list of what she wanted to do. Make her home base in New Jersey. No matter what happened, her mind hadn't changed about that. And she was definitely going to buy a place. And set up an office offshoot.

Her business? She still hadn't decided whether to sell or not. But she knew she wanted it to continue to be secure, not just for her but also for her staff, and she wanted the flexibility to run it how she wanted. Could Marty give her that? She planned to find out.

Which left Scotty. If she committed to him, it meant accepting her future would be tied to him. Whether or not marriage was in the cards, this commitment was certainly for as long as they both should live. That didn't sound scary. In fact, it sounded pretty good.

Did she love Scotty? The fact that she was prepared to join her life to his suggested she did. The misery that had grabbed her soul when they split was another clue. She missed him, she didn't want to be without him and her life was fuller, more complete, with him in it. He made her feel good, both inside and out.

If that wasn't love, she didn't know what it was.

The realization caused warmth to spread from her chest to her whole body, filling her, making her feel like she'd been chilled for a long time. Too long. And with that warmth came happiness and a sense of rightness. She hugged herself, then twirled round and round until she collapsed on her bed giddily.

"I love Scotty," she said aloud, then giggled at her silliness.

She had to get him back.

Sapphie sat on the bed cross-legged and looked at her list. It was a solid plan. It would bring her everything she wanted. Make her life how she wanted it to be.

Yet something was missing. It felt as empty and cold as her body had.

Why? What was wrong? What had she forgotten?

The more she stared at it and at the other charts covering the walls, the more she began to feel like those walls were closing in on her. It was all too controlled. Too tightly constrained. There was no emotion. No heart. No joy.

She couldn't fail, couldn't lose anything, but she couldn't soar either. And for all her planning, the one thing that stared out at her was that everything on that final chart was for her alone. It looked lonely.

What was missing was Scotty. He was on the list, but he wasn't a central part of it. He wasn't integral to each point.

Because her biggest fear wasn't just of losing what she had but of losing herself.

That was when she knew how important Scotty was to her. Because he was the one man who wouldn't let her lose herself. He'd be her lover, her partner, her sounding board, her conscience and her anchor. He'd also be her inspiration, her motivation and her champion. Committing to Scotty wouldn't take from her but would give to her. And she'd do the same for him. Together, they would be more than they would be alone.

That was love.

Suddenly, Sapphie knew how she could prove her love to Scotty.

She pulled the charts off the walls, tearing them up until only the action list remained. Taking a red marker, she put a cross through her list.

In the space at the bottom, she drew a big heart with "S + S" inside. Then she took the page off the wall and folded it carefully and put it inside her purse.

Finally, she grabbed her phone and dialed Marty's number. When he answered, she said, "I can't make the soccer game on Saturday, but I'll be back for Monday's meetings. I have to attend a funeral."

CHAPTER FIFTEEN

IT WAS RAINING ICE.

For the first time in his life, Scott hated the stuff.

He glared at the steel-gray heavens and cursed the cosmic irony as frozen rain clattered off the mahogany casket. He welcomed the biting pain as ice chips hit his face. It matched the pain in his heart.

The small-town cemetery was filled with big men wearing suits covered by parkas and overcoats, standing awkwardly. The hockey world, especially the parts that Bullet had touched, had turned out in force. The whole Ice Cats team had come, including the backroom staff. Representatives of all the teams Bullet had played for and of the leagues those teams belonged to stood side by side with his family and the townsfolk.

Knowing Cam, he'd have rolled his eyes at the fuss. Off the ice, he'd never liked being the center of attention.

A low keening sound broke the silence.

Laurel, who had been stoically dry-eyed throughout the funeral, faltered as Bullet's coffin was lowered into the dark earth. Supported by her two sons, brawny young men who looked like their father, she reached a pale hand toward the crossed hockey sticks—worn, taped and marked with Bullet's name and number—that adorned the lid.

"No-o." Her cry echoed around the bleak cemetery when the casket disappeared from view. "Please, no."

It took both sisters to hold her back, grabbing her tightly around her waist, when she tried to throw herself toward the deep hole. When the funeral director offered her a wooden box of earth and a small shovel, Laurel shook her head. Instead, she kissed the red rose she'd clutched all day and let it drop onto the coffin.

Scott's chest tightened; his eyes burned.

Beside him, Grey swore under his breath. "Damn it, Bullet. How could you do this? Why didn't you call?" His voice cracked.

Scott laid a hand on his friend's shoulder. He'd asked the same questions over and over. He'd carry the same heavy load of guilt for the rest of his life.

Still, in a quiet voice, he repeated what Laurel had told him last night. "Cam was sick for a long time. The medication wasn't helping and he hated the side effects. He wasn't in pain, but the growing debilitation was eating away at his pride and, emotionally, it was slowly killing him inside. He knew the prognosis wasn't good—he wasn't going to get better—and he tried to put on a brave face for so long."

Grey sighed heavily. "It's hard to believe there's nothing we could have done. That this was the only way he could end his suffering."

"And ease the burden for those who loved him."

"Like any of us cared about that," Grey muttered fiercely.

"I know. But he cared." Scott swallowed, trying to ease the lump in his throat. "Much as we hate it, we have to accept this is what he wanted."

The funeral director, who had been passing through the mourners, stopped in front of them, offering the box of earth and the shovel. Grey went first, said his silent goodbye, then tossed some soil into the hole.

Scott winced at the hollow thud it made when it hit the casket. Then he did the same. "Rest in peace, bro."

He shifted uncomfortably. "We should pay our respects to Laurel and the boys, then get the hell out of this miserable place."

"Yeah. Bullet wouldn't want us moping around a graveyard when we could be toasting him." Grey's lips managed a semblance of a half smile.

Both men found it hard to take that first step away.

Around them, the crowd began to disperse. Mourners made their way to the waiting line of cars at the gate. Grey and Scott held back, letting everyone else go. Even though there were plenty of people to look after Cam's wife, they wanted to be there for her.

Finally, Laurel's sons and her sisters walked a short distance away from the grave site, leaving her to pay her last respects to her husband. She dropped to her knees. In a low voice, she spoke for a few minutes. When she'd finished, the sky appeared to brighten and a small patch of blue appeared, at odds with the sleet that still fell around them.

Scott and Grey walked over to Laurel and helped her to her feet.

She thanked them. "You know, even with all the problems, I wouldn't change a second I had with him. I'll treasure every moment, always. He was my man, my heart. Our time together was far too short, but I know he loved me to the end. He still does."

She hugged Grey, then Scott. "Don't let the way he left us color your memories of him. Honor him by living and laughing and, most important, loving."

Laurel blew a kiss toward the small patch of blue in the sky, then gave them a watery smile before joining her family. Her back straight and her head held high, she didn't turn once.

Grey and Scott gave one last look at the grave, then followed behind slowly, their footsteps crunching on the salt-covered path.

"You know, that cloud kind of looks like the Stanley Cup." Grey pointed to the right of the rainbow.

Scott's gaze followed the direction of his friend's finger.

He stopped suddenly, almost slipping on the icy surface.

Not because there was indeed a cloud that, with a lot of imagination, was shaped like the famous silver chalice. But because a familiar, far more precious figure stood on the path ahead.

Sapphie started toward him. She faltered a few feet away, looking uncertain.

"Don't blow this, bro," Grey said softly. Then, a little louder, he added, "I'll catch a ride with Kasanski and Chance. See you at the house."

He stopped to hug Sapphie, then strode away.

Sapphie continued toward Scott, halting in front of him. She didn't meet his gaze.

He cleared his throat, trying to shift a knot the size of a boulder. "You came."

Talk about stating the freaking obvious.

"I'm sorry I'm late." She twisted her fingers together. "Flight delays because of the bad weather. Then it took forever to get a cab to come out here… I didn't think I'd make it."

"I'm really glad you did."

She finally looked up and gave him a tentative smile. "I know we're not— I thought you shouldn't be alone. I hope that's okay."

"Definitely. It means a lot." Jeez. Could he sound any lamer? "It's good to see you."

There was so much he wanted to say, to ask her, but fear of screwing up had him tongue-tied. He hoped it was a positive sign that she seemed lost for words, too.

The sleet stopped. This wasn't the best place for the conversation he wanted desperately to have with her, yet he was afraid that if they didn't talk now, the moment would be lost.

"Do you want to walk?" He nodded toward the memorial garden, where a winding path meandered between the snow-covered statuary to a gazebo.

"I'd like that."

Relieved, he managed a smile. "Will you be warm enough?"

She considered her long black coat and fur-trimmed boots. "I think so."

She slipped her gloved hand through his crooked arm. He flexed his fingers in his coat pocket, debating, then laid his hand over hers.

As they strolled, their breath misted the frigid air.

Unsure where to start, he blurted out, "I can't believe you're here."

Sapphie bit her lip. "I'm sorry. There should never have been any question of me being with you today. None of the excuses I gave mattered a damn. I know I missed the—"

"You came. That's what counts."

"You have Marty to thank for this."

His eyebrows shot up. "I do?"

"He gave me hell. Said there are times when those we love are more important than anything else. We do what we must to meet our work obligations, but we don't let those we care about down."

"He said that, huh?" Scott focused on the key four-letter word in the midst of her explanation, hoping it was true.

"Marty was right, as usual." Sapphie gave him a chagrined smile. "I've done a lot of thinking and realized that I was putting obstacles in our way. I thought I'd dealt with my baggage from the past, yet I was allowing it to dictate my present, and future."

The blame wasn't all hers. "I'm just as guilty of letting the past hamstring me. We were both trying to prevent any more pain."

"Instead, we hurt ourselves and each other even more."

They'd reached the gazebo, which provided some shelter from the snow that had started to fall. The bench inside was dry, so they huddled together on it. Scott put his arm around her shoulders, she rested her head on his chest and they sat silently for several minutes.

Then she sighed and straightened while still remaining in his embrace. "You were right, too.

You made a lot of allowances for me, but I didn't do the same. I was so set on my rules about not having a relationship—to protect myself—that I ignored the fact that we were already in one. Until we weren't."

Hope grew. She was saying all the right things. "I was as bad. I tried to hold on too tight. Force-fit us into an ideal that I knew couldn't work. Hell, it didn't work before. You'd think I'd learned. Instead, I pushed harder and pushed you away."

Sapphie caressed his face. "We've both been stubborn and made mistakes. Cam's death was a harsh wake-up call—one that forced us to face up to those mistakes. But it also helped me recognize that because life is short, you have to grab happiness where you find it. That you can lose more by doing nothing than by taking the risk and making the tough choice."

She grimaced. "I'm babbling again and not saying this very well." She opened her purse, pulled out a folded piece of flip-chart paper and handed it to him. "This is for you. My present for the holidays."

Scott opened it. On it was a list of actions for her life, like the one he'd created. Only, hers had a big red cross through it. Beneath the list was a heart containing their initials.

He gripped the cold wooden arm of the bench. Did this mean what he thought? He hoped so. Yet he'd been wrong about so much that he was afraid to assume. "You're early. Valentine's Day isn't until February."

"I like to be ahead of the game." Her laugh was a little shaky. "I told you I'd done a lot of thinking about what's important to me. I started to list what I wanted to do about them. Then I realized it was meaningless."

"It was?" The items she'd written seemed pretty important to him. Especially as they fitted closely with what he wanted. Did the cross through them mean she'd changed her mind?

"Of course. Because I was writing the list by myself. Where *I* live, what *I* do with my business—these things aren't only important to me. They affect us both. Our future together. I can't make those decisions on my own. I should be making them with you."

Her words lit him up inside, filling him with happiness.

"I'm sure we won't agree on everything, but there will be compromise. I want to make it work." Sapphie looked at him uncertainly. "Unless it is too late and you don't want that."

He surged to his feet, taking her with him, and wrapped her in his arms. "Trust me, I want that very much."

"Thank goodness." Sapphie puffed out a breath. "Unfortunately, we can't do that today. I only have enough time to go to the wake for an hour before I have to head to the airport for my flight to England. But we can do it when I return in a couple of weeks."

"Actually, we won't have to wait that long." He took out his phone, tapped the screen a few times, then showed it to her. "That's my ticket to go to England, tonight."

She looked up at him. "Really?"

"I wanted to show you how important you are to me. That I'm prepared to make tough choices to make things work for us." He twisted his lips. "I'm sorry I was such a jackass, insisting you come to the funeral. I shouldn't have used it as emotional blackmail. If the situation had been reversed, I'd have reacted like you did."

She framed his face with her hands. "You were in a mess. Your head wasn't on straight."

"That didn't give me the excuse to behave the way I did. I wanted to put that right. I thought about missing the funeral—Laurel would have understood. But I couldn't not be here. So I arranged the next best thing."

"I'm glad you didn't miss Cam's funeral. You needed to say your goodbyes." She smiled softly. "And we'd have wasted a lot of time, going in opposite directions."

"True." He lowered his head and kissed her, deeply and thoroughly.

In that moment, Scott felt complete. Being with Sapphie would never be easy. But the smooth would make the rough worth it and, man, he'd enjoy the making up.

When they started to head out of the gazebo, arm in arm, the snow switched to hail. It was so violent they had to dash back under cover.

"It's as if Mother Nature thinks we aren't done yet." Sapphie laughed.

"Perhaps she's waiting to hear the words," he said carefully.

Her gaze narrowed. "I don't want to spoil everything, but please don't pop the question."

He shook his head. "Those weren't the words I meant. We don't know if marriage is or will be on your—our—list. And, just so you know, I'm happy either way."

"Thank you. I may get there, someday—"

He kissed her. "For now, this is enough."

"Then which words do you mean?"

Hoping this wouldn't have the same reaction as a potential proposal, he said, "I love you." He added hurriedly, "I know you're probably not ready to say it, or even hear it. And I don't expect you to say it to me until you are, no matter what weather Mother Nature throws at us—" He sighed ruefully. "Guess I'm the one babbling now."

She said nothing for several seconds, making Scott nervous. Then her expression cleared and she wound her arms around his neck. "I love you, too. Very much."

Their kiss, achingly tender, sealed their love.

Outside the gazebo, the hailstorm eased and the pounding ice became softly falling snow.

Fingers firmly entwined, Scott and Sapphie walked out of the cemetery. Whatever the future held, they would face it together.

And win.

Four months later

"THIS ISN'T THE way to the apartment." Sapphie frowned as Scotty took the wrong exit off I-95 on their way from the airport.

"It's a new route home." He grinned.

She'd just arrived from a few days in LA, where she'd signed the papers selling her business to Antonelli Holdings for an obscenely large amount of money. Of course, that alone wasn't what had convinced her to sell. Marty had made her an offer she couldn't refuse.

She and Scotty had discussed the pros and cons and had decided the security the deal provided, for Sapphie and her staff—not to mention the opportunities for expansion and growth—were too good to resist. Sapphie still ran the business—which now had three full-time bases, in New Jersey, LA and Chicago—but because the offices were managed by VPs she'd selected, her time had been freed to work on only the projects she wanted.

The flexibility meant she could have the best of both worlds—the challenging job she loved and more time with the wonderful man beside her, whom she loved even more.

It was still early days, and there were plenty of issues for them to overcome, but it was working out well. More important, they were facing those issues together.

"Where are we going?" she asked as he turned into an unfamiliar leafy suburb.

Scotty sighed and shook his head. "You really want me to tell you?"

She'd never been a fan of surprises, but he looked so eager that she didn't want to spoil his fun. "All right. I'll be patient."

"You won't have to wait long to find out. In fact, we're here." He pulled into the driveway of a traditional-style brick house.

Everything about it was exactly as she'd imagined months ago when she'd thought about the kind of house he'd have. From the wraparound porch to the colorful shutters and gingerbread trim to the wide expanse of yard.

"It's lovely, but what exactly is *here*?" she asked as they got out of the car.

"Possibly our new home."

She looked at him through narrowed eyes. "What do you mean?"

They'd started living together, last month, when Scotty had moved into Sapphie's New Jersey apartment. She still had her other apartments for when she traveled to her offices. Scotty had given his ex-wife the house, which had suited everyone, including his kids. Angela wasn't antagonistic anymore and there was even the occasional sign she might be warming to Sapphie. It helped that both Wayne and Angela's boyfriend liked Sapphie.

Living with Scotty had taken some getting used to, but that was the benefit of their occasionally long-distance relationship—it gave them space to adapt to this new phase in their lives.

They'd talked about finding a place they could buy together. Sapphie hadn't expected it to happen so quickly. Her stomach tightened with apprehension as her old fears resurfaced. A house was a major commitment. Was this too soon? Would it be a step too far?

Sensing her nervousness, he leaned forward and kissed her. "We're getting a chance to see this house before it goes on the market. I promise there's no commitment to buy, but I thought it was too perfect to pass up the opportunity to check it out."

He held out his hand, palm up. "We can have a look, or we can turn around and leave. Your choice."

Just that easily, Sapphie's fears subsided. Because she knew Scotty meant what he said.

She placed her hand in his. "It *is* very nice. I don't suppose it would hurt to see if the inside is as good as the outside."

"I think you'll like what you see." They walked down the path toward the front door. "I know you'll like the deck and the backyard. It's filled with trees and has a stream running through it."

When they reached the steps, Sapphie stopped and smiled.

She slipped her arm around Scotty's waist and said, "I have a feeling this house is going to be perfect."

* * * * *

Be sure to check out the rest of the
NEW JERSEY ICE CATS *books*
by Anna Sugden:

A PERFECT DISTRACTION
A PERFECT TRADE
A PERFECT CATCH
and
A PERFECT COMPROMISE

Available at Harlequin.com